For the Ones Who Remain

R. Collins

Samsara Fleet | Book One

Books By Riley Collins

To learn more about Riley Collins, see an updated list of titles, and join his mailing list go to his webpage at https://www.rileycollins.info.

Samsara Fleet Series

Book One: For the Ones Who Remain
Book Two: For the Ones Who Are Forgotten
Book Three: For the Ones Who Rebel

ISBN: 1-7359029-1-8
ISBN-13: 978-1-7359029-1-3
Print Edition

Cover Art by: 17 Studio Book Design
Editing by: Garity Editing and Rosaire Publishing LLC

For ML

Love BAP

Chapter One

The drugs surged from the small ampoule and into Kal's system. It was a torrent that carried away pain and memories, leaving nothing. His head lolled to the side as his doughy body slid down the wall and he fell onto the soft mattress beneath. Unable to close his eyes, Kal studied the room as thoughts flitted through his mind.

The bar's clientele fit within one of two categories—miners taking a break after their shift or traders passing through, like Kal. Most of the miners were Kurz, the dominant species in the system, but the traders were an assortment from throughout the galaxy. Kal was the only Human in the place, something he had long since grown accustomed to in his years as an independent merchant.

The Miner's Pit truly lived up to its name—dingy, dark, and potentially lethal, it could have been almost any of the other chem bars that Kal had been frequenting over the past decade. Found mostly on dead-end worlds and stations, they allowed people like Kal a way to forget reality, to take whatever they needed to survive and make it through to the next day.

The patrons at the bar were in various states of consciousness, depending on their drug of choice. Two Kurz, stood to one side of Kal, talking softly in their high-pitched language while a group of five Tounous were engaged in a boisterous conversation at nearby table. The squat creatures gesticulated wildly with their bifurcated arms. They spoke

1

over one another, their chirping voices overlapping so fast that Kal's implant was having trouble translating the conversation.

Kal, like almost every other Human, had a neural implant embedded in his brain when he became an adult. The small chip performed a variety of tasks that made his life easier. It translated almost any known language to Human Standard, interfaced with computer systems, communicated, connected to local nets, and a host of other activities. Kal would've been lost without it.

Kal's muscles relaxed as the drug, Kuaile, saturated his system. The sensations of time and place began to disappear. He drifted in and out of consciousness, somehow both aware and oblivious of what was going on around him. He felt numb, exactly how he wanted. The shadows of the bar's patrons ebbed and flowed as the shifts changed in the mines, marking the passage of time.

The Miner's Pit was in a small mining station, Kirkira, nestled in an asteroid belt in the Gamamedes System. The system was at the edge of Kurz space, almost a week's travel from Humanity, and consisted of a single uninhabited planet and the dingy station. It was a bleak, lonely place filled with creatures that were drifting through the galaxy, looking for their next credit or hit.

How many times have I been here? Kal chuckled to himself. He'd spent the last decade of his fifty-odd years hauling cargo from one cesspool to another and ending up on the floor of chem bars like this one. It would have been sad if it hadn't been so funny.

One of the Tounous at the nearby table turned to look at him. "What's so amusing, Human?" The short creatures were not known for their humor, especially if they thought they were being insulted.

Kal couldn't help himself. "You are. You're talking so loud I can't help but listen—not like I want to." The Tounous flattened their ears back against their heads, letting Kal know that he had hit a nerve.

They slid from their stools and staggered toward him on their three legs, clearly affected by whatever they'd been drinking. Two of them broke from the group and made a show of rotating their arms and torsos back and forth. They were bristling for a fight. Kal pushed himself off the floor as they approached and lunged toward the closest one as it came close, his fist cocked back. His body failed him, and he missed completely, falling, face first, on the cold floor. The sudden impact to his chin caused an explosion of colors to dance before his eyes.

His opponents didn't give him any time to recover. They kicked him in the face and body until he could feel and taste the blood pouring from his head. They picked him up and began carrying his limp body across the room. Kal saw the dingy glass door of the Pit as he was tossed into the corridor outside. Thankfully, he didn't feel a thing. He turned over and examined the lights above him as pedestrians continued to walk over and around him, paying little attention. With another dry chuckle, he closed his eyes and drifted off.

Kal wasn't sure how long he'd been unconscious. There was no true sense of time in a mining station—everything was based on the worker's shifts. He pushed himself up, wincing from the knives of pain stabbing into his ribs. The occasional pedestrian shuffled by, skirting to the side of the grime-filled passageway to avoid him. There was significantly less traffic than when he had entered The Miner's Pit.

Must be the middle of a shift, thought Kal. The mines had three shifts each day. During the change, the corridors would be filled with miners.

The walk back to the middle of the station was a tour through the underbelly of the civilized galaxy. Brothels, pawn shops, and chem bars littered the sides of the walkway. Kal could hear the low hum and creaks of the station's ancient infrastructure around him. Kirkira Station had been operating for much longer than the original builders had intended.

As he neared the center, it became more crowded, and the establishments changed into small merchants and cafes. He had to weave his way around several large Kurz as they walked down the path. The huge creatures looked like a mixture of demon and insect, with large compound eyes and an almost Human mouth. Their enormous claws, which extended from their wrists past their hands added to their nightmarish appearance. Although they looked savage, Kurz were in fact highly intelligent and disciplined. They were an older species than Humans, with a much more advanced military and far more colonies.

Continuing through the more respectable center, the streets became less hospitable again by the time Kal reached the loading bays. Workers scurried around, loading and unloading ships, almost all of them dingy private merchant vessels like his. The large galactic corporations didn't see the need to send their ships to stations like Kirkira except to pick up minerals. Slapping the entry lock of his ship, *Annie*, Kal walked up the rear cargo ramp as it finished lowering to the ground.

The inside of the ship was a mess—food casings, broken electronics, and assorted junk lay strewn about. Registered as the *Queen Anne's Revenge* fifty years ago, the thirty-meter-long Shreen Voyager was a bit of a relic. *Annie* was designed to operate both in atmosphere and in space, which gave it a more streamlined appearance than many other merchant ships. Since he had purchased it a decade earlier, Kal had religiously avoided providing any upkeep other than the basic maintenance to prevent it from spontaneously exploding. The one exception was a small chamber he'd had installed for contraband.

Kal climbed the ladder to the upper deck and headed to his cabin. The ship had two, he'd claimed one as his personal quarters and used the other for storage. The lower deck had a galley, cargo bay, and crew quarters, which he used for surplus cargo storage. As he entered his cabin, Kal brushed his fingertips along a picture of his family attached to the hull—a souvenir from happier times. A familiar sense of wistful longing crept through his body.

Kal brought up his personal financials on the desk monitor. As a retired Earth Defense Force officer, Kal still received a small pension. He normally spent all of it on alcohol and drugs within the first few days of the credits hitting his account—anything to take his mind off reality. When he recovered from those binges, broke and still alone, he had to scramble to find whatever job he could. The cycle often put him in dangerous and unpleasant situations, not that he cared much anymore.

Every planet and station had a local net that allowed citizens to communicate with each other. They also contained news, job postings, entertainment, and alerts. Smaller stations, such as Kirkira, had only one, whereas large planets, like Earth, had thousands which were all accessible from any computer or neural implant.

"Let's see what we got," Kal said to himself as he browsed the job boards, looking for a shipping contract. He preferred something that would let him head back toward Human-controlled space but he wasn't in a position to be picky. Backwater Kurz mining stations normally didn't have shipments outside of Kurz space.

The job boards were relatively empty. There were contracts available, but most of them were to other planets in

Kurz space. Others required a larger ship, specialized equipment, or credentials Kal didn't have.

Kal sighed. *Damn, I may need to use the Alliance.*

He'd applied to become a contractor for the underground group a few years back, when credits had been *very* tight. The Alliance was an organization that specialized in less-than-legal commerce, as he had heard someone tell him once. They ran almost all the smuggling and illicit drugs in the galaxy.

Kal stood up from the computer and caught a whiff of his own body odor. He jumped in the mist shower, grabbed some meds for his hangover, and climbed into a fresh set of clothes.

Feeling marginally better, Kal stepped off the *Annie's* ramp and back into the bay, with a small chit in his hand. The thin metal card allowed him to find the Alliance front on any planet or station. The Alliance only conducted business in person.

The glowing arrow on the card led him to Lax El Dem's. The dilapidated store was tucked into a small side corridor in the bowels of the station. It had a single rusty door and a large window that was clouded with age. A holographic sign next to the entrance flickered intermittently, causing Kal's headache to creep back. As he entered, the automated door opened smoothly, belying its aged appearance. The store was a low-class pawn shop, with rusty metal shelves containing the belongings and heirlooms of those who'd needed credits quickly and had nowhere else to go.

"Hello!" Kal called out. The place reminded him of some of the horror holos he'd seen. He was half ready for someone to rush at him with a plasma cutter.

A grimy attendant bot appeared from behind the desk and greeted him with a small beep and a nod of its head. Kal pressed a button on the Alliance chit and a hidden door slid open behind the bot, revealing a shaft of warm light. At the same time, a thick metal door slammed shut over the store entrance, preventing anyone else from entering—and Kal from exiting.

As he made his way past the bot and through the door, he felt like he was entering a completely new world. It was decorated in the same ostentatious style as all the other Alliance fronts he'd been in. He was at one end of a creamy white hallway with gilded chandeliers hanging from the ceiling. An elaborate burgundy runner led down the hallway to a platinum-covered door—clearly reinforced to protect against weapon fire.

On the other side of the platinum door was a sumptuous but sparse room with a couple of plush chairs in the corners. A top-of-the-line service bot stood in the middle of the room on its single large tread. A holographic display on the top of the bot flickered to life and an attractive woman's face appeared.

"Hello Mr. Norman, how may we be of assistance today?" The bot's female voice was clearly synthetic.

"I'm looking for some work. Don't care what it is, 'cept it needs to take me back to EDF-controlled space."

"I see you're piloting a Shreen Voyager. Is that correct?"

Kal nodded.

A brief pause. "We have one contract available."

"What is it?"

"Transport of a package to the New America system."

Kal waited for the bot to continue. "And?"

"I am sorry, but we cannot disclose any more information about the contract. It has been identified as highly sensitive."

"Well, how the hell can I know if I should take it? Could you at least give me a rough idea of what I'd be transporting?"

"Sir, I am unable to divulge more information unless you take the contract."

This was unusual, even for the Alliance. They were extremely secretive—it was necessary for their line of work—but were usually upfront with what was being transported. Pilots needed to know what they were putting into their cargo bay. Some items could be dangerous or might require special precautions or storage.

"Well, what's the commission?"

"One hundred thousand credits, sir."

Kal took a deep breath. That was more than he had ever made in a run, more than he made in most standard months. More than he was comfortable with; a bunch of credits with no information could only mean some serious problems down the line.

"Do you have *anything* else? I'll even take something going in the general direction of Human-controlled space," he pleaded.

"No, sir."

Kal shook his head, he needed a drink. Maybe he should take that commission. *You remember what happened last time you did something like that,* Kal thought to himself. *You swore never again.*

"Well, thanks for nothing," he said. "Good luck finding someone." He'd have to be desperate to take the contract. He barely had any credits and still wasn't willing to do it. The Alliance operated outside of the law and paid well. But contracts that paid *that* well could be lethal.

Kal walked out of the building and headed back to the landing pad. Jobs were sparse in a colony like this one, but there would be more—eventually. He just needed to be smart with his money and wait until something new came up. In the meantime, he could relax, update the ship's software, and try to find a local security gig while he waited. He wasn't in a rush to get anywhere.

Chapter Two

Kal spent two standard weeks cooped up in the *Annie*, trying to keep himself occupied and away from the dark thoughts that clung to the edges of his mind. He spent several hours each day updating the ship's systems. *Annie* was old, and despite not wanting to spend any money on her maintenance, he needed to keep the software up to date so she could perform basic functions like docking and communication. After a few hours of work, he'd browse the job listings, then leave the ship to scrounge up some drinks or Kuaile and go back to his cabin. Next thing he knew, he was picking himself off the floor and repeating the routine again.

By the end of the second week, Kal felt himself going stir crazy. He'd completed all the updates he could, watched every minute of holos in the ship's memory banks, and walked every single passageway of the colony multiple times. Places like Kirkira were designed for miners, creatures who worked half the day and partied the other half, day in and day out. He was burning through credits at the chem bars, and his accounts were getting very low.

Kal visited the Alliance every day, but they still only had the one contract available. The alert he'd set up to notify him of jobs posted on the local net never went off; there weren't even local security openings available.

Kal sat on his bunk and looked out the viewscreen on the bulkhead. The electronic displays showed three-dimensional images of activity outside the ship, replicating the feel of a window. Like almost every other ship, *Annie* had no windows, not even in the cockpit. But the viewscreens made it seem like Kal was looking through one.

He saw a group of four Humans walking past, smiling and laughing as they talked. They looked young, perhaps twenty years old, and seemed to not have a care in the galaxy. *Was I ever like that?* Kal wondered. He watched them enviously as they sauntered across the landing bay and through a large portal to the station proper. Before he had time to think, he grabbed his jacket off the chair and was running down the ramp to catch up with them.

He slowed to a walk as he spied the group ahead of him, flitting in and out of his line of sight as they cavorted through the crowd of merchants. The group circled up in front of a bar, clearly deciding whether to go in. The Canary was one of the more upscale establishments on the station. The faux wood façade was clean, with clear windows and animated holographic displays around the door.

"Hell no," said a tall woman with her brown hair tied in a bun. "I'm heading back to Earth soon. No way am I going to screw up my life before it even begins." Her accent gave her away as being from New America, one of Humanity's four colonies.

"Come on Sandra, one last time. In a few weeks you're going to be sitting at Base Camp, polishing boots, wishing you had partied while you had the chance." The other woman was tall as well, with ebony skin and black hair that fell to her shoulders in cascading waves.

The two men in the group were standing slightly back, clearly trying to stay out of the conversation. *Wise move*, thought Kal.

"Klarissa, there's no way I'm going in there. Those places are for outcasts and losers. Nothing good can come from it. Let's head over to the observation level." Sandra turned and started walking away.

"We already did that—twice. How can we really explore the galaxy if we don't explore all of it? Once you're in Base Camp, your life will change. When's the next time we'll be together? This may be our last chance." Klarissa pulled on her friend's arm, trying to lead her into the chem bar.

Base Camp was slang for the Earth Defense Force's Basic Course. It was a civilian's first entry into the EDF—training them in the basic skills a soldier needed to survive. Kal knew quite a bit about Base Camp, having served as cadre there in his prior life. He knew that recruits were expected to be in excellent physical shape and have a clean background for the security clearance they would need. Drinking and taking drugs at chem bars on alien mining stations probably wouldn't help.

"Congrats on going to Base Camp," Kal said loudly as he stepped into the circle. "That's really impressive."

"Hey," said one of the men in greeting. He was taller than Kal with a solid build, dark skin, and black hair falling down his shoulders in dreadlocks. "I'd given up on seeing another Human. It's been weeks, and all we've seen are these ugly things." He gestured at one of the Kurz walking past.

13

The kid obviously had never been off a Human colony until recently. Many people forgot that the "strange" aliens they met in their travels were easily able to understand their conversations—they had implants as well. He wasn't unusual though. Although Humans could now travel the stars, it still took a lot of time and money—most people never left the planet where they were born.

"Shut up, Ekon," said the man next to him, shorter and with straight black hair. "You know they can understand you."

Kal leaned in and said in a low voice, "Probably not a good idea to say things like that too loud. Kurz can be pretty violent when they're insulted." It wasn't really true, but it never hurt to teach some manners. "I know what you mean, though. It can be rough. After a while, you feel like you're the only Human left in the universe."

Ekon's eyes widened and his eyes darted around, trying to see how close the surrounding Kurz were. Kal knew they were all too busy to care what some Human thought of them.

"I delivered some parts here a few weeks ago and am waiting for a new contract. Haven't seen any fellow Humans for ages either." He motioned towards the door. "I served in the EDF for over two decades and would be happy to tell you all about the force and Base Camp."

Klarissa looked at him skeptically. "What a coincidence. Unfortunately, we don't know who the hell you are."

Kal pulled out his EDF chit and held it up, showing the image of him next to his retired status and former rank of colonel. He always carried it with him, figuring it would come in handy if he got into real trouble. Security patrollers tended to be more careful if they realized that someone was affiliated with the EDF, even if they *were* retired.

Klarissa puckered her mouth. "Okay, okay. Appreciate the offer, but we are traveling as a group. You understand. We just want to spend some time on our own."

Ekon grabbed hold of Kal's shoulder and pulled him close. "One more can't hurt. Let's give him a chance, we haven't talked to another Human for weeks."

"I can go." Kal put up his hands. "I don't wanna intrude. Just thought you might want to grab a drink together. I'm traveling alone, so I don't get too many chances to talk to other people."

Sandra frowned. "That's gotta get lonely, being on your own." She turned to Klarissa. "If he comes, I'll grab something at the bar with you guys—but only if he comes."

"Fine, fine, I'm overruled," Klarissa conceded with a smile. "Name's Klarissa. That's Sandra." She pointed to the brown-haired woman. "We've been best friends since we could walk. These two guys"—she gestured at the men—"are Ekon and Li Wei. We all went to school together back on New America."

"Introductions over, let's go inside," said Li Wei hurriedly. Kal noticed he was continually fidgeting and rocking back and forth, a ball of nervous energy. He took a second look—the guy clearly was either on something or suffering from withdrawal.

"After you." Kal gestured toward the bar and followed the group through the entrance. A wall of vapor, noise, and pungent aromas slammed into him as he stepped through the doorway. The clientele was like The Miner's Pit—mostly Kurz, with some other species mixed in.

Li Wei ran ahead of the group and found a table. As they slid into their seats, a Hrush waiter walked over to them. The top of its head was covered with antennae that it used to communicate. Kal's implant seamlessly translated their undulations into Human Standard and piped it directly to his auditory nerves. Hrush were often hospitality workers; their calm demeanor made them ideally suited for the job.

"Welcome to the Canary. So glad you could join us today. Whether you're here for a quick bite to eat or want to forget your troubles, our establishment is here to serve."

The menu on the table's viewscreens was split into three separate sections—food, chems, and companions. Each line had a price next to it in credits.

Sandra and Ekon both ordered beers. Taking his cue, Kal ordered the same.

"A vial of Rapturium, pretty please," Li Wei said with a wink. Kal felt his stomach sink. *That's* what was wrong with the kid. Rapturium was a designer drug that was popular throughout the galaxy. For many species it was like nicotine—addictive with a slight buzz. For Humans, it was highly addictive and extremely dangerous. People routinely overdosed, losing control of their minds and becoming comatose. The United Earth Government had tried to get the substance banned throughout the galaxy, but since the negative effect was almost exclusively limited to Human biology, it remained on the market on any planet or station not controlled by the EDF.

"So Kal, what's a retired EDF colonel doing here?" asked Klarissa after the waiter left.

"Just tryin' to make a few credits." Kal shrugged. "I was in for twenty years and got to see the stars. The EDF is great, don't get me wrong, but I was tired of military life, so I decided it was time to make a change."

"Do you ever regret leaving?" asked Sandra.

"Sometimes," admitted Kal. "I miss the people." He missed the camaraderie and sense of purpose; but that was too cheesy to say to complete strangers in a chem bar. "But overall, no, I was ready for a change. The service takes a lot out of you, and I had no more aspirations. I had done what I wanted to." He wasn't willing to talk about the *real* reason.

"Were you in the war?" asked Ekon, leaning across the table. He was referring to the Torgham War, a conflict between Humanity and the Torgham almost twenty years ago.

It had been Humanity's first interstellar conflict, and almost a giant defeat. The Torgham had wrought huge casualties upon the EDF, and they had still been recovering when Kal retired. The intervention of other species had been the only reason they were able to retain control of all four of their colonies. Kal shuddered to think about his time on Wudexingqiu, trying to prevent the Torgham from capturing the system.

"Yeah, I was in it. Not a time I like remembering." Images flashed into Kal's head, unbidden.

"My mom was a soldier in the EDF when she was my age. She got out after her term of conscription ended, but always talked about it. It's funny, she said it was horrible but also that she missed it sometimes." Sandra blushed. "Sounds stupid, but I figured I would join up to see the universe, simple as that."

"Not stupid at all. That's why I joined too. You get to see and do things that you never would get to as a civilian." As part of the EDF, Kal had been to all five Human planets as well as several alien ones. That part of the recruiting pitch was true, you got to see the galaxy.

The server came back with their drinks and Li Wei's Rapturium. The young man grabbed the vial and pressed it against his neck with a gasp of pleasure.

"To new friends." Klarissa raised her glass. Kal raised his own and then drained it, slamming the empty mug on the table.

"So, given any thought to what you want to do in the EDF?" Kal wiped the foam from around his mouth with his sleeve and turned back to Sandra.

"Well, I am thinking of becoming a pilot eventually. Maybe start out as regular infantry and work my way up."

"Nah, you should go Tac-I," said Ekon. "Those are the *real* soldiers."

Tactical Insertion Specialists, or Tac-I's, were the elite of the elite in the EDF. Their mission was to board enemy ships and stations as well as conduct stealth reconnaissance. Tac-I's had to be trained in a variety of fields—customs, disguise and camouflage, and assault operations, among others—as well as have top physical conditioning. Less than one percent of soldiers in the EDF became Tac-I's. In Kal's experience, around ten percent of soldiers *said* they were a Tac-I soldier and half of all the new recruits wanted to become one—with the other half wanting to be pilots.

In his opinion, pilots were the true lifeblood of the EDF. Despite advances in artificial intelligence, even the most advanced AI was prone to making disastrous errors in some circumstances. During long trips a computer could manage to keep the ship on course, but during departure and landing, as well as in any sort of emergency, a pilot was vital. AIs were also susceptible to interference and enemy hacking—as the EDF had found out in the war against the Torgham.

"Both are essential," Kal said diplomatically.

"What about you? What did you do?" Sandra asked after taking a small sip from her glass.

"I was a logistics officer." He could see the disappointment in their eyes. "With an organization as big as EDF, you live or die by your ability to get supplies and materials where they need to go."

"I can totally see that." Kal could tell Sandra was humoring him.

Kal took advantage of the lull in the conversation to ask a passing server for another drink then turned back to the table.

"So, what brings you here? Why not stay in New America before joining up?"

"Well, Klarissa suggested it," Sandra replied. "I thought it would be good to go out and see the universe a little bit before Base Camp. We got a few credits from our parents when we graduated. We asked Ekon and Li Wei along because, well, we figured it would be good to have someone else with us."

"Who would have known they would be such morons." Klarissa smirked, giving Ekon a playful shove.

As the night wore on, Sandra peppered Kal with questions about his time in the EDF. He tried as best he could to answer them truthfully, while not making his career as a logistics officer seem *too* boring. His stories about the Torgham War were especially well received, but he left out many of them—some things were too painful to talk about. Sandra's enthusiasm was infectious, and Kal found himself pining for his time in the service. The three travelers told Kal stories about growing up on New America. From what he could tell, they'd had a pretty standard, if sheltered, childhood. Li Wei was silent, the effects of the Rapturium evident.

Their server ensured that their glasses remained full and Kal's beer changed to Krz'katoor, a strong local liquor. After several hours, Kal's head was clouded with drink, and he was having trouble stringing his thoughts together. He was listening to the two Sandras before him talk about practicing flying with their brothers when his seat moved out from under him and he fell to the floor.

"Kal, you all right?" the Sandras both looked concerned. They abruptly fused together, becoming a single young woman again.

"Ha, the old guy might have had a bit too much," Ekon snickered.

"Hey, do you have somewhere to stay? I can help get you a place to sleep." Sandra put her arm around his waist, pulling him off the floor.

"You think that's a good idea?" Klarissa's eyes widened and she nodded to the table. "We already lost Li Wei; I don't want you wandering off." Their friend was face down.

Ekon had his arm around Klarissa's waist and scoffed. "Don't worry, she'll be fine."

"Exactly. I'll be fine," repeated Sandra. "The guy's a mess." Kal wanted to defend himself but was having trouble forming any words. "He's hurting and probably doesn't know anyone around here."

In the corner of his mind, Kal knew he should be able to take care of himself. He focused on speaking. "You...stay with your friends. I can...can...find my way."

"Are you sure?" The two Sandras were back. And they both looked concerned. "You don't look too good."

"Of cour—course I'm su—sure." Kal raised his arms as he backed away from the table. "Not a probl—"

Kal's feet tangled with each other. His hands flew up, trying to grasp onto something, but to no avail. A buzzing sound rang in his ears as his head hit the metal floor of the bar and then he sensed nothing but muffled voices as his mind faded away.

Chapter Three

Kal woke with a start and looked around. He was in some sort of hotel room—a relatively cheap one from what he could tell. The small, cream-colored room had a bed, end tables, a small desk, and few cheap pictures hanging on the walls. The viewscreen on the far wall gave the illusion of looking directly out into the asteroid field around the station.

The previous night began to return in a trickle and then a painful flood. His face beat with shame as he thought about what happened. His self-destructive streak continued to reign. He'd lost count of how many times he had woken up like this, with an aching head and a heart full of regret. Sandra was snoring in a chair near the bed, her feet splayed out on the floor and her head crooked down into her breasts. Kal dropped his face into his pillow and closed his eyes, hoping to hide from his shame.

When he woke again, Sandra was awake and staring at the monitor on the desk surface. Her eyes were wide, and her mouth was slightly open.

"Uh, good morning," he offered tentatively.

"You…you should check this out now," Sandra whispered, not moving her eyes from the screen.

Kal painfully got up and walked behind her to study the monitor. It was a holo—of the Sol System, according to the banner at the bottom—from the perspective of a satellite or ship somewhere near the outside perimeter. The camera zoomed in as a fleet of four black vessels appeared. The ships

23

looked to have been grown rather than built, with each having a different irregular, almost bulbous shape. Small nacelles were scattered around the surface of the ships, reminding him of the seeds on a strawberry. Brilliant streams of energy began to shoot from two of the ships into the sun. There was no immediate effect, but then after a few seconds, the sun began to grow brighter and change hue—turning from a bright yellow to a dirty red color. And then it expanded, engulfing planets and sending an explosive wall of fire through the system. The ships disappeared, folding away. The point of view of the holo switched to another point even farther out as the original camera was consumed by the explosion. Finally, the monitor went black as the final camera was destroyed and the devastation complete.

A voice narrated the events unfolding on the holo, the announcer's voice sometimes breaking with emotion. "At 0934 Standard Earth Time, a fleet of unknown vessels entered the Sol System. They were unresponsive to EDF forces and immediately fired on the sun, destroying the entire system, with a complete loss of life. The EDF has transferred command to their forces on Wudexingqiu, and are mobilizing to respond to this unprovoked attack. We take you now to a live briefing from the EDF forces commander."

Kal tried to grasp the enormity of what he'd just seen. Besides being the capital and home planet of Humanity, Earth contained about a third of the species. The loss in lives was unfathomable. Outside of the lives lost, thousands of years of Human history had been obliterated in just a few minutes. As far as Kal knew, this type of disaster had never happened to any sentient lifeform on this scale. Humanity was now an orphaned species.

Who would do this? Kal wondered. The ships weren't familiar and Kal didn't know of anyone that would destroy an entire system without provocation.

The picture on the holo shifted to an image of an EDF general standing behind a podium. His eyes were bloodshot, and his uniform was crumpled, as if he had just picked it off the floor. Kal would have known the face anywhere—General Roger Kinkaid had been his platoon commander back at the academy.

Kal looked at the time stamp on the holo, it was over a week old. Although Humans could fold through the galaxy faster than light, there was no way to transmit signals that fast. Communications occurred through a network of probes that travelled between planets. There were tens of thousands of these probes traveling the galaxy at any time, delivering news and messages. They could take days or weeks to reach their destination, meaning that any news from outside of a system was always going to be dated.

"Fellow citizens of the United Earth Government, today is the darkest day in the history of our species. We have been attacked, without warning, by an unknown aggressor with devastating results." General Kinkaid stopped for a moment, gathering himself. "The EDF has sent exploratory probes to the Sol System and found no sign of life remaining." He paused again. "We do not know what evil force is behind this, but we will find out and we will destroy them. Acting Secretary General Anikulapo-Kuti has called for immediate conscription of all able-bodied men and women between twenty and fifty years of age. You are to report to the closest EDF station for in-processing. We will need every bit of Humanity's strength and resources to meet this threat. But do not doubt that we will recover, we will rebuild, and we will win."

Kal wondered what had happened since the general gave his speech. When he'd been an EDF officer, he had always been frustrated in the delay between when things happened and when he heard about them. Whoever caused this carnage, they almost certainly weren't done, and may have already moved on to their next target. Where that was, he didn't know.

He dropped down onto the bed and used his neural implant to check what other news there was on the local net. It was more of the same—Sol had been attacked, with devastating results. The other four Human colonies were on high alert and asking for their citizens to return immediately. It was painful for Kal to think about the people, the families, the children who had been vaporized in seconds on Earth. He thought of his old house and the neighborhood his kids had played in when they were stationed on Earth—all gone. The amount of devastation was unfathomable—billions of lives wiped out in an instant.

Sandra hadn't said a word but kept staring straight ahead at screen. Finally, she turned and looked at Kal.

"I can't believe it," she whispered.

Kal nodded.

"All those people, gone. The UEG, gone. Our history, gone."

Kal nodded. Humans no longer had a home—they may still have their other planets and cities, but their past was destroyed, cut off.

"I mean, what are those things? Why would they do that?" Sandra asked. Kal didn't bother to give an answer.

Sandra sat up in her seat. "They may be going to New America."

If so, they're probably already there, thought Kal.

"So, what do we do now? I mean, we need to go home, to get out of here." She looked at him with her wide eyes.

"Yes, we do," Kal agreed. "We need to leave *now*. I'm not sure what those creatures will do next, but I want to be with my own species when they do it."

"How are we going to get out of here?" Sandra asked, her face streaked with tears.

An alert chimed on Kal's neural implant. He activated the attached holo and played it on the desk monitor. It was eerily similar to the one they just watched—dark ships folding into a system, destroying the sun, and then departing. Only this time it was in the Kurz's home system of Khrdir.

The holo was more recent, taken a few days after the attack on Sol. Kal guessed the creatures must have more than one fleet, since no known species could travel between the two systems that fast. It seemed they were waging a war of annihilation against every civilization in the galaxy.

"What are they doing? Why are they doing this?" Sandra whispered.

"No idea," Kal answered, "but we need to get off this station, now. We have to get back to the UEG. I have my ship in the landing bay, ready to go. Are you able to reach your friends?"

Sandra's eyes went vacant as she activated her implant to contact the others. After a couple of minutes, they refocused and she looked back at Kal. "Klarissa and Ekon are here at the hotel. No one knows where Li Wei is."

"Not surprised. I hate to say this, but your friend probably won't make it back to New America. How long has he been using?"

"Only a few days. We told him not to do it, but he said he didn't see the harm in just trying it once or twice."

"Once is enough with Rapturium. We all need to get out of here. The Kurz will be on full alert and will most likely lock down this station. Who knows how long we'll be stuck if we don't get out now. Do you have a ship?"

"We were supposed…to be traveling back on a United Universe freighter in a couple of standard days…though who knows if that's going to happen." Sandra hunched over, hyperventilating.

"Look, my ship is a piece of crap, but I can squeeze you all in if the freighter isn't coming. I just gave you access to contact me on the neural net. Check with your friends and pack up anything you've got. I'm sending you the info on the ship, so you know where to meet me." Kal sent her the location and hull number of his ship.

"One sec," Kal said. He accessed the net. The free merchant message boards were in chaos. No one knew what to do. He did see an alert from the Kirkira Station command that all non-essential departures had been restricted. The station was locked down. "Damnit."

"What is it?"

"They're not letting ships depart. I need to make a few stops to see if I can get us out of here. Get the others and meet me at the ship."

Kal didn't like the idea of them seeing the inside of *Annie*; it painted a sorry picture of the state of his life. He had no desire to share his ship and pathetic personal life with four strangers, but he wasn't going to let four kids rot on a podunk station in the middle of nowhere.

"Also, about last night—" Kal started.

"No worries." Sandra stopped him quickly before he could finish, giving him a weak smile. "Nothing needs to be said. It happens to the best of us."

"Right. Meet me at the ship."

"We will." He could see the gratitude in her eyes.

Kal rushed out of the room and headed towards the bowels of the station. Kurz security patrols marched through the corridors, clearing them of vagrants and debris. It was a beehive of activity with all kinds of species frantically running through the passages.

Lax El Dem's looked as dingy as ever as Kal walked through the door. After his daily visits over the past several weeks, he could swear the bot was starting to be annoyed at his presence. He pressed the button on his chit to activate the hidden door, then headed into the secure back room.

"Any new contracts available for me?" Kal asked the bot.

"No, sir. There continues to only be one available."

"If I take this job, can you provide me access to leave? The Kurz have locked down the station." It was his only chance.

"I will need to check with upper management, sir. Please wait." The bot froze and a sign reading *PLEASE WAIT* replaced the pleasant holographic face.

The sign disappeared and a different voice came out of the bot. The intonation and tone made it clear that this was some sort of sentient creature, though the voice was modulated so Kal couldn't tell what species.

"Listen Human, we need to get this package delivered immediately, and you need to get the hell out of there. Seems like we have the perfect makings of a deal. We can probably get you out. But you need to leave now."

"What is the package?" Kal asked.

"Does it really matter at this point?" asked the voice.

"Probably not, but I like to know what to expect."

"All I can tell you is that it's a who, not a what. You want the job?" The voice was speaking quickly and clearly annoyed.

"Yes," Kal admitted.

"Great, head back to your ship. Wait for a bot to arrive in half a standard hour. It will have the package. If you're not ready when it arrives, this entire thing will go to shit. You got it?"

"Yeah, I got it. I'm setting a timer now and will be ready in exactly a half hour."

"Good, precise. I like you ex-military types. Now get out."

The bot's synthetic voice returned. "Sir, your account has been wired with half of the credits for this delivery. You will receive the other half upon acceptance of the package at the destination. As a reminder, the penalty for any malfeasances on an accepted contract is forfeiture of your life. Have a pleasant day."

Kal ran out of the building and contacted Sandra via implant as he rushed down the passageway to his next stop. *Sandra, you good?*

No, we're still missing Li Wei.

Kal swore to himself. *I'm sorry but you might need to leave him. I got us a way off the station, but there's not a lot of time.*

We can't do that, Sandra said. Even though the voice he heard came from her implant and was therefore emotionless, he could picture her face, with tears still streaming down her cheeks.

Kal slowed to a walk, swearing loud enough that several passersby turned to look at him.

Fine! I may know where he is. Meet me at the ship in twenty minutes.

Okay.

Sandra. Do. Not. Be. Late. Kal poured as much emphasis on the words as he could despite knowing her implant wouldn't translate it.

We'll be there. Sandra cut the connection.

Kal changed direction and ran to the station's landing bay. It was in complete chaos. Kurz patrollers, in full combat gear were posted near the entrance. Merchants and pilots crowded around them, pleading for them to open the bay so they could leave. Maintenance crews and bots rushed to and from the ships.

Kal worked his way around the crowd and hopped into *Annie* to grab his sidearm. He hurried to his cabin, opened the safe, and pulled out his pistol. One's type of weapon was a matter of personal preference among soldiers and mercenaries. Some swore by energy weapons, with their variety of settings and higher shot count, but nothing beat kinetic as far as Kal was concerned. A five-gram depleted uranium slug traveling at three times the speed of sound did an amount of damage that an energy weapon just couldn't match. After checking the charge level and ammunition, Kal ran back out the ramp, toward the drain.

Every backwater space port and station had a place that Kal liked to call the drain. It was where all the worst elements of society ended up. Places like these were where the true animals, the true savages of the galaxy lived. They were places where the authorities chose not to patrol and where gangs, druggies, and others roamed with impunity.

Due to his wanderings the past two weeks, Kal found the drain on Kirkira at the bottom of the station. The area was supposed to be only used for utility ducting and atmospheric and gravitational generators, but criminal elements had taken it over and set up their own anarchic realm. The dim corridors were littered with drug paraphernalia and unconscious addicts, some who seemed to already be dead. Kal kept one hand on his weapon as he walked through the narrow passageways, slowly scanning the makeshift structures, looking for a Human. His eyes lit on something—a body stripped naked and draped over a large pile of refuse.

Kal approached slowly; anything in the drain could be a trap. As he got closer, he confirmed it was Li Wei, and it looked like he might still be alive. His skin was pallid but lacked the waxy sheen of a corpse and his bare chest rose and fell uneasily. Kal kicked him in the ribs with his boot, causing the young man to groan slightly.

"Get up!" Kal yelled.

"Ughhhh…"

"Get up, now! I don't have time to explain, but we have twenty minutes to get to my ship or you're going to be stranded here, alone, for a very long time."

"Ughhhh…Ugh!" Kal kicked him in the ribs again, this time with a lot more force.

Li Wei turned himself over. A dried crust of vomit trailed down the side of his face and his eyes were bloodshot. It was hard for Kal to tell, but he was pretty sure the kid had pissed himself while on the refuse pile.

"Where is everyone?" Li Wei looked around and then slowly started to cry.

Unfortunately, this wasn't Kal's first time dealing with someone waking up from a bout with Rapturium. If he had ever thought about doing the stuff, seeing the after-effects had cured him of the desire. He was satisfied to ruin his life with alcohol and less destructive drugs instead.

"I can't explain now, but you need to get up." Kal caught movement out of the corner of his eye. The locals were starting to investigate.

"Hey, whatcha doin' over there?" A large Kurz walked over from one of the side corridors. His skin was almost the color of moss—a definite sign of drug use—and one of his legs had a large gash that looked to be infected.

"Don't know whatcha doin' down here, but this one is mine. He's a new client. I was gonna have some fun with him." The creature opened its mouth, revealing an inner beak.

"Nope, we're getting out of here. Or haven't you heard what's going on?"

"Oh, I heard, and no one is leaving here. So you might as well sit down and join him. We got everything you could want here."

"No one except us." Kal pulled out his sidearm and aimed it at the alien. "Now step back."

The Kurz jumped towards Kal, its claw-tipped arms poised to stab him in the chest. Kal took quick aim with his weapon and pulled the trigger. The round tore through one of the Kurz's arm, severing a claw, before punching through a conduit in a shower of sparks.

The creature's high-pitched howl rang out through the corridor, almost sending Kal to his knees. Kal pulled Li Wei up and slapped him, hard. He grabbed Li Wei's shoulders, pointed him down the corridor, away from the Kurz, and pushed him along. He stumbled but started to rapidly stagger forward.

The dilapidated doors lining the passageway opened and eyes peered out from windows, looking to see what had made the noise. Kal continued to alternate between supporting and pushing Li Wei along, keeping an eye behind them to see if the Kurz was following. It was still crouched on the street cradling its mangled arm as they turned the corner.

Kal thought they might have gotten away when two more Kurz appeared in front of them with their plasma rifles pointed at the Humans. Before the Kurz could react, Kal quickly got off two shots, hitting one in the chest and the other in the head. As he was falling, the second was able to get off a shot that grazed Kal's ear.

"Ah, crap." Kal could feel blood dripping down the side of his head.

"You okay?" Li Wei asked. He was limping along under his own power now.

"Just keep going. It's fine. We just need to get to the main levels."

They arrived in the central nexus of the station and continued running through the crowds. By the time they arrived at the landing bay it was even more chaotic than before. Spacers and merchants shouted and shoved one another as they rushed to their ships and pleaded with the large contingent of Kurz patrollers. Kal could see the three other Humans pressed together next to his ship, fearfully eying the anarchy around them.

Kal slapped the access panel and the back ramp lowered, letting them in. As soon as everyone was aboard, Kal closed the ramp and checked the time in his neural implant—five minutes left.

"Get him to the storage room on the second deck and tie him down on the bed. The computer can tell you where I keep restraining bands." Kal pointed toward the ladder leading to the second deck.

"Restrain him?" Klarissa asked. "Why?"

"Rapturium, it isn't something you can just stop. He will tear this ship apart once he starts to go through withdrawal."

"Hold on, you aren't doin' anything of the sort." Ekon stepped forward.

"Look, get your friend on the table and strap him down now or else you can find some other way out of here."

"Okay, okay." Klarissa started leading Li Wei toward the galley.

"Hey, you can't just restrain him like some sort of prisoner. He's our friend and we've known him a helluva lot

36

longer than you." Ekon stepped forward and looked down at Kal, their faces only inches apart.

"I don't have time to argue with you. You can either tie your friend down now and let me get us out of here, or get off my ship. There are no other options. We don't know if or when whatever destroyed the Sol and Khrdir systems will be here, and I don't intend on finding out."

Ekon stepped back, his eyes still narrowed. "Okay, okay, we play by your rules."

"Sandra, you know how to fly?" She looked shaken, and Kal needed to get her moving. He could see the signs of shock as she was still processing what had happened.

"I've only flown atmospheric. Did a little bit of training on fold drives to get ready for Base Camp, but that's about it."

"Good enough. Take this tablet and keep going through the preflight. I need to go outside and wait for a package."

"What package?" asked Klarissa as she stepped out of the galley.

"The package that is going to allow us to get out of here," Kal replied, deflecting the question.

He hit the access panel and stepped onto the pad. As his feet touched the ground, a large utility bot peeled to a stop in front of *Annie's* ramp. It was a nondescript gray rectangle with thrusters that kept it a couple of centimeters off the bay floor.

"Authorization needed," the bot instructed.

Kal pressed the tab on his Alliance chit, and the back door of the bot slid down, revealing a large storage compartment. Inside was a rectangular stasis chamber. The chambers were used to keep creatures stabilized and unconscious, usually in the case of severe trauma or injury, until they could be seen by the appropriate medical professionals. Normally they were transparent to allow medical personnel to see the patient. The windows on this one were opaque so it was impossible to tell who was inside.

The stasis chamber floated out of the storage bot, hovering at waist level. Kal contacted *Annie's* computer with his neural implant, and a simple loading bot rolled down the ramp and started to move the chamber into the bay.

"So, how do we get out here?" Kal asked the bot.

"Additional instructions are provided in this chit. It will destroy itself once accessed." A small door popped open in the front of the bot, and Kal grabbed the chit inside.

"Thanks." As he turned and started to walk back up the cargo ramp, alarms sounded throughout the shipyard. Kal's walk became a run as he continued through the ship's cargo bay, up the ladder to the second deck, and into the cockpit.

Sandra stared at the main viewscreen with a horrified expression as Kal entered the cockpit. *Annie* was tied into the Kirkira's external video feed and sensors, and on the main viewscreen was one of the alien ships that had wiped out the Sol system. It was on the outskirts of the asteroid belt but closing on the mining station *fast*.

Chapter Four

"It just...folded into the system," Sandra said, her breath coming out in short bursts.

"Did you do all the preflight checks?" Kal jammed the Alliance chit into a reader in the cockpit computer.

"Well, the ones I understood," she replied. "Why would they be attacking this station right now? We're in the armpit of the Kurz system."

"This station, as crappy as it is, provides about 20 percent of all the rare minerals for the Kurz. You capture that and you make it very hard for them to fight back." Kal knew that the minerals found on Kirkira were used for shipbuilding and more importantly in creation of armaments and fuel. If these creatures were attacking the station, then they were planning for a drawn-out war or occupation. Kal pushed his thoughts to the side and focused on how they were going to escape the station before it was destroyed or captured.

He pressed a button on the cockpit computer to activate the Alliance chit. A holo appeared on the viewscreen and a voice started to broadcast through the cockpit speakers. "Thank you for your assistance to the Alliance. The package you are currently storing must be delivered to our office on Caracas Station, New America with utmost haste. In order to facilitate your departure, we have primed a logic bomb to disable the station's defensive systems. It will render the system temporarily inoperable exactly four minutes after the completion of this message." A timer appeared on the secondary viewscreen, counting down from four minutes.

"What have you done?" Sandra looked at him, her eyes wide.

"I didn't do anything!" Kal couldn't help the sense of guilt that twisted his stomach as he spoke. "I didn't know they were going to do this, and I sure didn't know that this alien ship was going to be here."

"But there must be something we can do—there has to be." She trailed off.

"Look, I didn't know that this was going to happen. But when you make a deal with the Alliance, there's no going back—what's done is done. We can either leave or stay here, but I have no way to stop the bomb from going off." The timer on the piece of malicious code must've been set in motion when the chit was activated.

Sandra looked defeated. "What are you doing with the Alliance, anyways? I mean, I thought you used to be an EDF officer. What happened?"

"Lots. But I don't feel the need or have the time to justify myself to some kid I'm saving from an almost certain death."

Sandra's mouth snapped shut and slunk down in her chair. Kal started to go through the hot start routine with the tablet that Sandra had been using earlier. While he activated the main engines, a viewscreen in the cockpit displayed a stream of diagnostic data on the ship's systems. The Alliance timer continued to count down—less than a minute until the logic bomb went off.

"Everyone get to the cargo bay," Kal called out over the intercom. "You'll find jump seats on the bulkhead—get in one and strap yourself in. It's going to be one hell of a ride."

Sandra started to get up, but Kal pulled her back into the chair next to him. "Please stay here," he requested. "I need a co-pilot. Besides, as a future EDF pilot, you'll need to know how to do hot starts if the shit hits the fan."

Sandra sat back down and strapped herself into the co-pilot's seat, her face a mask. She carefully watched Kal as he continued to adjust the settings on the computer.

The Alliance timer reached zero, and Kal stopped what he was doing, waiting for something to happen. Abruptly, all the systems in the landing bay went out. The artificial gravity disappeared and the energy clamps holding the ships to the pad floor released, causing vessels and personnel to start floating inches off the ground. The energy field covering the bay door disappeared and the station's atmosphere shot out into open space. *Annie*, along with every other ship, item, and creature in the bay, was sucked into the void.

Kal tried not to look at the bodies floating past, at first writhing in agony, then quickly becoming lifeless. He focused on the cockpit panels in front of him, trying to plot a path out of the asteroids and away from the alien ships. Sandra let out a small whimper as the corpses drifted past, some of them writhing in agony before the cold void of space put them out of their agony.

Pushing the throttle to its max, Kal turned the ship away from the bay door, trying to avoid the debris. To his relief, he

41

saw some of the other ships that had been in the bay had the same idea and were starting to move away as well. At least there would be *some* survivors.

"Find the nearest somewhat safe fold point," Kal instructed Sandra. "We don't have time to be picky, so let me know if you see anything with a survival rate above 90 percent."

The fold drive allowed ships to open a wormhole through space and instantly transport a vessel from one location to another. The drives were highly susceptible to interference, particularly gravitational interference. The ship's fold computer calculated the chances of success when a ship folded based on sensor readings. The normal standard was eight nines, or 99.999999% but Kal was definitely willing to go with much less. It could also plot out points for the ship to fold from that would maximize their chances of success.

He focused his attention on making their way through the cloud of debris outside the landing bay door and into the asteroid field surrounding the station. The gravity of the station and asteroids made folding impossible until they were farther away. As they shot away from the station, small particles of dust and rocks from the asteroid belt began to hit the bulkhead shields of the ship, buffeting it slightly despite the inertial dampeners.

An alert rang out through the cockpit, and Kal saw small assault ships flying out of bays on the side of the large alien vessel. Kal turned *Annie*, trying to fly away from the station and the alien vessel. The assault ships slowed down and landed in the open landing bays of the mining station. Thankfully, none of them chased the fleeing civilian ships.

"They're taking over the colony," Sandra said.

"Yeah, looks like it." Kal nodded in agreement. "At least some ships got out of there before they landed, us included."

The enormous capital ship didn't launch any fighters. Instead, it engaged the fleeing ships with its point defense system, plasma cannons, and anti-ship missiles. Thankfully, the asteroids acted as a shield, saving several ships—though not all. Kal shuddered as he saw one of the civilian ships panic and try to fold out of the system. It never stood a chance this close to the asteroid belt and exploded in a ball of white light.

"I got it!" Despite everything, Sandra sounded almost triumphant. A series of coordinates popped onto the monitor in front of Kal. He quickly entered them into the ship's nav computer and turned towards them.

The strange ship was almost between the *Annie* and their new fold point. The capital ship was moving fast, but they should reach the fold point before it got close enough to fire on them.

Alarms blared through the cockpit again. "We have incoming!" Sandra shouted. "They launched three missiles at us. They're coming in fast."

Kal swore. The *Annie* was a simple merchant ship. It didn't have the advanced countermeasures or shields of a military vessel. Their only option would be to fold point before the missiles reached them. He had the computer display the fold survival rate of their current position on the main screen and the distance between them and the missiles on another.

"Looks like we're going to have to eyeball this," Kal said, his attention flitting between the two screens.

"What do you mean?" Sandra asked nervously.

"No way we're going to reach the fold point before we're hit. I'm going to hit the fold drive before the missile gets to us. Maybe, with luck, we'll get above ninety percent before that happens."

The survival rate bounced up and down but had a general upward trajectory as they flew toward the fold coordinates. It was at around forty percent and steadily moving towards fifty. Kal's hand hovered over the button to engage their fold drive.

"Missiles are about thirty seconds out," Sandra called out.

Their survival rate suddenly spiked to eighty percent, a result of some gravitation abnormality in the asteroid belt. Kal knew it was their best chance and slammed his hand down on the fold button. Instantly, the stars in the main viewscreen blinked as the ship's location instantaneously changed. They were now a light week or so away from the station. Their forward trajectory continued but was immaterial compared to the vast distance that they had just crossed with the fold drive.

Kal let out a sign of relief and looked over at Sandra with a weak smile.

"We did it," he breathed.

She nodded her head in agreement and let out a breath as her body slumped down in the co-pilot's chair. Sweat was still beading on her forehead.

Looking at the viewscreen in front him, Kal realized tears were rolling down his cheeks. He thought of the ships and bodies floating through space and felt guilt wash over him in waves, knowing that people had died so they could escape. He tried fruitlessly to reassure himself that he'd had no idea what would happen and that the bomb may have actually saved lives by allowing other ships to get away before the station was attacked. However, the sickening ball of guilt remained firmly lodged in his mind.

"Hey." Kal waited for Sandra to look over at him. "Thank you for your help. I didn't know that was going to happen. I—I'm sorry."

Sandra said nothing as she slowly pushed herself out of her chair and walked to the doorway. She turned around, as if to say something, then shook her head and walked out the door, leaving Kal alone.

Chapter Five

Kal felt a stinging pain across his cheek and woke to find that he couldn't move. His hands had been restrained behind his back, probably with the same bands that had been used on Li Wei. The faces of his three companions stared down, studying him like a puzzle.

Kal cursed himself. After their narrow escape, he'd been overwhelmed, and had told the others to get some sleep before heading back to his own cabin. Waiting for him was his emergency stash—he'd had it in case the next port or station didn't have a chem bar. There'd been no time to bring any supplies for the trip, so it was all he had. He'd gone through the whole thing in a matter of minutes—he was lucky he was still alive.

"Wakey wakey," Ekon said in a sing-songy voice. Kal guessed he was the one who'd slapped him awake. "We need answers, Kal. I just saw thousands die, and it looks like you're the one responsible." Ekon's eyes drilled holes into Kal's head. He could sense fear and anger in the man's voice.

"What happened on Kirkira?" Klarissa asked. "How did we escape when everyone else died?"

"Who are you really? What were those things? Why are you working with the Alliance? What is going on?" Ekon crouched down as he spat out the questions. His face was inches away and his breath, hot and humid, washed over Kal.

He had found Kal's pistol—Kal must have left it out in his stupor—and seemed to know how to use it. Sandra and

Klarissa stood behind him, hands on their hips, eyebrows raised expectantly while Li Wei slouched in a corner of the room, wringing his hands methodically.

"I already told you who I am—you saw my ID," Kal said. "I retired from the EDF several years ago and started working as a freelancer. As for those ships, why the hell do you think I know anything about them?"

Klarissa bent down. "It certainly seems to be a lucky coincidence that we left right as those ships arrived to take over the station."

"It was. If you think I'm working with whatever those things are that just wiped out Earth, then I don't know why we are having this talk."

"We don't think you caused it, but you seem to know more than you're letting on," Sandra said. "You've admitted that you're working with the Alliance. What sort of things do they have you doing? Are they part of all this?"

"That's not how the Alliance works," explained Kal. "It's not like I'm some sort of criminal mastermind. I took a contract with them so we could get off Kirkira. The Alliance doesn't have the power or motivation to destroy star systems. I don't know what you've heard about them, but most of the ones I've heard are bull. All I know is they hire people like me for small, less-than-legal jobs."

"Sure," Ekon laughed, "that's why we have a body in the cargo bay and there are corpses littering the space outside of Kirkira."

"What he's saying makes sense," Klarissa admitted. "I don't think the Alliance would have any reason to commit genocide. They want credits, right? Where are the credits in that?"

"They're still responsible for the deaths at Kirkira." Sandra looked white as a sheet.

Kal looked each one of them in the eye, trying to understand where their heads were. Sandra was still in shock, and Klarissa kept looking around, uncertain as to what to think. Li Wei hadn't moved from the corner and now was crouched in the fetal position. He was already suffering the first stages of withdrawal. But Ekon looked angry more than anything. Kal knew from experience that some people had to project their grief and guilt on others, that things couldn't just happen, *someone* had to be responsible. For Ekon, it was Kal who was responsible for everything, even if he didn't know why or how.

"I get it. I get why you're worried and don't trust me. But none of this is my fault, and I have no more idea what's going on or why it's going on than you. Look around you. I'm barely scraping by, even with my pension. I'm not a galactic criminal mastermind." Kal motioned around the dingy cargo bay with his head.

"I just don't understand how someone could go from being a Colonel in the EDF to…this." Sandra's voice betrayed her disappointment. "What happened?"

"A lot happened. None of it, almost none of it, criminal. And none of it is your business." Kal felt his patience running out as his mind tried to handle his hangover, his capture, and the events of the past day. He used his neural implant to send a series of commands to the ship. "Now, I've been patient with you restraining me on my own ship, but that patience is about to run out. *Annie* is tied to my neural implant, and I have shut down the ship's life support systems. There's no bypassing this, and even if there were, I doubt you have the abilities. Either you can let me go and we can talk like adults, or else we'll all die in the next hour."

Ekon kicked him in the ribs. "You son of a bitch."

"Ekon, come over here." Klarissa motioned to the hallway and the three of them walked through the door, whispering to each other.

After they were out of the room, Li Wei slowly dragged himself to where Kal lay on the floor and bent over him. "Hey, did you tell them where you found me? What I was like?"

"No, but you're going to need help. There is no Rapturium out here, and it's outlawed in Human-controlled systems, for reasons you've probably figured out first-hand. I had you tied up for your safety and ours. Most don't survive the withdrawal from Rapturium if they aren't restrained."

Li Wei looked down at himself and then at Kal. "I don't feel *too* bad right now. Why do people die if they aren't tied down?"

"They usually kill themselves or others," Kal responded matter-of-factly.

"Oh." Li Wei froze as he processed the information. Rapturium withdrawal was brutal. The addict would feel okay for the first several hours and then would go downhill quickly. People often went manic, trying to find anything for a fix. Kal decided not to mention that even when restrained, many people's minds did not survive the strain of withdrawal.

"I have some treatments that can reduce the symptoms, and we can strap you down with at least something to watch—that may help. You must have already started to feel the hunger, the urge, coming back. It will only get stronger over time," Kal said.

Kal heard Ekon shout in frustration outside the door and the three others walked back into the room. The two women looked at Kal nervously while Ekon stood behind them, fists balled.

"So, what happens if we let you loose?" Sandra asked.

"We go to Caracas Station outside of New America. That'll be where we part ways, thankfully."

"After all that's happened, how do we know we can trust you?" asked Sandra.

"I could ask the same of you. You three are the ones who put me in restraints. After all that's happened, we have to trust each other at some point. There are bigger things going on than just us four."

"What happened?" Li Wei asked as he looked at their faces. Kal realized that the man was blissfully ignorant of the devastation of Earth. In his state, Kal doubted that Li Wei even understood completely what had happened at Kirkira station.

"Release me, let's talk," Kal instructed. The four looked at each other until Sandra finally bent down and released the restraints.

Kal stood up, the pain in his head growing exponentially, and held his hand out to Ekon. "Thanks. I meant what I said—you can trust me."

"We'll see," Ekon muttered, slapping the pistol into Kal's outstretched arm.

For the next several minutes, the group explained to Li Wei what had happened to Earth. He was confused at first, not able to understand that the entire planet had been destroyed. Then he seemed to think there'd been a mistake. As Kal told the story, he had a hard time believing it himself, and he'd seen the holos and the ship with his own two eyes.

"So, do you have any idea why these…things are doing all of this?" Li Wei asked after he finally accepted what they were saying was true. "I know you're not involved, but surely you must have some thoughts, being former EDF and all."

"Nothing helpful. Whoever these people are, they were prepared, and they seem to be making plans to be here for the long term. They struck quickly, cutting off our command and control. Then they started to capture the industrial base with places like Kirkira Station. Most likely they're already working on consolidating power. The problem is, we don't know how many of them there are or how many planets and stations they've destroyed or captured. Our only move is to head back to Human space and see what we find."

51

The group sat reflecting on what Kal had said. The only sound in the cabin was the hum of the ship's systems.

"Restrain me," Li Wei said quietly.

"What?" Klarissa looked shocked.

"Restrain me. Now," Li Wei said looking each of his friends in the eye. "It needs to be done. With everything going on, I can't be a liability. I'm thinking somewhat clearly now, but who knows how long that'll last."

"You'll be fine man, you got this. You don't need to be restrained like some prisoner." Ekon slapped Li Wei on the back.

"The entire time you were talking—the entire time, I was thinking about how much I want Rapturium and what I would do to get it." Li Wei stifled a sob. "So many people are dead, and all I can focus on is my next hit."

"It has to be done," agreed Kal. "If we don't do it now, we'll pay for it later. Li Wei, I have something I can give you to help you sleep. At least for a bit. I've heard it's like hell when you're awake though—I'm not gonna lie."

Li Wei nodded. He slowly pulled himself off the floor and shambled across the hallway to the storage room. The rest of the group followed solemnly behind him. Li Wei set himself down on the metal table along the bulkhead. Sandra and Klarissa took a set of restraints off the floor and looped them around the table at his chest and calves. They pressed the button on each one, causing them to snap tight.

"Will this hold me?" he asked. "Feels loose."

"Yeah, the restraints tighten whenever you struggle. They only feel loose now because you aren't resisting," Kal reassured him.

"Thanks." Li Wei gave a weak smile. "Before we start this, something has been buggin' me. I kinda remember you finding me, and it was like a holo. I've never seen anyone shoot like that. Are you some sort of operative?"

"Nope, logistics all the way." Kal smiled back. "When I was first starting in the EDF I oversaw small arms procurement. Got pretty into them and started taking classes. Eventually I got good enough that I was on the EDF combat shooting team and even taught some advanced courses in Base Camp. You know some of the best shots in the galaxy have never put on a uniform."

"I thought you might have been Tac-I or something and just weren't telling us."

"Nope, just practiced a lot." Kal adjusted the galley monitor so that Li Wei could watch some of the holos in the ships memory banks when he woke. Then he pulled out a small med kit and injected him with a sleeping agent and pain medication. "I'll be back to check on you."

Kal left Li Wei with the others and went to the cockpit to update their flight plan. The trip from Kirkira to the New America system would consist of thousands of folds that he would need to plot out via the ship's computer. During transit, the only evidence they were moving would be the stars shifting on the viewscreen every few seconds.

Klarissa sidled into the cockpit and sat down next to him. "Kal, sorry for what happened back there. It's not that we don't trust you, but—"

Kal looked over at her. "It's exactly that, you said so yourselves. But I get it, you got a hell of a lot more than you bargained for when you met me on Kirkira. It isn't my fault, but with everything that has happened, it's understandable you'd be angry or afraid. Like I said, you'll have to learn to trust me. At least for a bit."

"I know, I know." Klarissa nodded. "You know, I had never even left Tiradentes before this trip." Tiradentes was the capital and largest city on New America. "Prior to meeting you, it had been different than I expected—not bad, just different." She chuckled.

New America was made up of several humongous metropolises. Each one was really a combination of multiple cities that merged into one large aggregation of Humanity. As a result of this planetary structure, most New Americans stayed within their own metropolis, the time and effort to leave not worth the effort.

"Where did you go before Kirkira?" Kal asked.

"A couple of worlds. We went to Norto and saw the royal palace there." Norto was the home planet of the Qudoru, a vaguely slug-like species. "Also headed over to Vernouth and climbed the glaciers." Vermouth was a Tounous colony.

"Why were you on Kirkira station anyway?" Kal asked. "Sounds like you had been to some amazing planets. A backwater mining station doesn't seem to be the best place for a vacation."

Klarissa gave an embarrassed smile. "Yeah, that was Ekon's idea. He said we needed to see all of the galaxy and not just the touristy spots. We picked it randomly when we were on Vernouth since it wasn't too far and there was a ship leaving that day. We were supposed to stop over for a few days and then head back to New America."

"Sounds like you were ready to go home," Kal observed.

Klarissa shrugged. "Yeah, I missed it. Sounds stupid, but it's true. Though now I wonder if there will even be a home to go back to. It's a cliché, but nothing will be the same again, you know?"

"Then maybe it's time to figure out if you're going to be the same as before."

Klarissa remained silent and quietly watched the stars blink on the cockpit viewscreen.

Chapter Six

The stars shifted a final time and New America appeared in front of them. The fold landed them as close as they could get to the planet, but it would still take them a half hour to land.

A chime went off, indicating they were being hailed. Kal felt a sense of relief as he saw a significant number of EDF fighters patrolling the system. During their ten-day journey to New America, he had privately wondered if they would get there too late and the planet would be surrounded by the monstrous black vessels, or even worse, not there at all. "They're on high alert. Not surprising."

Although he wouldn't say they were friends now, he'd gotten to know Sandra and Klarissa much better during their trip. When a ship was folding, there wasn't much to do. No one wanted to think about what might be happening as they traveled. Instead, they tried to find anything to occupy themselves. Kal spent most of his time with Sandra and Klarissa rewatching the holos stored on *Annie's* computer. When they'd exhausted all of them, they watched the ones the women had on their personal data chits.

Periodically, one of them would check on Li Wei. He spent most of the flight under sedation, but they would occasionally wake him up to check his cognition, change his catheter, and inject nutrients and pain meds into his system. The worst of the withdrawal symptoms were over, but Li Wei had clearly lost several kilos and his skin had turned sallow as his body did its best to destroy itself.

Ekon spent as much time as possible by himself in the crew quarters. Sometimes he would walk to the storage cabin to check on Li Wei or sit with the women when Kal wasn't around, and talk about their lives on New America. When Kal would tried to talk to him, Ekon responded with a grunt or ignored him.

Kal pressed the button to hail the planet. "This is Human registered ship *Queen Anne's Revenge* arriving from the Mining Station Kirkira. We're requesting access to Caracas Station."

"Roger, change course immediately to landing bay charlie. There you will be boarded and inspected. Upon arrival, your vessel will become property of the Earth Defense Force but will be returned to you upon cessation of hostilities." Kal was disappointed, but not surprised, he'd have to give up his ship. The EDF would need every single resource they could find if they were going to win.

"Acknowledged." Kal adjusted the onboard computer to change their heading. The computer would take it from there and automatically land in the station.

The heightened security made him nervous. Normally, a ship as small as *Annie* would simply land on the station without any inspection. He was reasonably confident that the Alliance documents accompanying their cargo would stand up to any scrutiny, but he couldn't shake the doubts in the back of his head.

Caracas Station was the main port for New America and the largest Human station now that Earth had been destroyed. It was an elongated prism, with landing bays making up each of the four large sides of the station and defensive cannons dotting the two ends. The large vessels that carried most of the goods in the galaxy were not able to enter a planet's atmosphere. Instead, they offloaded their cargo on the station and stevedores transported it to the planet via smaller atmospheric ships.

"We should probably get the others and let them know we're almost docked," Kal told Sandra as he headed out of the cockpit and down to the lower level.

Ekon and Klarissa were already waiting in the cargo bay. "We've arrived in the New America system. Security is tight, but those things haven't been here. We have about a half hour until we land on Caracas Station. Once we land, they'll inspect the ship for any intel and contraband. Looks like they are also going to confiscate my ship for the war effort."

Ekon hid a smirk by turning to study the stars on the bulkhead viewscreen.

"So, bottom line, grab your stuff and get ready. I wouldn't pack it up since they may tell us to lay it out for inspection," Kal advised. "I'm going to check on Li Wei."

Kal climbed up to the second level and entered Li Wei's cabin. The smell of body odor wafted into the hallway as the door opened. He was awake, watching a holo on the viewscreen and turned his head to look at Kal as he walked in.

"Howdy, Colonel." Kal hated the fact Li Wei used his former EDF rank. "I'm starting to feel a little less like crap. Have you seen this show? It was filmed back on Earth actually—in a city called Johannesburg." He frowned. "Guess there won't be any new seasons."

"Glad to see you feeling better. We're in New America and are maneuvering to land on Caracas Station. We need to get rid of those restraints—they may invite questions that we don't want to answer."

Kal pressed the button that released the restraints and pulled them off Li Wei. With a grunt and Kal's assistance, he was able to maneuver himself to a sitting position. He sat motionless for a few seconds, then fell off the table and vomited into a nearby waste bucket. Kal was glad Sandra had thought to put it there.

"Thanks for this." Li Wei said with a wry smile, still hunched over the bucket. "Honestly, I was in a bad place. I'm not right, don't know that I'll ever be, but at least I'm better than I was."

"It's a start," agreed Kal. "At least you're over the worst part of it. You'll need to go and get treatment as soon as you're back on planet. There are places that handle this kind of thing discreetly."

"Not sure what I'm going to tell my mom."

"Lie. That's what I always did whenever I did something stupid," Kal advised with a smile. "Now we need you to stand up and try out those legs. You haven't used them for a while, and your body has been through hell."

Kal put his arm under Li Wei and helped him slowly stand up. After several falls and stumbles, he was able to walk at least a few meters without hanging onto anything. While Li Wei continued to pace back and forth, Kal set about cleaning up the room and removing any trace of the temporary infirmary they'd set up.

He finished with a quick wipe down, then climbed back down into the cargo bay to find everyone had their gear laid out with varying levels of precision. He walked to his cabin and pulled out the few meager belongings he wanted to take with him. Kal pulled his tattered family photo from the wall and tucked it into his pocket. After some quick checks for anything out of place, he stepped back to the cargo bay to find that Li Wei had made his way there as well.

"One last thing," Kal said. "The package we're carrying is a high-ranking Human official who was hurt on Kirkira—a tragic accident involving a mining laser." He held up a chit he'd retrieved from a compartment in the stasis chamber, that had a forged bill of lading stored on it. "He's a diplomat from the Human embassy on Gorash who was touring the station when there was an accident. We're handing him over to the UEG here on Caracas for further treatment." He cleared his throat. "Everyone understand?"

"Not sure if I can remember all that. What if I forget?" Ekon asked with a wide-eyed look of innocence. "What if I accidentally say that we don't who's in there, but we were hired to smuggle them by the Alliance?"

Kal held his breath while he waited for the surge of anger to pass. Ekon had been more passive aggressive in the past few days. The fact that Kal had been spending a lot of time with Sandra and Klarissa probably didn't help anything. He knew he was being baited, so he tried to answer in as calm a voice as he could muster. "Well, then I guess we would all be accomplices in Human trafficking, a pretty serious crime. They'd lock all of us up for sure."

Ekon's smile faded.

"In fact," continued Kal, "the trials for these sorts of things last years, sometimes. And the defendants spend that time rotting in some cell—they're too much of a flight risk otherwise."

Ekon grunted and looked past Kal with an empty expression, a clear indication he'd tuned them all out and was looking at something on his neural implant. His bluff called, he decided to once again ignore Kal.

Minutes later, all the passengers of the *Queen Anne's Revenge* stood in the cargo bay as three EDF security guards went through their belongings. They were precise, starting from the cockpit and working their way back to the cargo bay. Two patrollers checked for contraband, opening drawers and looking under objects, while the third kept watch over the passengers and checked their IDs. Occasionally one of the inspectors would motion to another and they would confer over something that they'd found, eventually putting it back where it had been. Finally, they stopped in front of the stasis chamber, scanning it with a small handheld device to determine the contents.

"You have the documents to go with this?" asked the inspector.

Kal handed them over, keeping a pleasant smile on his face. He watched nervously as the inspector loaded the chit into a small tablet and inspected the contents.

"You got some dignitary in here, huh?" asked the man.

Kal nodded.

"Why are *you* transporting them? Seems like they should be on an EDF ship."

Kal quickly tried to think of a reason, but his mind was blank.

"There were no EDF ships in the area," volunteered Sandra. "The UEG hired us since they said time is of the essence. Said that he might lose the lower half of his body if they didn't get him back here as soon as possible."

Kal made a note to thank her later. He especially appreciated the made-up details; it added an air of authenticity to the story.

After a final look at the stasis chamber, the guard handed the chit back to Kal. "Okay, you're free to go. Make sure that you take any personal items with you. We can't guarantee that you'll get them back when we return your ship."

The patrollers walked down the cargo ramp. As soon as they were gone, everyone in the bay let out a small breath of relief.

Kal picked up his personal artifacts and stuffed them into his polymesh go bag, and slung it over his shoulder. He took one last look around *Annie's* cargo bay. She'd been a worthless pile of metal, but she'd been *his* worthless pile of metal. All five passengers slowly walked down the ramp, with the ship's cargo bot pushing the stasis chamber behind them.

The landing bay was enormous and was almost filled with ships of various makes and manufacture. Two large bay doors dominated one wall and several smaller openings dotted the wall opposite. Pilots, crew, and loading bots scampered around the bay floor, unloading ships under the careful watch of EDF soldiers. Each of the three main landing bays on the station was designed to hold several hundred ships. The fourth bay was for smaller atmospheric transports that ferried people and cargo between the station and the planet's surface.

"So, I guess that's it." Sandra fidgeted with her bag.

"Guess so." Kal wasn't too sure what to say.

Klarissa reached over and gave his arm a squeeze. She looked around the bay. "I can't believe we're back. When I left this station almost two months ago, I had no idea what we were in for. It feels strange returning, like visiting a place you used to go to when you were a kid. Familiar but smaller than you remember. I'm not quite sure what to do now."

"Go see your family and let them know you're okay. There isn't anything more important than that right now," Kal replied, his mind on the picture he had put back in his pocket.

"Maybe we'll see each other again. But if we don't, you know how to reach me, to reach us." Sandra dropped her bag and reached her arms around him in an embrace.

Li Wei reached out his hand and Kal gave it a shake. "Thanks for everything, Colonel. Truly."

"Just make sure you get the help you need." Kal was impressed with Li Wei's strength in his recovery and hoped he would see it all the way through.

Kal picked up his bag and then met Ekon's eyes. "I know we've had our disagreements, but I really do wish you the best."

Ekon grunted and walked toward one of the exits that led to the planetary transports. After a pause, the others turned and followed behind. Kal took a final look at his home for the past decade, then walked toward the exit that led to the commercial section of the station.

Unlike Kirkira, Caracas was relatively new. The hallways were well-lit and clean, with information kiosks at each intersection for lost travelers. Kal made his way through the crowd, almost all of them Human, with the stasis chamber floating behind him. He used the Alliance chit to navigate through the station. Eventually he found himself in front of an establishment called Ray's Souvenirs at the end of a deserted corridor. Kal entered the shop and used his chit to gain access to the back room.

"Hello sir, how may I help you today?" The bot was identical to the one on Kirkira, even using the same attractive Human face.

"I have a contract to take this"—he motioned to the stasis chamber—"to your office."

The PLEASE WAIT banner appeared above the bot's head.

"Well, we didn't think we would get the package when we heard Kirkira had been captured," said a distorted voice. "This is indeed good news. Based on recent events, we'll need this delivered immediately. I'm sending the drop off location to your implant. You need to head there right away." Kal heard a small tone in his head indicating he'd received a priority message.

The only information in the message were coordinates on the station. He was a bit surprised by them—they led to one of the levels reserved for EDF and UEG personnel. Kal had never heard of the Alliance betraying their couriers but couldn't shake the feeling he was being led into a trap.

He walked out of Ray's and took a lift to the command level. Kal watched the freighters and EDF capital ships docking and departing the station on the lift viewscreen. He found himself searching the stars, afraid to find the deadly black vessels coming toward them. *As if I would see them with my naked eye.*

The lift stopped near the top of the station and Kal stepped into a bright white hallway. He was definitely in EDF territory now—the advertisements and clamor of the lower levels had been replaced by the quiet hum of service bots going about their tasks. The walls were blank except for viewscreens placed at regular intervals, displaying standing orders or internal meeting schedules.

Kal finally arrived outside of what looked like a small utility room. He peered into the doorway. The room was featureless, the four off-white walls empty save for a single viewscreen, which was blank.

I don't like the look of this. Kal peered around and weighed his options. *Nowhere to go but forward.*

As soon as both he and the stasis chamber were fully in the room, the door shut behind them and a door on the opposite wall opened with a hum. A group of EDF soldiers rushed in, weapons drawn, and flanked Kal on both sides. He raised his arms above his head. The small sense of unease exploded into a major stomachache as he saw the phalanx of uniformed soldiers.

Behind them strode an EDF officer, a major general from the stars on her collar. "Colonel Kal Norman! What are the chances?" Major General Shreya Ahuja practically beamed at him. "When I heard you would be delivering this package, I almost crapped my pants. I mean what are the odds? Sorry for this little show," she waved at the soldiers with their weapons pointed at Kal's head, "but since you've been cavorting with the wrong element for so long, we couldn't take chances."

"Shreya, how are you?" Kal eyed the guards. "Maybe you can tell them to stand down."

"Of course, of course." Shreya snapped her fingers, and the soldiers lowered their weapons. "So, how's retirement treating you?"

"I think you already know." Kal lowered his arms slowly.

"Yeah, gotta be pretty desperate to take a contract from the Alliance," she said with a conspiratorial smile. "But you also gotta be desperate to hire them too."

"So, what's in this?" He nodded his head toward the chamber. "Seems like you went through a lot of trouble to get it. Why is the EDF working with the Alliance?"

"So many questions, so little security clearance." Shreya gestured toward the door behind her. "Follow me." Kal followed the general through the door. On the other side was another passageway, this one filled with uniformed EDF soldiers. The room they had been in was a sort of gateway between the publicly accessible area of the floor and the more tightly controlled and populated inner corridor.

"A while back we reached a sort of agreement with the Alliance. We had begun to make a dent in their operations, but it became apparent we didn't have the reach to get to all their assets, especially outside of EDF space. Although they don't play by the letter of the law, they don't cause too much of a problem for us. The Alliance offered the Secretary General a deal—they would stop their more illicit activities in Human-controlled space and provide their services at a discounted rate, and we would stop trying to take them down."

"A deal with the devil," Kal said.

"Perhaps," conceded Shreya, "but a very useful one."

Kal followed her through a reception area and into a rather impressive office. The room was lined with synthetic wood and contained a large desk filled with souvenirs of a long career of service, a seating area, and a viewscreen that looked out onto the planet. From this distance New America looked like a quilt-divided into large zones, each dedicated to a different purpose—living, commerce, manufacturing, and so on.

"We've been able to use this deal to get intel and items that would have been very difficult to get otherwise." Shreya sat down at the desk. "One of them is the package that you brought here. Although we had no idea how valuable it would be when we originally heard about it."

"What is it, or should I say, *who* is it?" Kal examined the plaques on the wall—each was a memento from a previous unit or fleet she had served with. It was a common custom among senior military officers to have offices filled to the brim with keepsakes from their career.

"Tsk, tsk. Like I said, so little clearance." Shreya noticed the plaque that Kal was studying. "Ah, home fleet. That seems like forever ago." The smile disappeared from her face. "Back when there was a home fleet."

She continued, "It was a shame to see you go, but we all understood why you left. With everything you went through, it was no surprise."

Kal turned to face her. "Doesn't feel like I'm the only one who has gone through tragedy anymore, though. Now we've all lost something."

"Yes, we have," Shreya agreed. She stood up from the desk and walked to a small credenza nestled against one wall.

"Still drink brandy? Perk of being a flag officer is you get the best liquor. Maybe if you'd known, you would've stayed in."

She poured two glasses, handed one to Kal, and sat down in the seating area taking the bottle with her. He took the seat across from her and raised his glass.

"To old times, as they say."

"Indeed." Shreya downed the liquor unceremoniously. "So, I'll cut to the chase. You saw what happened to Earth. You can imagine what we are going through now. The EDF lost half its strength in seconds, and now we're fighting an enemy that we know nothing about. We need people—more specifically, we need you."

"I've been out almost a decade," Kal said. "Doesn't seem like I have a place in all this anymore. I mean, I spend most days either consorting with the scum of the universe or else recovering from a hangover."

"But that is exactly why we need you. Humanity is not going to defeat this enemy on its own or by sticking to the rules. We're going to have to work with other species. We're going to have to work with people we may not normally want to, like the Alliance, or worse. But that's where you come in. We don't have people with your skills and who've also been immersed in these alien cultures. Hell, my top foreign affairs officer has spent a total of six months outside of EDF space."

Shreya's eyes had taken on a steely look. "Not to mention that you are one of a handful of people that has actually seen one of these ships with their own eyes and lived to tell the tale. We're not going to win this war with what we've got now. And this isn't just a war—it's survival." She leaned forward in her chair. "I can't force you to join; you're too old for us to conscript. But what else are you going to do, sit on this station and watch from the sidelines? I know you better than that, Kal. I saw you when you were at your best. If you agree, I'll swear you back in right now and give you provisional security clearance. You can be back in the fight. Hell, I'll even throw in the brandy." Shreya picked up the bottle and made a show of offering it to Kal.

He leaned back and slowly turned the crystal glass in his hand. He knew what his answer would be, what it had to be, but found it hard to say the words. "So, what exactly would you want me to do if I did come back in?"

"Well, for now, what you used to do. I never met someone who was better at getting people what they needed, and right now we need a lot of things. You in, or what?"

"Yeah, I'm in. God help me."

"Congratulations, Colonel Norman. Here's your brandy." Shreya put the amber bottle into his hands.

"Thanks." Kal put it down on the table in front of him. "So, what's next?"

"Well, for now, get yourself cleaned up and get a uniform. I'll have an aide help you with all the admin stuff. Do it quickly, though—no time to rest."

Kal finished his glass, set it on the table, and stood up. "You keep the brandy," he said. "You're going to need it more than I do."

Shreya smiled. "Ain't that the truth."

Chapter Seven

After the meeting with Major General Ahuja, an aide escorted Kal to his new quarters. He unpacked his bag and looked around the suite; it was much more luxurious than anywhere he'd stayed for a long time. It had a decent-sized bed with the classic EDF gray covers, a small couch, and his own private bath. Even on enormous stations like Caracas, space was at a premium, and the room was large enough that it was probably intended for a general. Shreya was either short on senior officers or trying to butter him up.

Giving the room a final once-over, Kal used his neural implant to locate the fabrication facility. This was where many items for the station were created using metal, plastic, and other raw materials. The fabricators could create simple items quickly, although there still were many complex items that had to be made by a dedicated facility. The onsite replicators scanned him to take his measurements and then fabricated a complete set of EDF uniforms in a matter of minutes.

Kal had always disliked the EDF uniform. Comprised of a pair of gray trousers, white dress shirt, and tight-fitting gray coat, it made him feel like the concierge at a high-class hotel. Three diamonds rested on his shoulder boards, signifying his rank of colonel. The rows of ribbons on his chest detailed his accomplishments and the campaigns he'd been a part of.

Kal walked back to his cabin to drop off his new uniform. Once there, he couldn't resist trying it on. He studied himself in the viewscreen, frowning as he noticed the toll the past decade had taken on his body. His midsection bulged against the uniform, and his black hair was tinged with an ever-increasing peppering of gray. Seeing himself, now old, wearing an EDF uniform felt both familiar and vaguely unsettling. He had worn it through some of the darkest periods of his life. It was a reminder of both what he had lost and how far he'd fallen since then. When Kal left the service, he hadn't looked back; in some ways the uniform made him feel like he was regressing. Shaking his head, he left the uniform on and walked out the door. For the first time in a while, he had bigger things to think of than himself.

He walked across the corridor to the technical support station and integrated his neural implant with the EDF system. It allowed him access to restricted networks and equipment, as well as allowing them to track his movements.

A chime sounded in Kal's ear via the neural implant summoning him to Shreya's staff meeting. It appeared she was putting him to work immediately.

It was only a few minutes' walk, through the central command and control corridors to get to the briefing room. Most of the higher-level officers had quarters in the same zone so they were available in case of emergency. Their quarters, support facilities, offices, and meeting rooms were all located nearby, making it easy to travel and complete errands without having to get on a lift. Walking the hallways, Kal noticed the soldiers he passed still seemed to be adjusting to their new reality. It had been three weeks since news of Earth's destruction reached New America, and everyone was still processing what it meant for them. Soldiers sometimes paused in what they were doing, staring off into space, or looking at blank viewscreens, their bodies still as statues. Several of them in stained and wrinkled uniforms that had not been changed in what appeared to be days.

Major General Ahuja's briefing room was rectangular with a large, faux wood oval table in the center. Much of the staff was already in the room, seated around the table in sleek metal chairs. Junior officers and enlisted sat in a second ring of chairs that lined two of the walls of the room. A viewscreen took up the entire wall opposite Kal and displayed a live feed of New America. He quietly took a seat against the wall, next to a young female captain whose nametape read Chen.

"So, what's this meeting all about?" Kal asked the captain. "I just got an alert to be here."

"It's General Ahuja's morning brief, sir," Chen responded. "Ever since the incident, we've been holding full-staff briefings twice a day." She paused. "Are you here as part of an offensive?" She looked hopeful.

Kal shook his head. "No, nothing like that. Just an old fart who was in the wrong place at the wrong time." Chen smiled. "Pleased to meet you. Name's Kal. I'm not exactly sure what I will be doing here, but glad to be part of the team." He held out his hand.

She hesitantly shook his hand with a surprised look on her face. "Pleased to meet you...sir. Pardon my saying so, but you don't look familiar. I thought I knew every senior officer on General Ahuja's staff."

"You must be intel."

Chen cocked her head. "Why do you say that?"

"You ask so many questions." Kal laughed. "I'm new to Caracas Station, just arrived today in fact. General Ahuja recommissioned me into the EDF after being out for a decade." He clapped his hands together. "So, when will this little shindig get started?"

"Now." Major General Ahuja walked in front of Kal and sat down at the head of the table. "Let's begin, everyone. Before we do, I want to introduce you all to Colonel Kal Norman. He's an expert in alien cultures, mostly from getting kicked out of every dingy bar in the galaxy." She chuckled at her own joke. "Additionally, he's an expert logistician, which will come in *very* handy since our supply lines from Earth are gone. I need not remind you all how important things like food, fuel, and ammunition are in a war. Colonel Norman will be invaluable in getting those things for EDF forces."

Ahuja paused. "Also, he's the person who delivered the prisoner from Gorash."

All eyes in the room turned toward Kal. He sensed Chen looking at him with a newfound curiosity. He raised his arm and feebly waved around the room.

"So, what or who did I deliver to you anyways?"

"She was a former United Earth Government attaché at the embassy," Chen explained. "Someone attempted to take her life, right before Earth was attacked. We know that she was funneling information to them, though we don't know what she told them or why."

"Captain Chen, what have you learned from the prisoner?" Ahuja asked.

Chen got out of her chair and walked to the front of the room and stood next to the general. The holo on the viewscreen began pulling out to show the entire New America system, then several star systems, and finally a significant portion of the galaxy. Each major system had a lightly shaded halo surrounding it, the color indicating which species controlled it. The Human sector of the galaxy was a grouping of forest green. Kal could see the neighboring species: the Kurz, Torgham, Qudoru, Tounous, Goro, and X'Ado, each highlighted in a different color. Small symbols also hovered next to each star, indicating key bits of information such as estimated forces, habitable planets, minerals, and other pieces of strategic information.

This tactical map of the galaxy was something Kal remembered from his days in the EDF. However, leaning forward, he saw that there were several systems that had a red cross superimposed over them, something he had never seen before. Both Sol and the Gorash system had these crosses over them, which Kal realized was an indication the system had been destroyed. Shocked, he realized the same crosses were over the Norto and Gedorhan systems, the capitals of the Qudoru and Tounous respectively. Additionally, there were several systems with a solid red circle surrounding them, which he took to mean they had been captured.

"Wait," Kal interrupted. "Are Norto and Gedorhan destroyed?"

"You didn't know?" Ahuja shook her head. "Damn, of course you didn't. You've been folding here for what, ten days?" She didn't wait for a response. "Captain Chen, please fill Colonel Norman in on everything that has happened since Earth was destroyed."

"Yes, ma'am," Chen responded and turned her body slightly to face Kal. "As you know, an unknown fleet of ships entered the Sol System and destroyed Earth twenty-six days ago. Approximately three days after that, Norto, the capital of the Qudoru, was destroyed. The next day, Adoran, capital of the X'Ado, was wiped out. Two days later Gedorhan was obliterated, and then Gorash two days after that."

"Do we even know who did this? What are these creatures?" Kal ground his teeth in frustration.

"We don't have much—nothing, really. Our commanders have started to call them the Ukhel, an ancient word for death. We don't know where they come from or what they want. It appears they intend to stick around though."

"Why do you say that?" Kal asked.

"They've begun capturing colonies and mining stations rather than destroying them. Our mining station on Homestead was captured after a brief skirmish. The Qudoru have lost two mining stations as well as one of their colonies, Trako. The Ukhel also captured the Tounous colony at Rhokel. Finally, we recently received word that the Kurz mining station Kirkira was also captured."

"I can confirm that last one. I was there," Kal affirmed.

Chen raised an eyebrow. "Very interesting, sir. I'll need to talk with you later about what you saw. Also, your ship's sensor data could be very interesting." She continued, "Unfortunately, the Ukhel are destroying communications probes as they enter the systems they capture, preventing us from learning anything about what they're doing with these planets and stations."

"It's also disrupting the entire probe network," a major added. "The network wasn't designed to handle a situation like this. The probes are preprogrammed to automatically follow a specified network path between planets and stations. The Ukhel are eliminating the links in the network, causing delays and loss of communication."

"With both the communications network being slowly decimated and several home worlds destroyed, the flow of information has been brought to a complete stand still," Chen continued. "We're operating almost completely blind at this point."

"Any updates on where we think they are or what their next move is?" Ahuja asked.

"Nothing specific, ma'am. We expect them to continue to capture additional systems." Chen sighed. "But without more information, we can only guess where they'll go next, but they seem to be moving rapidly to consolidate their power." Chen gave a small shake of her head.

"What about New America?" asked Kal. "This system must be high on their priority list."

The other people in the room looked around nervously. "Yes," replied Ahuja, "that's something we've considered. As you probably noticed, we have all forces in the area on full alert."

"We're using every single resource available to make sure they won't capture the planet," said a general seated at the table.

"So, back to the prisoner Captain Chen. What's she been able to tell us?" Kal could tell Ahuja was frustrated as she asked the question.

"The asset that Colonel Norman delivered has provided us some interesting intelligence—though she has proven to be less valuable than we hoped. She was able to confirm that the Ukhel have been watching us for years at least, gathering information about the politics, fleets, and cultures of Humans. All communication that they had with her went through an intermediary, so she never talked directly to the Ukhel. We do not know what they look or sound like, but they certainly seem to be meticulous in the way they operate."

"They've been watching us, waiting, and then just attacked out of nowhere?" Kal thought back to what he had been doing for the past few years and shuddered to realize these creatures had been planning Earth's destruction while he was getting wasted in chem bars.

"Exactly." Chen nodded. "Based on what the asset has told us, information from other species, and their method of attack, we think the Ukhel have been making indirect communication to spies across multiple interplanetary governments, the UEG being no exception."

"Was the prisoner able to tell us why they attacked? Why us or any of the other species?" a general sitting next to Ahuja asked.

"Unfortunately, no, ma'am. Right now, our best guess is that they saw this portion of the galaxy as vulnerable to attack." Chen gave an apologetic look. "A target of opportunity."

"So, we still don't know anything." Ahuja gave a snort of frustration. "Is there anything more the prisoner could tell us? Where they come from for example? There's no record of these ships in existence."

"Again. Unfortunately, no. Our best guess is that they're a nomadic species that's been making their way across the galaxy."

"That doesn't seem to align with what you just said," said a colonel. "They're capturing stations and planets. Nomads wouldn't do that."

Chen balled her fists. "That's true, sir. But it's the only explanation we have so far. We just don't have the intel we need right now."

"So, we have a superior enemy force and we don't know where they are, what they'll do, what their goals are, or where they're from. Does that about sum it up?" Ahuja asked.

Chen bit her lip and nodded.

"Just fantastic." The general leaned back in her chair. "Atkins, what is the latest status on the defense posture for the New America system?"

General Atkins went through the intricacies of the patrols and inspections in the system. A succession of officers went after him, each briefing on a different aspect of the war effort. Kal closed his eyes. He had hoped that by being back in the EDF, he would be reassured, that he'd see some sort of grand plan. It was disappointing to find out that even at the highest echelons of the EDF, they were grasping at straws and operating blind.

After the final officer had briefed, Ahuja took a deep breath and then swept the room with her eyes. "Thank you all. Things look dark right now, darker than they ever have for Humanity. We all have lost people in our lives, people we cared about, at the hands of these Ukhel. Based on what we've heard, this enemy won't stop, won't parlay, and won't relent—so neither can we. Our focus is to continue preparing for an attack on New America. We will continue to commandeer all civilian ships and retrofit them for the war. We're operating blind, so Captain Chen, I need you to figure out a way to re-establish communications and figure out where the enemy is and what they're doing. Continue sending out communications and exploration probes to as many systems as you can. The fog of war is thick, and we need to disperse it."

Captain Chen nodded. "Yes, ma'am."

Ahuja stood from her chair. "Okay folks, we're one of the last lights for Humanity—hell, for the galaxy. You know your orders and what must be done. This is our last stand and we must win."

At the last word, Ahuja stood up and started to walk out of the room. As she passed Kal, she whispered, "follow me."

Kal followed her back to her office. Once the door slid shut, she collapsed in the chair behind her desk while Kal sat across from her. Shreya sat quietly, her mouth slightly open, and looked at the viewscreen with her back to Kal. He couldn't tell if she was using her implant or just taking a moment to recover. The enormity of her responsibilities was not something Kal envied.

With a deep sigh, Ahuja spun to face Kal. "I know it doesn't seem like it, but the prisoner you delivered was critical. Her name is Nicole Bergeron. She was a low-level military attaché to the Kurz government. Apparently, she was contacted by the Ukhel through an intermediary a couple of years ago. In exchange for some credits"—Shreya's mouth twisted—"she began funneling them information about our diplomatic relations, military plans, and anything else she could get her hands on. Immediately before the destruction of Sol, the Ukhel attempted to assassinate her. They also carried out several other assassinations across the galaxy that we assume were other informants. Nicole was the only one who survived, as far as we know. When our embassy staff learned of what had happened, they tried to extricate her back to Earth in the most discreet way possible—not knowing that the Ukhel were already moving to attack."

"Why would the Ukhel assassinate her if they were about to attack anyway," asked Kal. "Seems like a waste of resources."

"You heard Chen's briefing—because they are utterly ruthless. Our guess is that once they had given the greenlight for the attack, they wanted to make sure we had nothing to go on. The very fact that she survived and can talk to us is a victory. She's already given us immeasurably more information than we had just a day ago—as paltry as it is. As far as traitorous scumbags go, the gal isn't half bad. At least she feels remorse for what she did. We have her on suicide watch now—turns out that her family was on Earth when it was destroyed."

That hit a bit close to home for Kal; he grimaced, thinking of his own family. Shreya quickly changed the subject. "How are you adjusting to military life again? I recall that you never really were all that into the 'yes ma'am, no sir' stuff. You've been out long enough that I'm surprised you even remember how to wear your uniform."

"Took me several hours, but I managed." Kal smiled thinly. "So now that you have me, what am I going to do?"

"Funnily enough, now that I have you, I am sending you away. We'd planned on putting you in charge of the logistics network here. However, headquarters is rightly concerned that New America is a priority target for the Ukhel, and they say they have a more pressing need for you anyways. Key

83

assets and resources are being reallocated from here to the EDF's secondary headquarters. With Earth gone, our most pressing concern is our supply lines. As you heard in the briefing, communications are crap right now and supply lines have also been decimated. We're having issues simply being able to feed our people, much less win the war."

"Lots of demand but no supply," said Kal. "Any chance other species could help us? Surely we can get some message to some who would be willing to help."

"Unfortunately, no. The other species that were attacked can't even help themselves and everyone else is standing firmly on the sidelines. We've been working with the Alliance to see what we can find, but they can only provide a fraction of what we need. This chit"—she pulled it from a compartment in her desk—"contains the coordinates and pertinent information for Kapustin Station. It's a research station that was also intended to be used as an alternate headquarters for the EDF, although I think no one really ever thought we would need it. You will be leaving tomorrow to meet up with General Sato's staff. He's the supreme commander of all EDF forces left in the galaxy."

Kal took the chit from her hand and placed it in one of the service pockets in his uniform.

"General Sato will give you more detail on your assignment when you get there, but in general your job will be to make sure our headquarters has the means to fight. You've gone from being a space bum to being critical to Humanity's survival. Quite the step up in a few days." She chuckled dryly. "A squad of recruits will be joining you tomorrow. Base camp has been relocated to the new headquarters for obvious reasons. One final thing—you'll be taking a security detail and Bergeron with you. I have told the security detail that you are to be given access to talk with her during the trip. See if you can get any more information. I think she has been forthcoming, but I know from my time in counter intel that there are always more nuggets of information...if you ask the right questions."

"Understood. I'm not looking forward to it, but I understand." Kal leaned back in his chair. "We'll be best friends by the end of the trip. What about you? I mean not only as the leader of the EDF around New America, but just you, Shreya. What are you going to do?" Kal remembered her as being extremely self-contained. A rock amidst chaos. That façade was starting to crumble.

She sighed. "I don't know, Kal. I try not to think of it. I mean I never had a family of my own like you, but still, almost everyone I knew or cared about was in the Sol System. Sometimes, I get the feeling a blade is inches from my neck, and I wonder what there's left to fight for. But then you know what happens? I get pissed. These Ukhel took everything from us, for no reason." She wiped a small tear away from the corner of her eye. "I say it is about time for us to start taking."

Chapter Eight

Kal was playing hide and seek with his daughter, Lan Fen, in the backyard of their home on Earth. Sunlight streamed through the trees, creating a wavering mosaic of light and shadow on the lawn. She hid in the acacia, giggling to herself as he pretended not to know where she was. He crept toward her hiding place, placing his feet carefully, gently pushing aside a branch, and jumping into the clearing to find it empty. Her faint giggles, which he'd heard seconds before, had disappeared.

Worried, Kal decided to ask his son and wife if they knew where she was.

He ran to the house and barged through the blue front door, calling for Stephen and Li Na. There was no response. The kitchen counter and dining table were covered with dust, the bright yellow paint on the walls was cracked and faded. Kal searched the house, calling for his family, and then in desperation, for anyone. As he climbed the stairs to the second floor, he heard faint crying. The stairs creaked each time he placed a foot on a step, echoing his own pain. The picture frames on the wall, which normally contained family photos, were empty and hung at odd angles.

He reached the top of the stairs and rushed down the hallway. The kids' rooms were empty. Their beds had been stripped to the mattress and their desks were bare. As he neared the bedroom he shared with Li Na, the cries grew louder, and he felt a painful stabbing in his ears.

Kal took a deep breath and placed his hand on the door. The cries separated, and the voices of Li Na and their children each became distinct. Kal took a deep breath and pushed the door open…

The wails slowly transformed into the peal of the alarm he'd set the night before. Kal opened his eyes, sat up, and staggered to the bio recycler. As he looked at himself in the viewscreen mirror, the face of an elderly stranger stared back. He studied the folds around his eyes, the wings of gray growing in his salt and pepper hair, the frown lines around his mouth. It was a face that had seen more than its fair share of sadness. The face of a man who'd been through hell and back. He splashed water on himself, trying to clear his mind, and pulled on his uniform, struggling to get it fastened around his midsection. His go bag, which contained the few things that he could still call his, was draped over a chair. He grabbed it and headed to the landing bay, putting the nightmare behind him.

From what Kal could tell, landing bay alpha was identical to charlie, where *Annie* had landed, except that it was only inhabited by soldiers and EDF ships, mainly fighters. Kal made his way to the sleek corvette that was to be his transport to Kapustin Station. The ship was about fifty meters in length, with a low profile and aerodynamic shape that told him it was also an atmospheric craft. Two large engines framed the rear cargo ramp of the matte-gray ship. Their safety lights blinked, indicating they were in the process of spinning up. A dozen new recruits stood in a loose formation at the base of the ramp. Kal sucked in his breath as he saw Ekon standing in the gangly formation.

"Group, attention!" shouted a large blonde-haired staff sergeant at the front of the group. It took Kal a moment to remember his military courtesies—after a decade away, these were the sorts of things that tripped him up. "Carry on!" he responded as he walked up to the sergeant.

He waited for the instructor to put the recruits at ease before speaking. "Good morning, sergeant. Everyone here for departure?"

"Yes sir, all present. The head pilot is Captain Garcia. He's going through the pre-flight checks with the other crew members. The prisoner is onboard. We've secured the smallest stateroom for her and will have an armed guard outside at all times."

"Thank you, Staff Sergeant…" Kal looked down at his nametape. "Jones. I'm going to stow my gear."

"Sounds good, sir. We should be leaving once the flight crew has completed their pre-flight checks."

Kal climbed up the ramp and walked through the cargo bay. After flying in *Annie* for so long, he was taken aback by the polish and technical sophistication of a ship that was not relying primarily on luck. Every inch of the interior screamed efficiency and care. After peeking into the galley and crew quarters, Kal made his way up the narrow stairs to second deck. He passed the doors to the two staterooms, one for him and one for their prisoner, before reaching the cockpit.

Walking through the door, he was greeted by the warm azure glow of a top-of-the-line navigation system. The three soldiers inside were calling out the various controls and systems to each other. A middle-aged woman with dark brown skin and warrant officer's insignia on the collar of her flight suit noticed Kal as she was turning to examine one of the displays.

"Howdy sir, welcome to the *Oruc*." As was custom, pilots were generally lax when it came to military courtesies. Frankly, it was something that Kal didn't mind at all. "I'm Chief Taisha Kanumba, this is Captain Karl Garcia, and this is Lieutenant Jae-ho Park."

The other two gave quick nods and continued with their work. They were clearly in the middle of a process they had done many times before, efficiently going through the ship's systems and speaking in the strange slang that was unique to pilots. As a pilot himself, Kal took a moment to appreciate the ship and gave silent thanks that he hadn't seen it before piloting *Annie*. Otherwise, he never would have been satisfied with her.

"Captain Garcia, all passengers accounted for and ready for takeoff," Jones's voice came over the ship's intercom.

"Sir, we're almost ready for departure, just a few more checks," Garcia said. "You can go ahead and make your way to your cabin to get settled in if you like. Out the door and the second right." Kal knew a polite dismissal when he heard one and appreciated the pilot's tact in delivering it. The man probably had dealt with high-ranking officers before and knew how to handle them.

"Thank you. You may take off when ready." Kal turned and walked toward his stateroom. As the highest-ranking officer, and commander of the ship, Kal had been assigned the largest stateroom. A guard stood across the narrow corridor, keeping watch over the prisoner in the other one. The remaining officers and Chief Kanumba would be in the three cabins while the recruits had bunks in the crew quarters.

The stateroom was much smaller than his quarters on Caracas Station, but larger than the cabin he'd lived in for the past several years on *Annie*. The wood and brass accents gave the room an almost luxurious feel despite the small size. Kal shoved the contents of his go bag into the drawers of the built-in dresser.

The ship lurched, causing him to stagger. He was surprised by the rather clumsy takeoff from the flight crew— he would have been smoother taking off in *Annie*. Kal lost his footing and fell to the ground as the ship shuddered violently. An alarm blared over the intercom system, followed by an automated warning filled with a preternatural sense of calm: "Attention all passengers, we are currently under attack. Please brace yourself for emergency maneuvers."

Kal rushed out of his stateroom and into the cockpit to find the flight crew frantically completing their take off procedures. They probably didn't appreciate the additional set of eyes, but he was only a couple days removed from flying himself and wasn't able to shake his urge to be at the controls.

Kal slid into the commander's console behind the two pilots and quickly brought up the tactical map. Four red icons, denoting Ukhel capital ships, had folded in close proximity to the planet. The ships had wasted no time in starting their attack and he could see the red dots of their missiles on the map as they flew at the EDF forces.

As opposed to when the Ukhel had arrived at Earth and Kirkira, the local security forces were ready and immediately engaged. They returned fire, letting loose with a barrage of plasma and kinetic weapons while fighters swarmed around the large enemy ships. The EDF plasma bolts splashed off their energy shields without making any sort of noticeable impact and the Ukhel point defense systems were proving equally adept at destroying the EDF missiles and picking off any fighters that came too close.

"How's it going?" Kal asked. He had to restrain himself from jumping forward and pushing one of the pilots out of their seats.

"Almost there," Kanumba replied.

Kal could see pilots running across the landing bay, jumping in their ships, and speeding out of the two large bay doors, racing to join the battle.

Eight EDF capital ships were also engaged with the attackers. Kal slammed his fist against his armrest as a missile made it through the Ukhel point defense and detonated against the side of the ship. The armor plating gave way and spewed atmosphere and debris into space. Despite the damage, they continued to maneuver and returned fire with a battery of plasma cannons, destroying several EDF fighters.

It quickly became clear that they were outmatched. One by one, the EDF battleships and carriers were disabled or destroyed by the superior firepower of the smaller enemy fleet.

"Do we have any weapons?" Kal asked. He shuddered to think of the lives he had just seen wiped out.

"Yes," Garcia replied, "but they won't make a dent in these Ukhel ships. Also, we've been ordered to stay in the landing bay in order to allow the fighters to launch." He clearly was also frustrated watching the action unfold without being able to do a thing.

"I guess we wait." It was the last thing Kal wanted to do.

He tried not to fidget as the Ukhel ships began to move towards the station. Six of the eight EDF ships were gone and the final two wouldn't last much longer. As two Ukhel ships continued to mop up what remained of the EDF forces, the other two focused their fire on the station. It became clear that they were targeting its shield and weapons systems.

Kal also noticed that the Ukhel did not have any fighters. It appeared their fleet consisted solely of the large capital ships as well as the assault craft he'd seen on Kirkira. Kal had never heard of a fleet without fighters, but the Ukhel clearly were different than any species in the galaxy.

"They're looking to take the planet and Caracas Station, not destroy it," Kal said.

"Looks that way," Garcia commented offhandedly.

They continued to watch the battle unfold on the cockpit viewscreens. Kal felt the large blast of a missile hitting a shield generator near them; the shock waves pushing the *Oruc* across the bay, embedding it in a mass of utility conduits. Kal was thrown from his chair and landed awkwardly on his shoulder. He heard a cracking sound and felt a stream of fire move down his side.

"Everyone okay? What's our status?" Kal asked as he pulled himself into a sitting position using his chair's armrest. Looking around the cockpit he saw that Garcia had a gash across his cheek, but both Park and Kanumba, although shaken, did not appear to have sustained major injuries.

"Sir, you okay? You hit the deck pretty hard," gasped Park.

"We have incoming!" Garcia shouted before Kal could respond. "They launched assault craft at the station—dozens of 'em, coming in fast."

"Missiles are inbound as well," added Kanumba. "Looks like they are prepping the invasion by taking out any personnel or fighters left in the bays."

"Which means we're going to have Ukhel soldiers here in about two minutes," concluded Park.

"Are we able to take off?" asked Kal.

"There's no major damage, but the shields and dampeners weren't up when we slammed into the wall. The electrical line to the maneuvering thrusters was cut. I'm going to need to get to the access panel on the outside of the ship to fix it." Park started to undo his restraints.

"Do we have any weapons?" Kal asked.

"Yeah, the weapons locker is directly behind us in the passageway," Garcia responded. "I need to stay here in the cockpit in order to talk with Park while he fixes the thrusters. Chief Kanumba, can you get some of the recruits from below and provide cover for Park while he makes the fix?"

"I'll go too," Kal offered. "I have five years as a small arms instructor."

Kal, Park, and Kanumba rushed out of the cockpit and pulled several weapons from the locker then made their way to the cargo bay on the lower level. The weapons all had dual fire, meaning they could shoot either kinetic or plasma bolts. As they descended, Garcia made a ship-wide announcement explaining their current situation and requesting a detail to help provide security.

They were met in the bay by Sergeant Jones, Ekon, and another recruit.

"Can't take most of the recruits out; they'll be more of a liability than anything at this stage," said Jones apologetically. "But these two said they've at least shot a weapon before. This one"—he nodded toward Ekon—"said he's seen the Ukhel before."

"I can attest to that," confirmed Kal. "I was with him when it happened."

Kal handed a rifle to each recruit—Jones was already holding one. The access panel where Park needed to make the repairs was on the port side of the ship. Based on the angle of the *Oruc*, the Ukhel would be landing toward the starboard side. Jones quickly gave each soldier instructions, placing one at the bow, stern, and port sides of the ship. He ordered everyone to lay low while the repairs were being conducted and only engage if they were discovered.

Jones quietly climbed out of the port side hatch and signaled for the others to exit. Ekon and the other recruit headed to the bow and stern respectively, while Kal crouched behind a sensor nacelle on the port side. Lieutenant Park and Chief Kanumba headed to another nacelle on the port side and immediately detached an access panel. The ship's landing skids provided a clear line of sight underneath, so Kal crouched down to see if he could watch the Ukhel as they arrived.

A small assault craft slowly entered through the landing bay's containment field and descended. It looked to be roughly a quarter of the *Oruc's* size, a miniature version of the larger Ukhel capital ships. Its course and velocity remained constant as it maneuvered, smoothly touching down on the floor.

Kal looked up to check on Park. His arms were almost completely immersed in the ship's hull and his upper shoulders rotated as he manipulated something within it. Kanumba stood behind him, directing a small light into the opening. A ramp opened on the rear of the assault ship, smoothly gliding down until it rested on the bay floor.

Eyes glued to the ship, Kal watched as what he assumed must be an Ukhel slowly walked out. It was Humanoid in shape, except for a tail or possibly third arm coming out from its back. The creature appeared to be wearing some sort of mech suit or armor that covered every inch of it and moved with a light grace as it walked down the ramp, each step and gesture fluid and smooth. The Ukhel held what Kal guessed was a weapon in its arms, sweeping the stick-like object slowly across the bay.

Three more Ukhel glided down the ramp and fanned out across the bay. They all moved with the same methodical, cat-like grace, stopping only to shoot any Human who still seemed to be alive. They made no discernible noise, potentially communicating through their suits, or in some other way that was indetectable to Humans.

Kal winced each time he saw one of the Ukhel's slugs rip through one of the people lying on the floor. Occasionally, he would hear one of them call out in desperation and had to clench his jaws to prevent himself from screaming.

How much longer? Kal asked via their neural net. *This is horrific.*

Sorry, not long, just a minute, Park responded.

I give us about two minutes, top, until they get to this corner of the bay, Kal said.

The Ukhel swept through the bay like angels of death, slaughtering any Human in their path. A report of a weapons or a cry from its victim occasionally rang out as they continued their gruesome march. Kal listened over the net as Park and

Garcia talked back and forth, checking if the repairs had worked. He prayed that the Ukhel would not be able to break into the encrypted military net that their team was using to communicate. Based on their movements, they seemed unaware of the *Oruc's* crew conducting repairs in the corner.

We have complete power, announced Captain Garcia over the neural net. *You can close her up and head back.*

One of the Ukhel had come across a young man, his legs trapped under cargo containers. He begged for his life but the Ukhel soldier standing above him only paused long enough to pull the trigger. Ekon let out a sob as a bolt of plasma vaporized the man's head. The four Ukhel looked up toward the *Oruc* and pointed their weapons at the ship.

Damnit, sorry, Ekon cursed over the net. He jumped from his position on the bow as a large blast went off at his feet, catapulting him forward like a rag doll and into the side nacelle of the ship.

"Cover me!" Kal called as he ran to grab Ekon's limp form. No need to use the neural net anymore since they had already been made. Plasma fire streaked through the bay from the soldiers around the *Oruc* toward the four Ukhel. The bolts splashed harmlessly against the personal energy shields protecting each of the aliens.

"Damnit, their energy shields are good," cursed Jones. "Switch to kinetic."

The Ukhel continued firing. Luckily, their rounds mainly hit the hull of the ship without inflicting heavy damage on any of the dismounted Humans.

Kal grabbed Ekon's hands and dragged him to the *Oruc's* door. When he got there, Captain Garcia was waiting and pulled the injured soldier up and into the ship as he screamed in pain. His legs had been shredded by the explosion, and all that remained were bloody streamers.

"Colonel, you and I need to provide cover," instructed Jones. "Everyone else, get into the ship on the double."

Park, Kanumba, and the recruit ran toward the door amid plasma fire and explosions from Ukhel grenades. Kal unleashed as much fire as he could on the four advancing Ukhel, focusing on volume rather than accuracy. The kinetic rounds had much more of an effect on the aliens, causing them to stagger whenever a round hit their armor. He cycled through his targets, aiming at whichever one was closest to the ship, trying to at least slow their advance and buy the team time.

"Get down!" Jones yelled as he lobbed a grenade over the fuselage of the *Oruc* and directly at the closest Ukhel soldier.

Kal dropped to the ground and turned his body away as the grenade went off. The shockwave momentarily disoriented him, but when he looked up, he saw the blast had knocked the Ukhel down and shattered the third arm off its body.

He took precise aim and directed the remaining rounds in his magazine into the downed soldier, aiming at the small hole where the arm had been attached to its suit. The Ukhel jerked as the slugs hit it, then stopped moving.

"We got one!" Kal shouted in triumph.

"Now let's get out of here," Jones yelled back.

Kal's triumph quickly wore away and he started to plan how he could get to the dead Ukhel. If they were able to capture one of the creatures, even dead, it would go a long way to helping them understand what they were against. Looking around the bay, he thought he might be able to make it if he sprinted.

"You can't make it." Jones grabbed his shoulder. "Sir, I know what you want to do, and it's suicide—we have to go *now.*"

Reluctantly, Kal nodded and sprinted towards the *Oruc's* hatch as the three remaining Ukhel continued to maneuver around their position, trying to encircle them. Jones climbed through the port door and Kal jumped in after him, rolling as he hit the deck of the cargo bay.

One of the recruits closed the door before Kal had a chance to get up. Racing back up to the cockpit, he found the flight crew efficiently going through the power-up sequence.

"Sir, Caracas Station is no longer responding," Captain Garcia said over his shoulder. "I think it is safe to assume that command has either been destroyed or captured by the enemy." Kal's mind went to Ahuja, another friend lost to he'd lost to these bastards. "We're going to go full thrust, so strap in."

"Strap in for combat departure in five seconds," Chief Kanumba called out over the ship's intercom.

Kal jumped in his chair and fastened the restraints across his body.

The Ukhel in the bay realized what they were planning to do and ran back to their ship for protection from the *Oruc's* main engines. Garcia activated their maneuvering thrusters and rotated the *Oruc* out of the conduits at the edge of the bay. As soon as they were free, he set the throttle to max, launching them through the bay door and into space. The momentum overwhelmed the ship's inertial dampeners and slammed Kal into his seat. He adjusted his console's viewscreen so he could watch the wreckage of Caracas Station as they sped away. It was clear the Ukhel attack had severely damaged it, but it was still in one piece and looked to be habitable based on the sensor feed they were still receiving from the station.

As the *Oruc's* speed leveled off, the pressure lifted from Kal's chest. He could see several green icons on the tacmap as other Human refugees tried to escape the area and fold away.

A klaxon sounded through the cockpit and warning beacons lit up on Kal's console as ten missiles launched from a nearby Ukhel ship. The missiles forked, with a pair heading toward the *Oruc* and the rest tracking the other fleeing ships.

Chief Kanumba began to deploy countermeasure drones. "The missiles are going to hit before we are able to fold," Kanumba advised. "I am deploying full countermeasures to see if anything works." The EDF countermeasures were automated drones that mimicked the heat, look, and sensor reading of the ship.

The missiles continued following the *Oruc* and were quickly catching up. One of them suddenly veered off course and exploded, fooled by one of the drones. The others remained locked on, continuing to home in on the *Oruc*.

The final missile detonated almost immediately behind them, spinning the *Oruc* along its axis and triggering a cascade of red warning lights. "We've lost power to all thrusters," called out Garcia. "Life support and essential systems remain functional, but we can't change direction, fire, or defend ourselves."

"Can we fold?" asked Kal.

"Roger, fold drives are miraculously still online and we're above ninety-nine percent survivability if we fold now."

"Then do it!" Kal called out.

Garcia hit the fold button on his console and the stars shifted as the ship was instantly transported out of the New America system and into deep space.

Chapter Nine

"Well, that was...interesting." Chief Kanumba sighed as she turned around in her chair to look at the others.

"I'm going to need to check our drives." Captain Garcia stood up and stretched. "We can still reach Kapustin Station, but we have no control over our speed or heading right now. I'll see what we can do to fix the systems."

Since folding operated independently of the ship's heading and velocity in normal space the *Oruc* would still be able to fold to the station even though they were spinning and unable to control their speed. After each fold, the ship remained at the same velocity and heading as it was immediately before the fold. Kal remembered how confusing this had been to him at the academy. It wasn't until he understood that when the ship folded there was no concept of velocity that it made sense—in one second it was at one location, and a second later, in a new location—everything else remained the same.

"Okay, let me know when you've figured it out," Kal replied. "I need to check on one of the recruits—he got hit by an explosive round when we were fixing the ship."

"Yes sir. This could take a while, though. It wasn't a direct hit, but it was damn close," Garcia warned. He turned around and began running diagnostics on the cockpit computer.

Kal walked out of the cockpit and ducked into his stateroom. He flopped onto his bunk and closed his eyes with a groan. Everything was happening so fast. Ekon's bloody wounds flashed through his mind. Kal had been through similar situations during the Torgham War, but that had been a long time ago and he'd worked hard to push those memories away. The horror of what he'd seen in the bay, the methodical and merciless killing of defenseless people, was something he'd never seen before, and it shook him to his core.

Damn, I could really use a drink, he thought as he drifted off to sleep.

Kal jerked awake and brought his hands up to his pounding head. He could tell he was suffering from withdrawal. It was the longest he'd gone in years without a drink or hit. There was no way to tell how long he'd been out. Hopefully not too long. A commander needed to be with his soldiers when things got rough. He pulled himself off the bed with an oath and smoothed his uniform over his frame with his twitching hands. He needed to see how Ekon was doing.

A makeshift infirmary had been set up in the crew quarters. Ekon lay on his bunk, clearly awake, with a blanket covering the lower half of his body. Sergeant Jones was examining the readouts on a mobile medbot that had been set up next to him. Several tubes and wires stretched from the bot and disappeared under the blanket covering the patient.

Every EDF combat ship had a medical bot onboard. They had a variety of drugs, organic compounds, and nano-bots and could handle most types of trauma and common ailments. Once initialized, the device would diagnose and treat the patient. They were a miracle of science, Kal had seen them heal people who he'd thought were dead.

The other recruits were on the far side of the quarters, pretending to be doing other things—but their eyes betrayed them by occasionally darting to the area around Ekon's bunk.

"So, we have good news and we have great news, Private Kimathi," Jones said with a smile. "The good news is that we have been able to control the bleeding and stabilize the area around the wound."

"The great news?" asked Ekon skeptically.

"Once we get to Kapustin Station, you'll be getting a brand-new pair of bionic legs, courtesy of the EDF." Jones patted Ekon's shoulder lightly.

"Uh. I guess that is good news," replied Ekon slowly, pain meds clearly clouding his mind.

Jones lightly patted his shoulder. "You'll be the first recruit to go through Base Camp having already been injured in combat. That's gonna make you a popular guy."

Kal knew what Jones was doing. He was keeping it light, trying to distract Ekon's mind from the horror he had just been through. Kal had heard a lot of people criticize what they saw as false bravado or a cavalier attitude by frontline soldiers, but he knew it was a survival mechanism.

"Staff Sergeant Jones, could you clear the quarters? I want to talk with Private Kimathi alone," Kal asked.

"Yessir." Jones turned around and addressed the recruits in a stern voice. "Okay soldiers, I want you out in the cargo bay, *now*. Just because we're in transit doesn't mean you get to sit around. I'm going to make you wish that we hadn't survived that last battle. I want everyone formed up in the bay for PT, now!" Another way to keep soldiers' minds off what they had just been through and get them used to what they'd face in Base Camp.

The recruits dropped what they were doing and almost ran over each other trying to make their way to the cargo bay of the ship. Kal wondered if they could detect the edge of affection and humor in Jones' voice. The cargo bay was the only place on the *Oruc* that was large enough for physical training. Whenever soldiers were folding on an EDF ship, it was standard practice for them to take it over for training. Every EDF officer and NCO knew that soldiers without anything to do inevitably ended up in trouble.

"How are you doing?" asked Kal, pulling a chair up to Ekon's bedside.

Ekon turned his head and studied Kal's face for a moment with a confused expression. "Doing great...sir." His eyes gained some of their focus as he realized that it was Kal sitting next to him.

"Ekon, I'm sorry this happened to you. I wanted to let you know that I'm grateful for your actions today. You helped get us off Caracas Station and likely saved every single person aboard this ship." As Kal spoke, Ekon's mouth curled into a sneer, and he could feel the contempt oozing off the man. He worked to keep his tone and demeanor calm.

"You done, sir?" Ekon asked.

"Yeah. Anything you want to say to me?" Kal continued to keep his voice calm through a small miracle.

"Nothing I can say to your face…sir." Ekon turned his head away.

Kal tried to keep his anger in check. He knew Ekon had been through a significant trauma, but Kal was suffering from withdrawal and tired of the man's hostility and passive-aggressive behavior. Even though this was a soldier who had been through hell, Kal couldn't take it anymore.

"Enough! I'm not sure what I did to you to make you this way. We had our issues on my ship, and you've had to face some tough shit in this last month. But everyone else has as well. I never asked for any of this, and I sure as hell didn't ask for you to be on this ship with me."

Kal stopped to take a breath and calm himself. But his anger was still eager to pour out of him—anger not just at Ekon, but at the entire situation. "But here we are. You want me dead, but guess what? So do I. Unfortunately, what we want doesn't matter anymore. I have to keep going, and so do you. We may not like each other, but I hate the Ukhel a hell of a lot more."

"Been practicing that?" Ekon turned his head and smiled. His hatred seemed to have focused his mind; the confusion was gone from his eyes and only anger remained.

"Screw you. What do you want from me?"

"Nothing, I just don't trust you and I don't understand why I'm a private sitting in this bed with no legs and you're leading this ship. I don't understand why you get to come into our lives, kill a bunch of innocent people, and then walk away. I've lost everything. My family is back there on New America and I'll probably never see them again. Right now, I can't even walk." Ekon tried to sit up in the bed and failed.

"At least you have a *chance* you might see them," Kal spat back. "I lost my family ten years ago, and I wish that I had the chance you have. Even captured by the Ukhel, you have a chance, some small chance to see them again. I have nothing."

Nothing but memories, he finished in his mind. Kal remembered his wife, Li Na. He'd met her in a dive bar in the Mariga System. He'd gone in with friends, fellow officers, expecting to grab a drink and then head back to his quarters. He'd ended up staying there for eight hours, just talking with her. They went on to have two beautiful children, Lan Fen and Stephen. Kal remembered them as being perfect now. He knew that they could be frustrating and often didn't listen, but all he remembered was their smiles and laughs. They'd been destined for great things, or at least that's what he had thought.

Ekon opened his mouth to say something, froze, then closed it. He studied Kal's face for a moment then averted his eyes and looked down at the small screen on the medbot next to his bed.

"My family died in an accident ten years ago. I had a wife and two kids." Kal pulled their picture out of his pocket. "I died when they did. The rest of my life I've just been biding my time."

"So, what's the point?" Kal wasn't sure if Ekon's question was directed at him, or rhetorical. "I mean after everything, what's the point of going on?"

Kal thought to himself. It was a question he had asked himself countless times over the past decade. He never had an answer. "I don't know."

Ekon continued to study the readout, not meeting Kal's eyes. "Do you think the others are still alive—Sandra, Klarissa, and Li Wei?" he asked.

"I like to think so. I have no idea what the Ukhel are going to do, but I believe they want to capture New America, not destroy it."

"Why do you say that?" Ekon directed his gaze back to Kal's face.

"They were trying to capture Caracas Station. Those weren't the actions of a force that wants to kill everyone."

Ekon bit his lip and dropped his head back down on his pillow. Kal figured the man had had enough. He quietly got up and walked out of the crew quarters.

As Kal walked toward the ladder to his stateroom, he smiled to himself as he saw the recruits in formation, conducting PT. Staff Sergeant Jones stood in front of the formation, barking out the names of various exercises while the recruits scrambled to keep up. Kal remembered being a recruit like them. He had always hated those PT sessions, never knowing what exercise was next or when they were going to be finished. As a senior officer, he now had much bigger things to worry about, but he had to admit to himself he still didn't miss it.

Kal had volunteered for the service immediately after finishing school. As a kid growing up on Mariga, he had yearned to explore the wider galaxy. He knew the EDF was the ticket off the icy planet. As soon as he got the chance, he had volunteered to join up. In the colonies, the EDF was not the beacon of hope that it was on Earth. Many of Kal's family and friends had seen them as occupiers or police, enforcing the will of Earth on colonies that were days away. Kal had never cared about any of that—he only saw them as his ticket off planet.

Base Camp had been tough for him. He wasn't a natural athlete and the training had been the most physically demanding thing he had ever done. He aced his intellectual aptitude test though, which qualified him for the Officer's Academy. Kal enjoyed the academy. The art and science of military study came naturally to him, and he loved spending countless hours in the library, reading through ancient military manuals and histories.

Kal shook his head and headed back in his stateroom, he loaded the chit Shreya had given him a day earlier into the desk monitor. It contained a treasure trove of information about Kapustin Station. The station was in deep space far from any significant system. Human-controlled space made a roughly spherical shape. Besides Earth and the four colonies, there were hundreds of other star systems the EDF patrolled, most of them worthless. It was a little less than a two-week journey by fold between the farthest two EDF-controlled systems.

Kapustin Station was at the edge of Human-controlled space. The six species that neighbored Humanity each had their own adjacent spheres of influence. Kapustin was right between the Human and Goro spheres. Since it sat in the middle of deep space, away from any system, it was almost impossible to find without the coordinates. Kal could see that resupply must be a substantial issue due to the remote location.

The chit had a brief history of the Kapustin—it was one of the newest Human stations, having been built only a few years ago. Due to its dual purpose of clandestine research and emergency headquarters, its existence was highly classified. Kal wondered how many of the remaining EDF ships knew about the base. With communications spotty at best, there had to be ships traveling through the stars unaware that there was still an EDF headquarters. With the attack on New America, he had to assume the other Human colonies also had fallen or would soon.

The information on the chit was mainly focused on the current supplies and logistics capabilities of the station. It had a significant amount of storage to compensate for the difficulty of getting cargo to it. It was designed to hold up, under normal circumstances, for up to five years without resupply. Unfortunately, circumstances were definitely not normal anymore, and the station was already over capacity with all of the additional personnel and equipment being rerouted there.

It was commanded by General Greg Sato—Kal had never met him, but knew his reputation. Sato was known widely for his courage, his dedication to the study of military art, and his leadership in a famous offensive against the Torgham decades ago. Hopefully the general's tactical skill would still be of use against an enemy like the Ukhel.

Kal sat back in his chair and ran his hands through his hair. He felt somewhat relaxed for the first time in days. Although they were currently adrift in space with no defenses, at least they were not in any immediate danger.

As he thought back on what had happened, his mind turned to Li Na. *Wonder what she would make of all this,* Kal mused. Li Na had been fiery on the outside, but a calm pragmatist on the inside. He remembered the fights they would have. When she got angry, her fury was quickly evident—cheeks red, hair rising to frame her face like the mane of a lion. However, when she calmed down, the transformation back was just as quick. Li Na handled the stresses of having a family and trying to make ends meet much more calmly than he did. She had the uncanny ability to take events one at a time without second guessing or worrying about the future.

I need to be more like her, Kal reflected. *I need to focus on what I can control and dismiss what I can't.*

Thinking back on the past days, weeks, and months, he realized how his life since her death had fallen short of what he knew Li Na would have wanted. *There is nothing I can do about the past, but maybe there is something that I can do for the future.* He ignored the cravings gnawing at him and turned his mind back to the task at hand, reviewing everything he could about Kapustin and trying to think about how they could fight the Ukhel.

Chapter Ten

"How's the prisoner?" Kal asked.

The young recruit outside the stateroom door snapped to attention. "Fine, sir, she's just been reading books and watching holos since we left." They had enabled the guard stationed at the door to see what was going on within the makeshift brig so they could keep track of the prisoner. The feed was monitored by both the soldier on duty as well as the ship's computer, which would alert on any suspicious activity.

"I'm going to go talk with her. No weapons or sharp objects," Kal told the guard.

"Go ahead, sir." The guard pressed his hand against the access panel to allow Kal entry to the room. It was almost an exact mirror of the stateroom Kal was staying in, albeit slightly smaller.

Nicole Bergeron sat behind the desk, looking at something on the monitor. She looked up as the door opened, her face unchanged.

The woman didn't look like what Kal had expected. To be honest he hadn't known what to expect, but certainly not the small woman sitting behind the desk in front of him. She looked to be in her mid-thirties, with pale skin, and long blonde hair that highlighted the angular features of her face.

"Nicole Bergeron, right? I'm Colonel Kal Norman." She stared at him; her eyes defiant as they met his own. "I transported you to Caracas Station while you were in the stasis chamber. Glad to see you up and about." Kal sat down in the chair across the desk from Nicole.

Nicole gave a small snort. "Thanks, I guess. So, what do you want?"

Kal ignored the rude tone. "Just checking in on you. You got what you need?"

"Well, freedom would be nice, but barring that, yeah I'm good."

"So, I have to ask—what made you do it?" Kal imagined a more diplomatic approach would have been better, but he couldn't help it. He shuddered to think of the damage that this woman had caused. What had possessed her to betray everyone and everything?

"Do you really care? What's done is done." She looked at him with a feigned indifference.

"You had a decent career as far as I can tell. Attaché to Kurz is a relatively plum assignment for the diplomatic corps, as I understand."

"Being an attaché isn't exactly a glamorous job, and the UEG isn't exactly the greatest employer either. I was a mid-level bureaucrat stuck on an alien world." Nicole took a deep breath. "Look, obviously I didn't know who was asking me for information or what they wanted it for. I had a shitty job. This Nordlok approached me in a restaurant. They said they were working for some local syndicate and asked if I would be willing to provide some information for them in exchange for a lot of money. Nothing big or classified, just a few items, memos, policies, that kind of thing." She sighed. "I don't know what changed, but pretty soon I was giving them more and more. And once you're in, there's no backing out."

She tilted her head to look him directly in the eyes. He could see the tears welling in them. "I never provided anything that was highly classified. Mainly, it was just stuff that confirmed rumors that had been going around for a while already. And I didn't know who was really getting the information—how could I have?"

"You should've thought it through. The information you provided might not have been strictly classified, but it aided our enemy. The Ukhel can use that information to figure out where to strike, what our general military strategies are, and understand our supply lines. Even if a single piece of information is harmless, when combined they can give the enemy a very comprehensive picture of how we operate. Besides, syndicates are some of the scummiest organizations in the galaxy."

Local syndicates were small-time criminal organizations that only operated on a single planet; anything larger would put them in direct conflict with the Alliance. They didn't have the capabilities or reach of the Alliance, but they tried to make up for it by having even fewer scruples.

"Yeah, I knew it was wrong. I also knew I had parents and a sister living in slums back on Earth. Attaché sounds glamorous, but it's really an over-glorified, underpaid drone. The money that the Nordlok gave me helped my family pay off their debts and get their own apartment, no more communal living."

"No more living at all," Kal deadpanned. He twisted the knife to see what would happen and immediately felt a pang of guilt and regret.

"Screw you. The UEG never gave me a thing and I didn't owe them anything," Nicole spat, a tear trailing down the side of her cheek.

Kal had an impulse to apologize, or at least temper his remarks, but held back. Didn't she deserve his venom, his condemnation? Or was what she'd done really that bad? He felt confused as to how he felt about her and her actions and didn't trust himself to speak. It was easy to condemn someone's choices from afar, but when you had to deal with them face-to-face, you realized that there were two sides to the story.

"You can work to make this better," Kal said. "Tell us everything you know and maybe we can figure out a way to kill those bastards."

Nicole let out a hollow laugh. "I *am* working to make it better, Colonel Norman. I've told you everything I know. I've told everyone who's interrogated me what I know. The truth is that there's no way to make this better…no matter how much I want to. Earth is gone."

She's telling the truth, Kal realized. She doesn't know a thing. No wonder she was on suicide watch. She'd lost everything in her life and she was the one responsible, or at least felt that way.

Nicole turned away and studied the viewscreen on the wall next to them, tears falling onto the desk between them.

Hesitating, Kal stood up from his chair, paused, then turned and walked out the door. He nodded to the guard and climbed down the ladder to the first deck. As his foot touched the floor, he realized that all he felt for Nicole Bergeron, was pity.

Kal sat at the galley table and waited for the other officers to join him. The galley on a ship like the *Oruc* was intended to be a meeting space as well as a place for meals. A large rectangular table was fixed to the floor in the center of the room and viewscreens and a food fabricator rested on the bulkheads. The machine took raw vitamins, minerals, proteins, fats, and carbohydrates and processed them into something like food. It was essential for deep space travel.

Kal had asked the other officers to meet him there so they could plan how they'd proceed. So far, Captain Garcia and Chief Kanumba did not seem to be very optimistic regarding the possibility of repairs.

While he waited for the others to join, Kal reflected on his exchange with Nicole. She seemed conflicted in many ways—remorseful over what she had done and resentful of the people she had betrayed. Kal knew little about the communal living dorms, or communes, back on Earth except that they were tough places: no privacy, rampant crime, and suffocating poverty. For Nicole to have made her way out was, in itself, a miracle. When he handed her over to the authorities on

Kapustin Station, that would probably be the last time he saw her. She would spend the rest of her life in a cell somewhere being interrogated until her mind or body gave out. Kal surprised himself by feeling a bit of remorse about it.

The other officers trickled in the room, grabbed a drink from the fabricator, and sat at the table. Everyone seemed to still be shaken by what had happened at New America. They looked everywhere but at each other as they waited for Kal to start the meeting.

"What's the latest?" Kal asked. It had been a day since they left Caracas, and the flight crew had been working hard to determine if there were any fixes that could be made to the ship.

"Well sir," started Garcia, "we've checked all the ship's systems and there's no way to fix the thrusters. The systems are toast, and the ship will need to go into the yard to get those back online. Weapons and shields are the same, unfortunately."

Everyone looked around uneasily.

"So, there isn't much of a choice to be made then," Kal concluded. "Seems like we are going to just have to fold to Kapustin Station and then hope we can figure out something."

"I think so, sir," Jones said. "There's no reason to sit here on our thumbs and wait. We don't have enough supplies to remain in deep space long, and keeping discipline, especially among untrained recruits, is hard in a situation like this."

"So, if we decide fold to the station, there's no way we'll be able to maneuver between each leg," Garcia said. "We'll maintain our momentum between each fold, so we could theoretically slam into a small asteroid or piece of debris. Small chance, but still a risk that you all should be aware of," Garcia offered.

Kal thought about what the pilot was saying. The *Oruc* was speeding through space, tumbling around. If they folded to Kapustin Station, they'd be making not one, but hundreds or thousands of folds in series. In between each one, they'd have no way of maneuvering around obstacles. There wasn't much in deep space, but the pilot was right, it was still a risk.

"A good point Captain Garcia," Kal said. "But the risk *is* low. Almost impossibly low considering our route. The bigger problem will be when we arrive at the station." He sighed. "Set a course to Kapustin. We'll need to lock down all equipment prior to the final fold since we'll be arriving out of control."

Garcia nodded, clearly expecting the order. "Will do, sir. I'll have Chief Kanumba plot the route and do our pre-fold checks. Once we are en route, Lieutenant Park and I will continue to try and figure out how we're going to get under control once we get to the station." He chuckled. "I'd like to see their faces when they see an out-of-control corvette hurtling at them."

❖

An hour later, Kal was in the cockpit waiting for the flight crew to activate the fold drive. He didn't need to be there but felt like he should be present since he was ultimately responsible for their fate.

"Sir, do we have your clearance to proceed?" Captain Garcia asked.

"As we have no choice … yeah. Proceed," Kal confirmed.

"Here goes nothing." Garcia activated the ship's fold drive, and the stars abruptly changed as it instantly transported them to another point in space.

"All systems reading normal," reported Park. "At the current rate, we should arrive at Kapustin Station in approximately six days."

"What we do then is anyone's guess," Kanumba said.

"Have faith, chief," Garcia laughed. "We'll figure something out. Maybe you can climb outside and push."

The engineer ignored him and continued to monitor the ship's systems while the stars on the viewscreen blinked again.

After a few minutes, Kal walked out of the cockpit and back to his stateroom. The ship was essentially on autopilot until they made their final fold and arrived at Kapustin Station. The computer handled all of the fold calculations, and they couldn't pilot or maneuver the ship anyway. He sat down on his bunk and brought up the chit with information on Kapustin Station. He wanted to be ready when they arrived.

If we arrive at the station, Kal corrected himself.

Chapter Eleven

Kal found himself, once again, pacing up and down the length of the *Oruc*. He paused in the cargo bay to watch Sergeant Jones showing the recruits where supplemental breathing masks were and how to use them. Last time Kal had stopped by, he'd been going over the emergency procedures during loss of environment or gravity. Kal also checked in with the Lieutenant Park in the cockpit—per regulations there was always a member of the flight crew stationed there in case of emergency.

Kal continued to find his mind drawn to their prisoner. Their conversation kept popping into his mind as he walked from room to room. He cringed as he thought about his parting words. He couldn't understand why he'd said what he had considering all she'd lost. Kal liked to think he would never have found himself in her shoes, but he wasn't confident of it. He knew he would do anything to see his family again—without any remorse or hesitation. Also, his comments weren't helpful in getting more information from Nicole; he needed to see if there was something they had missed, any bit of information that could help their cause. He believed her when she said she'd told them everything she knew. However, there may be details *she* had missed or forgotten.

"She awake?" Kal asked the recruit outside the door.

The woman quickly checked the monitor. "Yes sir. Would you like me to let you in?"

"Yes, but let her know I'm coming in." Kal could have walked in unannounced, but he was hoping to build trust after their first encounter had gone so poorly.

The guard announced Kal and waited for Nicole to give permission for him to enter before opening the door. He walked in to find her sitting on the bunk, peering at something sparkling in her hands.

"Eh, you're back," she remarked without looking up.

"Look…I wanted to say I'm sorry for how I left things." Kal stumbled over his words. "What you did was wrong, but you had no way of knowing what would happen. I'm not here to judge. I'm here to try and understand what happened to see if there is any information we can use."

"Okay, thanks," Nicole said in a flat tone.

Kal stiffened. "You can't say you're blameless. You can't pretend to be innocent in all this. You might not have known what the information was to be used for, but you knew it was wrong. Billions of Humans died, not to mention—"

"You think I don't know?" The words floated quietly across the room. "You think that I don't feel responsible?"

Kal stopped, her questions cutting his sentence off like a knife. She continued, "I feel responsible for everything. Why do you think they have me on suicide watch? I know what I did!" Nicole stopped and took a breath, trying to calm herself. "But I can't sit here and let myself be beaten down. I'll answer any questions, provide any help I can, and fight to undo just a little of whatever harm I did."

She put whatever she'd been holding on a shelf next to her. "But I won't be a verbal punching bag, listening to every soldier who comes through this door tell me what a piece of crap I am. I know it, and I am trying to do whatever I can to help. I joined the diplomatic corps to help Humanity, to help make things better. I messed up and I paid a heavy price for it…a *heavy* price. Now, either ask me a question or get the hell out of here."

Nicole stood and faced Kal, her hands balled into fists at her side. As she stopped talking, she abruptly dropped back on the bunk, and the air seemed to go out of her body. Kal studied the woman for a moment. She was pretending to look down at the tablet in her hands, slowly manipulating the screen but he couldn't see what was on it.

"What were they like?" He sat in the chair across from her.

"What…who?" Nicole was clearly taken aback.

"Your family, what were they like?"

"They were normal." Nicole's mouth twisted up. "A normal family. They didn't deserve what happened to them, not that anyone else did either. My parents both worked blue collar jobs on the landing pads on Earth. My sister was special, though. She had a presence, the kind that made everyone stop what they're doing and stare when she walked into the room."

Kal looked in her eyes, letting her know he was listening. "I had a family too," he confided as she paused. "They died years ago, but they were perfect, at least to me. It's funny, because I knew it at the time but never really stopped to appreciate it."

Nicole picked up the trinket she had been holding when Kal walked in and handed it to him. It was a small golden starfish pendant.

"You know what this is?" Nicole asked.

"A starfish. They have these on Earth, right?"

"Exactly. Starfish are pretty interesting. One of the only creatures that can regrow an appendage. You cut off one of their arms and it comes back."

Kal nodded.

"My sister Sylvie gave me this. Said it was something to remember her by while I traveled the stars. You know Sylvie wanted to join the EDF, said she wanted to see the galaxy." Kal handed the pendant back and Nicole placed it in her pocket.

"Sounds like me when I was a kid. I couldn't wait to get away," Kal confessed.

"Yeah, she always had one eye on the sky." Nicole wiped away a tear. "But you didn't come here to talk about my family. What do you want to know?"

"I don't mind listening," Kal replied. "I just wanted to hear the full story of what happened. Who did you talk to? Is there any information you can give about your handler? Did it ever give you its name or any other information?" Nordloks were genderless.

"No, it just asked me to call it Two," she replied, frustrated. "Besides saying it was working with a local syndicate it never told me a thing about who it was working for."

"Any specific types of information it was especially interested in? Like military capabilities or formations?" asked Kal.

"Well, it asked about those things, but I told it I wouldn't share any highly classified information. Over time, a lot of the questions came to be about production on Human and Kurz worlds—what was mined, produced, or grown where."

"Hmmmm. Sounds like they were already figuring out their lines of supply. Large fleets need fuel and food, and if the Ukhel truly did come from far away, they would have to gather materials here. They wouldn't be able to count on resupply from home." Kal rubbed his hair thoughtfully.

"How were they able to survive here for years then?" Nicole asked.

"They probably only sent a few ships at first and were able to buy what they needed from the private market. Now that their full fleet is here, they'll need a significant number of resources." If his hypothesis was true, Kal was impressed with the Ukhel's foresight. It seemed like they had been planning years ahead. They could immediately begin diverting supplies to their fleet as well as potentially sending some back to wherever they came from.

"You're the only person who's collaborated with the Ukhel and survived their purge. What happened? How are you still alive?" Kal decided to change the direction of his questioning. He would need to get a full list of all the

125

information Nicole remembered giving the Ukhel later. Perhaps their intel officers could get some idea of what they were thinking from it.

"Luck." Nicole shrugged. "One day, Two asked to meet up in an alley near the outskirts of the capital. It was way outside the city and completely isolated, but that was always the case for in-person meetings; they're always in alleys or dead ends, for obvious reasons. I was waiting, keeping out of sight, when there was an explosion. Luckily a disposal container blocked most of the blast, but I still got pretty messed up. Two was on the roof above and started firing at me. Apparently EDF counter-intelligence was already trailing me; some of the information I'd been downloading had been raising suspicions. They saw the explosion and took Two out." She sighed. "I guess they must've found something on it that indicated it was working with the Ukhel."

"So, they sent you back to Earth, and then rerouted you to New America when Earth was destroyed?"

"Guess so. They were probably concerned that someone would attempt to kill or free me." Nicole shrugged.

"A fair concern," Kal admitted. "What was your job at the embassy?"

"I was a commerce attaché. We had started to trade in military hardware and supplies with the Kurz. It was a program that was going to be a model for future relationships. The Torgham War showed that we were vulnerable because of our isolationists policies. Top leaders were very wary of treaties and mutual assistance agreements but felt we could deal with the Kurz because of their code."

The Kurz had a strict code of beliefs that dictated complete adherence to rules and policies. Breaking one's word was considered a cardinal sin, so treaties with them were considered absolute.

"Sounds like you were a big deal," Kal said. "We almost lost that war. I can imagine that the powers that be wanted more allies." The Torgham War had been a wake-up call to Humanity. Only the relatively advanced X'Ado entering the war had prevented a catastrophe. They worried about the regional balance of power and felt that if the Torgham were able to capture Humanity's planets and stations, it may shift too much in their favor. They demanded a ceasefire, which the Torgham had flatly refused. So, the X'Ado attacked, pushing the Torgham out of Human space. Since then, Humanity had been a sort of pawn between the two powers, reliant on the assistance of X'Ado, who had a vested interest in assisting the EDF in developing more advanced technology and fleets, but only sharing what they chose to.

"Sounds like it, but really it was just dealing with low-level bureaucrats. I thought it was a stepping stone for something bigger—eventually I wanted to be an ambassador." Nicole paused. "I was getting close to my time for a new posting. The next job would have been as a senior attaché, and I would have been responsible for an entire team. I figured that when I left the planet, it would be the end of the whole affair and I could forget that this had ever happened."

"How exactly did you get the information to Two?" Kal asked. "I would think the embassy has technology to prevent people from doing what you did."

"It had a micro-chit installed in my neural implant. The chit could be scanned, and the data removed by this device that Two had. The techs on New America took a look at it and said that they weren't able to find any forensic information on it, though. They did say it was like nothing they'd seen before."

"When we get to Kapustin, we should have someone look at it again," Kal said. "Perhaps there's something they missed."

"Maybe." Nicole seemed doubtful. "I want to make amends. So, if there is something I can do to stop the Ukhel, then I'll do it."

Kal nodded and stood up. He knew what a motivator guilt could be. As he left the room, he turned and saw Nicole had pulled the starfish pendant out of her pocket and was holding it in her hands, studying it again.

Chapter Twelve

Kal sat in his chair in the *Oruc's* cockpit watching Captain Garcia's hand float above his console, ready to activate their drive. They were about to take the final fold into the space around Kapustin Station. They would appear without any way to maneuver or control their speed and it would be up to the station's control team to figure out a way to stop them.

Jones had already ordered the recruits go through the ship and stow anything that could potentially be a hazard—using it as an opportunity to train them on the ship's equipment.

"Ready sir?" Lieutenant Park looked up from his console.

"Yeah, hit it." Kal braced himself since they weren't sure exactly where they would end up in relation to the station. Since it was not orbiting a planet or star, the station's precise location could be annoyingly unpredictable—even with the *Oruc's* advanced sensors and systems.

The stars shifted on the cockpit's screen as they folded and the flight crew immediately went into action, hands flying across screens, trying to determine their location with respect to the station. Kanumba sent out a general hail to the station, alerting them of the situation.

After several tense seconds they heard a response over the cockpit's speakers. "*Oruc*, this is Kapustin Station. We understand your situation and are working on a solution, stand by." The tone was indifferent, as if they had out-of-control ships folding next to them all the time.

As they waited for an update from the station, Kal tried to think of something they could do as the seconds ticked by. Suddenly, a thought occurred to him and he turned to face Kanumba.

"Wait, I have an idea," he said. "Ask them if they have any D class cargo freighters."

"Why?" the chief asked skeptically.

"They're large transport ships used for hauling storage containers. They're the only cargo ships with an atmospheric bay long enough to fit the *Oruc* in, fifty-two meters. If they have one, it could match our speed and pull us into their hull."

"Works, except the *Oruc* is *fifty-four* meters long." Park said.

"The front sensor cone is four meters long and designed to come off easily for maintenance and repairs. It would be a tight fit, but I think we would be able to make it." Garcia looked thoughtful.

"Best idea we got right now." Kanumba tapped the communications panel to hail the station. When the tech replied, she explained the idea to him. There was a pause and then another voice came onto the net.

"*Oruc*, we're going to try this. The transport *Madrid* is conducting emergency departure procedures and heading to your location."

A large container ship disengaged from the station and headed toward them. As it approached, the *Madrid* rotated so that its cargo bay lined up with the *Oruc*. The *Madrid* continued to speed toward the *Oruc*, though its tail was now facing directly at their ship as it approached.

"*Oruc*, this is *Madrid*," said a female voice. "We're going to be matching your speed and trajectory and then will pull you into our cargo bay. We'll need to begin decelerating and changing course once you are inside—it will be a bumpy ride."

"Acknowledged, we are ready and all personnel are in emergency brace position." Garcia responded. He muted the comms and then made a ship-wide announcement for all personnel to strap in.

As the *Oruc* continued to hurtle toward the station, the Madrid drew closer until finally it had matched their exact velocity and was hovering above them. The container ship was roughly three times the size of the *Oruc* with a large central cavity positioned directly above them. The *Madrid's* two bay doors, already opened, framing the *Oruc*.

"You know," Park smiled at Garcia, "my parents told me I should go into finance, less risky. I am kinda thinking they were right."

"Less glory. Who wants to sit at a desk?" Kanumba slapped him on the back.

A large robotic arm extended out of the bay of the *Madrid and* two large clamps at the end opened and grasped the mid-section of the *Oruc*. A shudder went through the ship as the clamps tightened around the ship, abruptly stopping its rotation. The arm retracted into the *Madrid's* bay pulling the *Oruc* with it. There was a large jolt as the front aerodynamic cone made contact with the underside of the *Madrid*. The arm continued to pull, trying to shear off the front cone like a razor.

Kal watched the screens, willing the cone to break off. Popping sounded from in front of them as the fastenings holding it to the ship were sheared off. As the *Oruc* was slowly pulled in, the inside wall of the *Madrid's* cargo bay filled the viewscreen, blotting everything else out.

"We've secured the *Oruc*," the commander of the *Madrid* announced over Kapustin Station's command net, "and are currently decelerating and will dock shortly."

A small cheer went up in the cockpit, and Garcia let the rest of the passengers know that the maneuver had been successful. Kal was surprised that he could hear the cheers of the recruits in the cargo bay.

After several minutes, the *Madrid* successfully docked with Kapustin Station, but it took another couple of hours for the station's cargo handlers to successfully extricate the *Oruc* and move it into one of the interior landing bays since the deceleration process had caused it to wedge itself into a bulkhead.

Once the docking process was complete, Kal grabbed his go bag from his stateroom. He had already packed his few belongings prior to their final fold. On his way to the cargo bay he saw that there was no longer a guard outside of Nicole's stateroom. *Looks like Intel wanted her fast,* he thought wistfully.

The recruits were performing their last checks of the crew quarters. Ekon had been moved into the bay and was waiting for the medical team from the station to arrive. A sheet still covered his lower half, but the man seemed to be in good health and spirits, laughing and chatting with the recruit assigned to wait with him. As Kal passed, Ekon gave a small nod—not exactly the warmest farewell but lacking the venom Kal would have expected a few days ago.

The interior of Kapustin Station was odd. As a career military officer, he had become used to EDF military installations. For efficiency and cost savings reasons, EDF facilities tended to have the same layout and characteristics, but this one was slightly off. Besides appearing almost brand new, there were minor differences in the layout and structure of the bay—small things like the exit doors leading into the rest of the station being larger than normal and the bay control cluster located in a different area.

A man that looked to be about Kal's age, with thick black hair and a beaming smile stood at the end of the cargo ramp. "Colonel Norman, welcome! I'm General Sato." His smile grew even wider as Kal took his outstretched hand. The general pulled him into an embrace almost causing Kal to fall down.

"Thank you, sir," Kal responded breathlessly.

"Eh, can it with that 'sir' crap. Follow me." Sato turned and Kal fell in at his side as they started walking. The general's aide, a woman who looked to be in her mid-thirties followed behind.

Sato led Kal out of the bay and through the station's corridors. "Our home planet is destroyed, we all have lost family and friends, and we are facing an enemy the likes of which we have never seen before. I think the time has come for a little informality, so just call me Sato when it's the two of us. Besides, you're a recently converted civilian as I understand. I'm guessing you're still getting used to all the 'sirs' and 'ma'ams'."

"It's been easier adjusting than I would have thought," Kal responded.

"So, I read through your file, former logistics officer. The work you did was pretty impressive in the Sol System. Looks like you've been off the grid for a while, but that actually serves our purposes pretty well." They reached an intersection and Sato stopped and turned to face Kal. "Before we talk shop, I wanted my aide, Captain Ruiz, to give you a tour of the station. When you're done, meet me in my office."

Ruiz's tour was given at a rapid pace. The ease with which she rattled off facts and figures indicated that Kal wasn't the first person she'd given it to. Kapustin was slightly larger than Caracas Station in volume, making it the largest EDF station now that Sol was destroyed. It was designed as four spherical nodes, called domes, arranged in a tetrahedron shape. In the middle was a central dome, about twice as large as the others. Huge corridors connected all of the domes with each other.

"This station is the most advanced structure our species has ever built," Ruiz commented. "Each separate dome is self-contained and self-supporting. Even if you were to sever all the corridors, the domes would still be able to operate independently if they were resupplied."

They walked past a large unoccupied medical facility. The soldier at the front desk looked bored out of his mind.

"We also have the best medical and science resources in the EDF on this station. Its primary purpose is as a research hub for work so classified that it couldn't be developed anywhere else. It has a secondary mission of acting as an alternate headquarters because of its isolation and secrecy."

"Sounds like you're pretty proud of the place," Kal observed.

"Yeah, I guess I am. If it weren't for this station, we'd have no chance against the Ukhel. This is the perfect place to launch our counter-attack against them. Destroy them as they have tried to destroy us. You're here just in time to take part." Ruiz looked him in the eye for a moment and then kept walking. Kal wasn't sure if she was a wide-eyed optimist or delusional, but he was betting on the latter.

Although each dome was self-sufficient, they had different functions—research, training, logistics, fleet operations, and command and control in the central dome. The layout of each depended upon their purpose, but they all contained housing, life support, and at least some rudimentary storage. The design was ingenious but clearly not EDF.

After an hour they arrived in the central dome and Ruiz stopped in front of a non-descript door. "These will be your quarters, sir. If you would like to drop off your bags and come back out, I can take you to General Sato's office."

Kal walked into the room, which turned out to be a suite. It had a sitting room as well as a bedroom with a proper bed and a desk attached to the opposite wall. The viewscreens played a live feed from outside the station, showing the view from the center of the station.

After taking a quick inventory of the room, Kal dropped his bag on the bed and headed back to the corridor to join Captain Ruiz. "Okay, let's go."

General Sato's office was close to Kal's quarters—it appeared that all senior officers were located next to each other, same as on Caracas. The general's nameplate was on a small plaque affixed to the wall next to a set of wood-lined doors. As Kal stepped close, the doors opened automatically and he walked into the office. The office was spacious and luxurious enough it could have been on Earth. The wood that lined the walls was like nothing Kal had seen before. Wispy strands of gold and silver ran with the grain and was highlighted by the dark hue of the rest of the material.

"Beautiful, isn't it?" asked Sato.

"Amazing. How was this station built? It clearly wasn't Humans who built it, or at least not solely Humans."

Sato laughed. "You're right. Takes most people longer to figure it out. This was built with aid from the Qudoru. They prefabricated much of this station in conjunction with our best engineers. It was supposed to be the first foray into an eventual alliance with them."

Sato walked over to a small table next to the wall that held several decanters filled with what looked to be different types of liquor.

"Anything to drink?" Sato asked.

Kal shook his head, he'd just gotten over his withdrawal. The general grabbed a glass from the table, poured in a generous amount of a dark blue liquor, and dropped in a cube of ice. He took a seat in the sitting area in the corner and motioned for Kal to join him. As he joined the general, Kal continued to marvel at the luxury of the office.

"As you know from the Academy, Humanity took a long time to get over our xenophobic tendencies," Sato continued. "When we first discovered there were other space-faring species, it shook us to our core, scared us to death. We kept to ourselves and tried to build up our strength alone. We didn't seek to understand these other creatures or build bridges. We refused to enter into any alliance for fear that it could embroil us in a war we could not win."

"Yeah, but the Torgham war showed the error in that." Kal responded. "The fault was that you cannot always choose when you will go to war—it isn't something you necessarily plan out."

"Very true," agreed Sato. "However, it did work for a long time as we continued to advance and develop. You have to at least credit the Torgham with teaching us that we couldn't be an island in this galaxy. The X'Ado were willing to help us defeat the Torgham but weren't willing to do much else."

"No reason to. They seek balance." Kal replied. The X'Ado had a particular belief in nature, that true harmony existed in gaining what they called a complete balance. Kal didn't understand too much of their philosophy on this, but knew it extended to every aspect of their existence.

"Thankfully our leaders learned from the conflict and began to reach out to other civilizations. We opened up dialog with all our neighbors, except the Torgham, trying to establish trade and technology-sharing agreements. Not a lot of citizens know this, but we had agreements with the Qudoru, X'Ado, Kurz, and Tounous. Mostly they were just words in a document; we didn't have much to offer in the way of trade or technology. This station was one of the first concrete outputs of that process." Sato sighed. "Unfortunately, it was too little, too late to stop us and all of our allies from being decimated by the Ukhel."

"We may still be able to recover some of what we lost," Kal said.

"I hope you're right." The general shifted in his seat. "Right now, I am, as far as I know, the most senior Human official left alive, military or civilian. We continue to send out probes and scout teams trying to locate survivors and figure out where the enemy is. So far, we've had no luck on either front. Your arrival brought us the first news of the enemy attack on Caracas Station and New America. It looks like after cutting off our head, they're consolidating control over what remains."

"So, you haven't heard of any other systems being invaded like New America?" Kal asked.

"No, not yet, but we expect to hear of more soon. The Ukhel's intentions seem pretty clear. They will invade and subjugate every system in this portion of the galaxy. The communications net continues to degrade as the Ukhel destroy any probes they encounter. We've sent out as many exploratory probes as we can, but they're unreliable, and we're seeing our losses mount. We also worry about the risk of one of our probes getting captured—if the Ukhel are able to decrypt the memory banks, they can find out the location of this base. Frankly, my information is, and always will be, at least two weeks behind what's actually happening now. We could be the only Humans left in the universe and I wouldn't know until at least fourteen days from now."

Sato sighed and took a large gulp from the glass. "I'll be honest. Motivation is at an all-time low, not only for the soldiers, but for me as well. All of us have lost friends and family; many of us have lost everything. We've had to put passcodes on the airlocks to prevent people from jumping out. I built my career, my ethos, on the concept of the attack. However, I find it hard to know what to do when we don't even have the capability to attack, and if we did, we wouldn't know where to go."

"Don't we still have ships out there?" Kal was disturbed to see the legendary General Sato like this. The initial warmth and enthusiasm from his greeting with Kal was gone, leaving him deflated.

"There are still a lot of ships that are unaccounted for. This station is known only to a select few. We've received some refugees, but I am sure there are many EDF vessels traveling aimlessly, not sure where to go or what to do next. I have several scouts traveling between systems, spreading the message for our commanders to come back here." He raised his glass and took another drink. "We have to be extremely careful though. Our only defense is our secrecy. The scouts are only allowed to give our coordinates in person, since we cannot be sure the Ukhel will not intercept our communications."

Sato placed his empty glass on the table in front of them.

"We know that some have heard the message, and we're seeing a trickle of Human ships. But that creates another problem—the station is already filled with more vessels and people than it was ever intended to hold. Our supply lines are gone and our materials on hand are dwindling."

"I'm guessing that's where I come in," Kal offered.

"Exactly. Our chief of logistics was in the Sol System when it was destroyed. Captain Ruiz has been doing the best she can in covering, but she's a Tac-I. Excellent officer, but I don't think she ever encountered a problem she didn't think she could shoot into submission."

"So, you want me to take over for her?" asked Kal.

"We need a professional to help us organize. Right now, I can't tell you how much we have of what or where it is. We think we're short on some critical items, but without a better understanding I can't tell you how short we are. Frankly, I come from the Captain Ruiz school—shoot first, and second, and then ask questions if you have time. But I've been in the EDF long enough to know that doesn't cut the cake. Most of the time, victory is based on a soldier's ability to eat, to have a ship to pilot, and weapons to shoot. That is something we are sorely lacking right now." Sato gave a wan smile.

"I'll have Captain Ruiz brief you on where we stand. Also, we have a daily staff meeting, and I would like you to start attending these. All of the resources and information of this station are now at your disposal." Sato stood up from his seat and Kal followed.

"Thank you. I promise that we'll get this situation fixed," Kal said.

"You had better, because we're Humanity's final hope." General Sato looked grim as Kal stepped out the door and into the hallway.

Chapter Thirteen

Over the course of the next several weeks, Kal worked with Captain Ruiz to figure out what supplies they had on hand and how they would get resupplied. They'd taken over an extremely complex logistics apparatus with the additional complication of requiring the utmost secrecy so as not give up the existence or location of Kapustin Station. Incoming deliveries had trickled to almost nothing, and the supplies they had received were stored pell-mell around the station without proper organization or inventory.

Although clearly a motivated officer, Ruiz was no logistician, and she still was hampered by the trauma of the Ukhel attack. Her notes were a mess and she freely admitted she hadn't placed the effort into tracking their supplies that she should have. Instead, she spent much of her time thinking how they would wage an offensive against the enemy.

Despite her logistical failings, Kal and Ruiz formed a friendship. She was a no-nonsense Tac-I officer from the Patagonia system. Her wife had died in the Ukhel attack on Sol, and she channeled the sorrow she felt into a white-hot rage. She continually talked about taking revenge on the Ukhel and the pain she would inflict upon them. Kal knew her plans for revenge were a fantasy but was smart enough to understand they were the only thing keeping her going.

During his off-time, Kal started to visit the gym to try and get back into shape. The EDF had muscular stimulation machines to help soldiers grow bulk through direct stimulation. However, he felt the machines were no substitute for a two-hour workout.

He also visited Ekon in sick bay and then Base Camp a couple of times. Ekon had been fitted with cutting-edge prosthetic legs, and after a week of recuperation and training with them, he was able to rejoin his squad in Base Camp. Ekon was never what Kal would have described as warm, but the passive aggressive attitude had been replaced with something else that Kal couldn't define. He didn't think Ekon particularly relished seeing him, but Kal felt an illogical sense of guilt over what had happened to him. He wondered if they would have become friends if they hadn't been through the horror of the Ukhel attack together. Ekon performed well in Base Camp, and as Kal expected, the instructors treated him with a certain reverence his fellow recruits didn't enjoy.

During his visits, Kal would also talk with Sergeant Jones. Despite everything they had been through, he continued to maintain a respectful distance from Kal. At first Kal was resentful, but he began to appreciate how Jones maintained his bearing as a non-commissioned officer and remained laser-focused on training the new recruits.

Base Camp took up a significant portion of available space on Kapustin Station. It had never been intended as a training facility, so the cadre converted any space they could into space for classrooms and drill. The training was accelerated due to circumstances but remained organized around four phases—military drill, ship operations, atmospheric combat, and zero gravity combat.

Kal remembered enjoying the military drill portion of Base Camp—especially learning the history of the Earth Defense Force. The current traditions of the EDF could be traced back to the space branches of the various countries on Earth, most of which had sprung from their armies or air forces. This lineage influenced much of their customs, terms, and hierarchy. There were still some terms from the old seafaring navies though. It made sense, as the large capital ships and mechanics of space travel were very similar to being at sea for months on end with no ability to communicate. It was ironic that the advent of the fold drive had at once decreased the distance between places while at the same time increased the difficulties in communication.

As a student of history, Kal saw many similarities between their current period and the nineteenth century. Vast planets were separated by the ocean of space, and ships, once underway, had no ability to communicate. In the period prior to the advent of the fold drive, all of Humanity was connected by an almost instantaneous network that stretched around Earth. They had taken the ability to communicate instantly for granted. When the fold drive opened everything up, space doctrine had to be completely rewritten.

That freedom came at a cost. Although not discussed often, Kal had learned about the prisoners and debtors that had been forced to be subjects as countries perfected the fold drive. Often, the tests were failures, destroying the ship and killing everyone aboard. Other times, the ships disappeared, never to be heard from again.

As a colonist, Kal also knew the distance and delay in communications made it difficult for the UEG to keep control of their planets. Only the threat of other species kept the colonies in line. They were resentful that they were seen as junior partners in the UEG, but didn't have the resources to hold their own against the other powers of the galaxy.

As he was walking around the station to clear his mind, Kal reflected on his conversations with Nicole aboard the *Oruc*. He had tried to see her in the brig, but General Sato had left strict orders forbidding visitors. He was ashamed to admit his initial disgust at her actions had faded, but he certainly wasn't about to tell that to the general.

Over the weeks, EDF and civilian ships continued to trickle in. Due to space constraints, station operations had to set up external gangways, since the atmospheric landing bays were filled with ships or Base Camp recruits. Luckily, Kal and Ruiz found they had enough supplies for the near future, even with the additional personnel. But morale continued to suffer as people grieved the loss of their loved ones.

When Kal had first arrived, the news of the Ukhel's attack had been fresh, and most people were still in a state of shock. As time wore on, the shock turned to depression. The station operations team tried to create activities to boost morale, but a general feeling of hopelessness and aimlessness continued to pervade the station corridors.

Even General Sato became despondent and depressed. The daily briefings felt almost rote in nature and he became less and less vocal in the meetings. In contrast, Kal felt himself become more driven as time went on.

He figured he had the advantage of being much further removed from his own personal tragedy. Kal had lost everything years ago, everybody else was just catching up to him. *I probably would have been one of those people walking out the airlock*, Kal thought to himself. The distance from his own loss acted to both protect him from it and to insulate himself from the new tragedy that had befallen all of Humanity.

Kal began to realize the entire leadership team of the station was paralyzed—whether by sorrow, fear, or something else. They went through the motions, as had been drilled into them during their time in the EDF, but there was no discussion or dissension; General Sato decided not to send out more probes or ships due to concerns over the Ukhel discovering their location, and soon, Kal and Ruiz were the only voices in favor of continuing the missions. Unfortunately, Ruiz often was more harmful than helpful, her fiery arguments cementing the opposition to her plan.

"We need to do something!" Kal found himself once again acting as the voice for action during the daily brief. "It's been ten weeks since I came to this station, and we have yet to do a thing."

"What would you suggest?" Brigadier General Santiago Lee asked. Lee was the station commander and had lost his parents in the attack on Earth. Luckily for him, his husband

and two small children were living on the station and had been spared in the attacks.

"Well, for one, we should be sending out significantly more scout ships. We've only sent five in the past week, and those were to systems we've already reconned. We know New America and Mariga were captured, but with the probe communication network completely down at this point, we have no reliable intel about the other two colonies, not to mention the non-Human systems that were attacked by the Ukhel. Also—"

"I think it is safe to assume that they have been captured as well," interrupted General Lee.

"Maybe, sir, but we don't know that for sure. We also have no idea what has happened since New America and Mariga were captured—we need to know what the Ukhel are doing to those planets." Kal bristled at the general's condescending tone.

"Every ship we send out has the coordinates to this base." Lee continued the same argument he used every time. "If any of them get captured, we may have just given up our location. We're not ready to face an Ukhel fleet, and we have over a hundred thousand people on this station."

"Sir, as I said before, we have two people on the crew memorize the coordinates and wipe the travel history from the ship. The Ukhel won't be able to find the coordinates."

"But what if they torture the crew? We don't know what they're capable of, and you're talking about risking Humanity's future." Kal knew Lee was concerned about his family aboard the station and couldn't blame him—he was one of the few people who still had something left.

"Granted, but we are never going to be ready to face them unless we take some sort of action." Kal had been through this argument so many times that the anger he used to have was slowly being replaced by resignation.

"I am afraid I have to agree with Lee," Sato started with his familiar refrain, "we can't just—"

The general was interrupted by a loud howl of frustration—Ruiz was on her feet, her face red with frustration. "I can't take this anymore. We sit here with our thumbs up our asses and just wait for something to happen to us. I thought you were a soldier, sir. What are we waiting for? We need to understand what the situation is, gather whatever forces we can, and then we need to strike back. I can't take this waiting around, this stalling. If we aren't going to do anything, then what's the point? What *is* the point of all of this? At least the people who are jumping out of airlocks are making a choice."

Ruiz walked to the door of the conference room and whirled around. "General Sato, sir, you cannot just sit here. We have to take action, and I am not coming back to this idiotic meeting until we do."

"Captain Ruiz, you are an officer in the Earth Defense Force and cannot—"

Major General Gbeho was interrupted by Captain Ruiz's laugh. "There's no Earth left! The EDF failed to defend it. There. Is. No. EDF. Don't you get it? Don't any of you get it?"

Ruiz stormed out the door, leaving a trail of silence in her wake.

As the quiet hung heavy over the room, Kal looked around the table at the assorted generals and colonels, their eyes wide like frightened animals. Ruiz's theatrical outburst exposed a truth they didn't want to admit—they were afraid. Gbeho's mouth opened and closed as she found the words. Finally, she blurted out, "General Sato, I call for Captain Ruiz to be reprimanded."

General Sato looked at her silently, a frown on his face, his forehead lined with thought. "No...no, she is right. We need to do something."

"Absolutely!" Lee leaned forward and looked around at the group. "But before we can take action, we need to map out all the courses of action."

"Quite right, we don't want unnecessary risk," one of the colonels agreed.

"Yes, a rash decision would be disastrous. I'll take the lead on the course of action development and analysis," Gbeho offered. "We'll need some time to develop the courses of action, so I suggest we postpone our daily stand-ups until a week from now when we will convene to decide on our next steps."

Kal's mind wandered as he listened to the officers contort themselves in order to prevent action. His hand traced over the monitor in the table, making small doodles, as he listened to them discuss the bureaucratic steps they would take, clearly meant to delay the day when they would have to make a decision.

After the meeting ended, Kal walked to Captain Ruiz's quarters. "Come in," she responded when he announced himself at the door.

Kal walked in to find the woman behind her desk, looking at something on the monitor. In one hand, she held her sidearm, and in the other, an open bottle. Kal could tell by the pungent smell filling the room that whatever it was, it wasn't water. He felt a spike of concern, Ruiz was dramatic, but this was excessive, even for her.

"Sir, what's going on?" she asked casually, her eyes red.

"You tell me," Kal replied. He tried to determine how quickly he could move to intervene if she decided to use the weapon on herself. He knew Ruiz well enough at this point to believe she wouldn't turn it on him.

"Eh, don't worry. I've done this every night since I found out about my wife." She shrugged. "Guess I just don't have the nerve to do it though. I just can't go through with it."

"Well, I'm glad for that. Just to make me feel better, can you put that down?" Kal gestured to the sidearm.

"This? You know it's a collector's piece. Beautiful weapon. Uses chemical propellant. They don't make these anymore." She smiled down at the gun.

"Oh, I know. I used to have one myself. It was a gift when I retired." He'd left it on the *Annie*.

"So, what happened after I left?" Ruiz put the gun in a drawer in her desk.

Kal told her about the staff's decision to develop a course of action analysis to determine what they should do next. She snorted when he told her about the call for her reprimand. When he detailed the halt in daily meetings until Gbeho was ready with her proposal, she laughed so loud Kal wondered if the sound could be heard in the corridor outside her quarters.

"Doesn't that beat all? They figured out a way to twist the situation so they could do even less. I swear that if I pointed that gun at Gbeho's head, she would ask me to wait so she could convene a meeting to help her decide what to do next." Ruiz nodded to the drawer.

"I think we've been going about this all wrong." Kal pushed the monitor back into its receptacle on the wall to clear the space between their faces. "Like you said, there really isn't an EDF anymore. We need to figure out what to do, and then do it—no more meetings or asking for permission. I bet you that they won't raise a hand to stop us. It would be too much work for them, too much risk."

"Oh, insubordination, I like it!" Ruiz's smile lit up her face. It was the first time Kal had seen her happy.

"Now we just need to figure out what to do and how we can create an excuse for our actions."

Kal and Ruiz spent the next several hours developing their plan. Despite constantly pressing General Sato and his staff to act, they found it difficult to figure out a realistic and achievable plan of action themselves that could make a difference against the Ukhel. They took solace in their belief that they couldn't make anything worse.

After they knew what they wanted to do, they had to figure out how. Although Kal doubted the General's staff would spend too much effort to stop them, he didn't think they would help them, or allow them to use their authority to make things happen.

"Okay, so I will go ahead and talk to Bergeron." Ruiz's mouth twisted, betraying her distaste of the imprisoned attaché. It took effort, but Ruiz finally saw the necessity of including her in their plan. Kal also had to admit he wanted her to have a chance to redeem herself.

"Unfortunately, we can't let her know everything. She's being monitored, and if Sato were to hear about this, he may just lock us up before we even start. Try and see if her skills are what we're looking for and if she is willing to help. I think she could be helpful on this mission, but her personnel file can only tell us so much. I'll talk to Captain Garcia." Kal concluded, "We'll need to get the pilots on board."

"Also, you need to talk to Jones," Ruiz reminded him. "We're both Tac-I, but I think he'll be more receptive to you. Seems to have a soft spot for you from what I can tell."

Kal was surprised. "Really? What makes you say that?"

"Don't you see how he scowls less when he sees you?" She elbowed him in the ribs. "Honestly, though I can talk to him—we're both Tac-I—but you've fought with him, and he respects you. That means something."

"Okay, I'll talk with Jones," agreed Kal.

"I have to admit," Ruiz said, "I care a lot more that we actually try and make this work than if it actually does work. I can't sit here anymore, and trying and failing sounds a hell of a lot better than not trying at all."

"Agreed." Kal stood up. "Now we just have to see if we can get others involved in our plan."

"Aren't mutinies fun?" Kal heard Ruiz chuckle as he walked out the door.

Chapter Fourteen

"Well, I gotta to admit, the other pilots are getting bored sitting here," Captain Garcia said. Kal approached him with their idea while he was relaxing on the pilot's deck, near the landing bays. "However, your plan won't work for two reasons.

"First, for what you want to do, only using scout ships won't cut it. They're fast, but they're also noticeable—if this is to work, you need to have ships that blend in. Second, you aren't going to get enough EDF pilots to sign on to your plan. Although I'm not sure if this is technically a mutiny or not, what you're talking about comes close enough that there are many who will flat-out refuse, or worse, report you."

"Good points. We can adjust the plan though," Kal said. "If we have your help, we can make it work."

"Go on." Garcia raised an eyebrow,

"If you talk with pilots you trust, and are *somewhat* tactful, we can avoid being reported. Also, there are a significant number of civilian pilots and ships that have been pressed into service. I think they can be brought to our side pretty easily."

"True, but how many ships do you need?" Garcia asked.

"We figure to need at least twenty to make this effective—though the more, the better." Kal looked Garcia in the eyes. "Now, are you in?"

"Of course I'm in." Garcia smiled. "I'm getting bored sitting here too."

Kal already talked with Staff Sergeant Jones, trying to get him bought into their plan. Part of it relied on the ground security that dismounted infantry soldiers could provide. Jones had initially been appalled by the idea, and Kal was worried that he might report what he and Ruiz were up to. After a few more visits, Kal saw the NCO start to soften. Finally, on his fifth trip to Base Camp, Jones relented in his opposition.

"Fine," the man admitted, "what you say makes sense. I don't like it, but I've seen what is going on in the fleet and among the soldiers. I'm getting tired of telling soldiers to wait for orders that aren't coming. I don't know any way to solve it other than what you've laid out."

Kal tried to hide his relief. Jones and the infantry were critical to making their plan work, and he didn't know who they would go to if they couldn't get him on their side. Kal had learned the sergeant was something of a legend among the soldiers. If he threw his weight behind them, they wouldn't have any problem getting volunteers.

"But," he paused, "you have to keep your promise. No action is taken until you have at least heard out General Gbeho's plan."

"I promise," Kal assured him. "In fact, we'd always planned on doing that. I don't want to go behind General Sato's back, but I don't think Gbeho will have much of a plan."

"I'm hoping that our leaders will do the right thing," Jones tried to reassure himself. "If we give him and his staff another opportunity, a last opportunity, then I think we would be at fault if we didn't do something."

"Exactly—we are doing this reluctantly." Kal was eager to agree. "But we can't continue to wait. Too much is at stake."

Kal continued to supervise logistics for the station while building support for their plan. Since going through a complete inventory, he knew there was little chance of their supplies running out anytime soon—fuel lasted a long time when you didn't send out any ships. It gave him reassurance that the station would still be able to operate if he left. Kal was busier now than he had been in over a decade, and he couldn't help noting the irony that his own state of mind was a mirror opposite of the people around him.

Captain Ruiz had been relieved of her position as aide to General Sato. It wasn't clear to Kal if anyone else had been assigned or if Sato had given up all pretense of needing an aide. But she took advantage of this lack of assigned duties to spend countless hours training the Base Camp recruits with Staff Sergeant Jones and the other instructors. As a Tac-I officer, she was an expert in combat—and battle suit training was the area in which she shined.

The gray battle suits completely covered the wearer's body, allowing them to operate in a vacuum as well as protecting against energy and kinetic attacks. There were several different models intended for different atmospheric and gravitational environments, but all were designed to increase the wearer's strength, provide an assortment of built-in weapons and equipment, and provide limited thrust capabilities. The standard-issue battle suit at Kapustin was designed primarily for planetary operations but was capable of operation in a vacuum for a limited time.

Kal occasionally visited Base Camp area to train on the suits with the recruits. When in the suit, the operator had a heads-up display that connected to the user's neural implant, displaying key information as well as providing almost-instant feedback based on the operator's thoughts. The suits were tricky to master, though, because they required the user to maintain strict control of their thoughts in critical situations. If the user panicked while wearing the suit, it could be disastrous. Kal got a perverse pleasure in watching the recruits crash off the station's bulkhead as they learned to control their thoughts. Although it was funny in training, it could be deadly in an actual combat scenario.

When the Base Camp instructors learned Kal was an expert shot, they asked him to guide the recruits in small arms. The simple task of training fresh and motivated recruits gave him a welcome respite from dealing with paperwork and the frustrating brick wall of inaction at the top levels. It also allowed him to make inroads with the soldiers he was trying to recruit. Marksmanship was ultimately an exercise in maintaining calm, controlling breathing and movement so that you were able to fire accurately.

Major General Gbeho took two weeks to develop her courses of action. During that time, Kapustin Station received dismal information from the probes that returned, adding to Kal's frustration. Their suspicions were confirmed—both

Wudexingqiu and Patagonia had been captured, meaning Humanity no longer had control of any of their planets. The EDF had crumbled, their stations had been captured, and all but a handful of ships had been captured or destroyed.

Most species were either occupied, in complete disarray, or had sworn fealty to the Ukhel. It was clear the invaders had done their homework, and their show of overwhelming force had cowed any species that were not already destroyed. What they didn't know, was how much resistance was truly left. Space was a large place, and it was easy to hide entire fleets and stations. He had to hope the Kurz, X'Ado, and the others had a station like Kapustin and were preparing a response.

In General Sato's briefing room, Kal looked at the attendees and the only word he could think of was deflated. They slumped in their chairs, their uniforms stained and unkempt, looking down as they waited for the briefing to begin. It was a group of people who would accept their defeat because they saw it as inevitable.

"Thank you all for your patience." General Gbeho began her presentation after the initial pleasantries were out of the way. "Based on our previous discussion we've identified three unique courses of action."

The viewscreen behind her flickered to a map of their section of the galaxy with Kapustin Station in the middle. Yellow circles surrounded a handful of planets and faint lines, indicting scouting routes, made their way between them, all of them starting and ending at the station. Almost all the planets were highlighted a deep red color, indicating capture by the Ukhel.

"The first course of action is to increase our scouting activity by fifty percent. It carries the increased risk of detection, but increases our intel capabilities. Of course, the scouts would remain on their current routes since we do not know where the Ukhel are and don't want to risk incidental or unwanted contact."

The map's overlay transformed. The web of circles and lines remained, but now there were several additional blue circles surrounding several major systems with blue lines connecting them to the station.

"Second, and I must say that this is the riskiest"—Kal snorted—"we can continue our scouting but develop an emergency resupply route. We would send several teams to scout ahead and determine planets we could use for resupply. They would only make contact if there was no evidence of enemy activity. If they saw anything they would fold out immediately."

All but a few of the circles and lines disappeared from the map.

"Finally, we can continue as planned, but develop a series of time gates to slowly and methodically increase scout traffic. Our working group recommends this one, as we still have at least six months of supplies thanks to Colonel Norman's work." Gbeho nodded to Kal.

The officers silently contemplated the options for a moment. Kal was disappointed but not surprised by the relatively conservative options Gbeho had laid out. He looked at Captain Ruiz, meeting her eyes, and could see she felt the same as he did. Sato and his staff couldn't act anymore, the briefing made it clear.

"I think before we talk there is pressing information that this group should know." Kal paused for effect. "One of our scouts, the *Lagos*, left for a routine patrol to Kurz-controlled space and has yet to return. They should have been back eight hours ago." A small lie, but one he knew would get their attention. The scout ship was in fact floating in open space, waiting for further instructions. If they were not contacted in the next twenty-four hours, they would return and report that they'd had technical issues with their fold drive.

The pilots they'd recruited were already getting their ships ready to depart, and the infantry and Tac-I squads were loading up on the ships as well. No matter what happened, a small fleet of fully loaded scout ships and civilian vessels would leave the station that day.

Their plan was simple, launch as many ships to as many different planets as possible to figure out what the hell was going on. To cover their tracks, they'd cooked up an emergency to get Sato to approve a small recovery mission. When a small fleet of ships left, the hope was that there'd be an initial wave of confusion which would prevent a response from the station. It would give the conspirators some plausible deniability that what they were doing went against Sato's intent.

These small fire teams would travel to as many planets in the galaxy as they could reach. They would spread word to as many Humans as they safely could about Kapustin Station, establish contact with any planetary or interstellar governments still resisting the Ukhel, scout out the location of enemy fleets, attempt to determine the status of the Human worlds and as many others as they could, and look for potential suppliers or ways to restore the supply lines to Kapustin. Then they would all rendezvous back at Kapustin and provide any intel they gathered. Kal and Ruiz just hoped Sato and his staff would be smart enough to use it.

The plan wasn't as audacious as they would have liked, but they had to operate in the reality they were given. It was certainly more than General Sato and his staff would ever directly approve.

Kal and Ruiz would be traveling on the *Oruc* with Nicole Bergeron. Their mission would take them to Kurz space to try to establish diplomatic relations with whatever remained of the Kurz government. As a sort of ally to the UEG, the Kurz were one of their best hopes for aid. The Ukhel had attacked them, but Kal hoped the more advanced Kurz had been able to secret away some of their fleet and resources. Nicole's expertise and knowledge of the Kurz made her critical to the mission.

Kal's news of the lost ship had the intended impact—the room went deathly silent, and the officers around the table

161

wore shocked expressions on their faces. General Sato scanned the room, searching for an answer or for someone to step up and say something. Instead, he found his own impotence and fear reflected back at him.

"Well, we need to do something. We can't let one of our scouts fall into their hands," Ruiz said, breaking the silence.

"Sending out anyone else will just increase the risk. We should be patient and wait." General Lee's suggestion wasn't something they had counted on. He truly was paralyzed with fear.

"Excellent suggestion, General Lee, but"—Kal let the word hover in the air for a moment—"they could also be stranded without a fold drive, and by leaving them out there we risk the entire station. The Ukhel may come across them and find our location."

Kal watched to see if he had gauged the audience correctly. He knew that everyone, except for Ruiz and himself, was only there to survive another day. They were sheep, waiting for someone to direct them—the concept of taking action had been utterly buried by their fear and loss.

"That's true," Lee conceded, "but what can we do?"

"Well, the scouts are already prepping a mission to find them." Kal knew he had to get this out quickly and move on. "There are some Tac-I and infantry squads available as well that are at full strength and ready to assist. Should we stop them, though?"

"Absolutely not," interjected Ruiz. "If we have the ships and soldiers already staged, we can take a small force with us.

However, if they are in Kurz-controlled space, we need someone who is familiar with their customs and culture."

Now was the most dangerous part of their scheme. Nicole Bergeron was a traitor to Humanity. As far as everyone around the table was concerned—with the exception of Kal and Ruiz—she would remain a prisoner to her dying day.

"True, if they find the *Lagos* in their space, it could be considered a violation of their sovereignty and our agreements. As we all know, the Kurz do not see these types of events in black and white." Kal wasn't sure that was true, it might be. But he was counting on the fact that neither did anyone else in the room.

Once again, the room went silent. "Well, there is Ms. Bergeron—she is an expert on the Kurz," a colonel seated at the far end of the table blurted out. Kal wanted to cheer. It was exactly what they needed.

"Never," General Sato said, scandalized. "The woman's a traitor. She sold secrets to the enemy."

The conversation turned to an argument regarding the merits of allowing Nicole Bergeron to assist in the rescue mission. Kal and Ruiz watched silently, occasionally making a small comment or asking a pointed question to change the course and stoke the fire of their argument. They wanted to keep them taking and wear themselves out without reaching a conclusion. It would make them more malleable in the end. The important thing was they were talking about the mission as a given, and only quibbling about the specifics of crew.

163

"We know Ms. Bergeron is not going to betray the UEG or EDF again. I have interrogated her personally and can say she has nothing but remorse for her actions. Not using an asset that would be valuable on this mission is putting emotion ahead of logic." Kal had no idea if his argument would work. If not, he and Ruiz had already agreed they wouldn't try to break her out but would instead do the best they could without her.

"Fine," General Sato said as he slapped his hand down on the table. He did not look pleased.

"I'll volunteer to take command of this mission." Kal knew that they had won and needed to end the conversation quickly, before there was second guessing. The officers in the room wanted to be absolved of responsibility, and he was happy to oblige.

"Well, I think one of our operational commanders should be the lead. No offense, Colonel, but this is what they are trained for." Brigadier General Lee perked up at the thought of a logistics officer commanding a tactical recovery mission.

The EDF had two classes of officers: operational and support. Operational officers were infantry, pilots, and the like. They were the ones who devised the plan of attack and led soldiers into battle. Support officers like Kal provided the materials, communications, and other tools that the forces needed to achieve their objectives. It was highly unusual and against EDF protocol for a logistics officer to lead any sort of tactical mission.

"Too true, but I have experience with the Kurz both in a public and private capacity. Another officer will not have that level of knowledge."

"Good point, Norman, but you need someone who has experience in combat operations." General Sato's demeanor had changed now that the pivotal decision had been made. "Gbeho, can you detail someone to be the operations officer for Norman? Norman, you will be leading the mission, but they can deal with the day-to-day navigation and take command in the case of any contact with the enemy."

Kal knew when he had been beat. "Yes sir, I'll work with the scout teams to depart as soon as possible. Can I have Captain Ruiz detailed for this mission? Her Tac-I background may come in handy."

"Yes, I think that makes sense." Sato sounded happy to send Ruiz away. "I'm glad we were able to work this out. Colonel Norman, we are counting on you to get our soldiers back."

Chapter Fifteen

Kal and Ruiz regrouped in his stateroom immediately after the meeting to go through their next steps. They were committed now. Their plan was reliant on speed, and getting off the station before Sato's staff had time to realize what was going on.

"Well, that worked out pretty well," Kal said.

"Yeah," Ruiz agreed, "now we just need to see who Gbeho assigns to this op. Depending on who it is, they may be a giant pain in the ass."

At that moment, Garcia and Jones walked through the door. "Hope you weren't talking about me, ma'am," Jones announced with almost a smile on his face.

"I wasn't, but it still applies." Ruiz smiled.

"So, we've got the green light. Garcia, can you confirm that the pilots are ready?" Kal asked.

Garcia had been grinning since he came through the door. Since agreeing to be part of the plan, the pilot had become their biggest supporter and thrown himself into the effort wholeheartedly.

"Yes, sir. We're ready. We've got thirty-nine ships prepped and ready to go—four scouts, with the remainder being civilian ships confiscated by the EDF. All have flight crews that have been briefed and understand the mission. The thirty-five civilian ships have been given their objectives, and we feel like we can cover about a hundred planets if everything goes smoothly. They'll scout out the area and will contact the locals, should the situation permit.

"The four scouts will depart together to rendezvous with the *Lagos*, which is waiting for us about a light year from here. Once we rendezvous, we'll split and each head to the space controlled by the other species the Ukhel have attacked. For each, we've identified the most likely secondary seat of government, so each team will start there."

"I have three squads of infantry and one squad of Tac-I, all with battle suits, ready to rock." Jones seamlessly picked up the narrative. "We'll be providing cover for landing parties on the scout ships as needed."

"The traitor," Ruiz said with a sneer, "will be with us on the *Oruc*. The other scout ships at least have someone familiar with the alien cultures they'll be traveling to."

"Sounds like we all know the plan," Kal said. "I want to make sure that everyone understands not only the importance of this mission but the possible repercussions, even if we are successful. We are essentially co-opting some of the very limited resources that Humanity has left. There's a good chance we could be branded as traitors should this not go to plan. Hell, even if it does go to plan." Kal wasn't sure what the reaction from Sato and his staff would be when they arrived back at Kapustin. Normally, they'd be thrown in the brig, but Sato and his staff didn't seem like the type that would go to that amount of effort.

"It's not like they were using these ships anyways," Jones said. Although initially hesitant, the sergeant was completely onboard now.

"The stakes are too high to sit around and wait for the Ukhel to find us. We need to start taking the fight to the enemy." Ruiz's eyes glistened for a moment. "They need to pay."

"I agree, but I want to make sure what we are doing is crystal clear to everyone. I am asking you all to risk your lives and potentially commit a capital offense. The EDF is gone, we're just people now. Every single person who joins us should be doing it willingly and with their eyes open."

"I explained it to every single soldier," Jones said. "We agreed it'll make a great story one day."

"If we get to tell it." Garcia raised an eyebrow.

"You gotta have faith, sir," Jones said as he gave the pilot a small shove.

Garcia laughed. "Just had to say it. Eyes wide open, right?"

"We've got an hour," Kal said. "Everyone knows what they need to do. Let's get to it."

Kal had a few things to do before they left—not the least of which was to meet the officer assigned to their mission.

He headed to the station's operations cluster next to the landing bays. Although the command center was where the orders were issued, the operations cluster was where they were created. The soldiers there tracked every mission, drafted orders, and conducted ongoing contingency planning. It also served as a secondary command center if the primary was destroyed. On most stations or ships Kal had been on, the operations center was a beehive of activity with soldiers running across the floor or shouting at each other across the room.

This one was eerily quiet. A skeleton crew manned the neat matrix of consoles in the center of the room. Their faces betrayed their indifference and boredom, eyes vacantly looking at their monitors or staring off into the distance. As Kal walked through the rows of consoles he noticed one technician was clearly using her neural implant, her eyes staring off in the distance while tears ran down her face.

Probably looking at family photos, he thought grimly.

He walked to the middle of the room, looking for the battle captain—the officer that supervised the day-to-day activity of the center. They were responsible for directing the technicians at the consoles and responding to any emergencies that came up.

Kal found the man stretched in his chair, slowly sipping out of a glass. He sat back with his feet propped up on his console and his mouth turned up in a feline grin. A young soldier leaned over his desk, smiling back, as if they were sharing a particularly wicked secret.

"Look, I promise you, the stuff will make you go places that you have—"

"Never been before?" Kal finished the captain's sentence.

He shot up and his grin vanished. Kal turned to dismiss the other soldier only to find she had disappeared as if into thin air. *Neat trick*, thought Kal.

"I'm Colonel Norman. I'm supposed to have an operations officer on my mission to recover the *Lagos*. General Gbeho said to come down here to brief them and pick them up." Kal didn't really care about the state of discipline. As far as he was concerned, most of the soldiers were right not to care—their leaders clearly did not.

The captain quickly checked his viewscreen. "Lieutenant Colonel Zhou will be joining you, sir. He's in the back office, over there." The captain pointed to a door in the corner and then leaned forward again slightly as if exchanging confidences. "Is it true that you're actually going to Kurz space? Like, are we actually making our move?"

Kal nodded. "Yes, we're heading to Kurz space. As for making our move, we'll see. I can promise you this though, we aren't going to sit around anymore."

"About time, sir. I haven't seen a ship leave the station in over a week. Feels like we're just waiting to die," the captain confided.

"Not anymore," Kal said. He rapped his knuckles on the desk. "Remember, you're an officer. You should be setting an example on this station. Not sitting around, hitting on soldiers."

The man blushed. "Yes, sir." It could have been his mind playing tricks, but Kal thought he sat up a little straighter in his chair.

As he walked across the operations cluster, he marveled at the technology on display. The room was two decks tall with a large viewscreen covering an entire wall. The consoles in the center of the room were clearly state-of-the-art, with large high-resolution holographic displays. The cutting-edge technology seemed out of place when he saw the laconic conversations and defeated postures of the soldiers operating it.

"Colonel Norman?" Lieutenant Colonel Zhou folded the monitor he was looking at into the wall and got up as Kal entered his office. "Pleased to meet you, sir."

"Hello, Colonel Zhou, same here."

"So, could you fill me in on the operation, sir? I understand we're leaving in less than an hour?" Zhou stood erect, his eyes trained earnestly on Kal.

Kal provided Zhou the official reason for the mission, emphasizing the grass roots nature of the effort to recover the pilots and the wisdom of General Sato's staff in sanctioning it. Zhou was a wild card in the mission, and Kal wasn't sure what the man would do when he realized their real intentions after they left Kapustin Station. Kal wasn't worried about him directly sabotaging the mission, but he didn't want the guilt of having to brig a loyal officer.

"Remember, this mission is a little non-standard," Kal said.

171

"I'll say. But I think it's exactly what we need to do. I'm looking forward to getting out there." Kal had the impression Zhou was putting on a show for his benefit.

"Maybe, but a small step if anything. Grab your stuff and meet me on the *Oruc*. Don't be late, as we aren't waiting around." Kal shook Zhou's hand and started turning to leave.

"Already prepped to go. I packed my go bag as soon as I heard. I will see you on the ship."

Kal nodded and stepped out of the office. Zhou was a by-the-book officer, that might be a problem. He checked the time on his implant. *About thirty minutes left, just time enough for my final stop.*

The brig was located on another dome, which meant he had to hurry. The problem with the station's redundant design had become clear to Kal as he found himself once again on a lift, traveling through one of the tunnels to another spoke. Travel was very inefficient; he spent a significant amount of his time travelling between domes.

The guards let Kal into the brig after a thorough review of his credentials and direct authorization from command.

"Wait here, sir," said a guard, leaving Kal alone in the interrogation room.

It was one of the few places in the station that was not well lit. The dark gray walls loomed in on him while a bright light shined on the chair opposite. The other thing that stood out as different to Kal was the empty gray walls, there wasn't a viewscreen or console in sight. He knew that there was a complete sensor array monitoring the room—measuring body temperature, heart rate, perspiration, and a host of other variables—but it was invisible to the naked eye.

Nicole walked in through a door on the opposite wall with a guard a few meters behind her, weapon pointed at her back. She sat in the chair opposite Kal and set her hands on the table. Her restraints unclasped and lay themselves flat beside her wrists.

"So, to what do I owe the honor?" She seemed tired and defeated. The fire Kal had seen previously replaced by resignation. "Your friend, Captain Ruiz, was in here a few days ago, asking me questions."

"Was she?" Kal feigned surprise. "I'll cut straight to the chase, we have a missing ship, and we think it may be stranded in Kurz space. You are, by far, the foremost expert on their culture on this station. We want you to go with us when we leave in the next thirty minutes." Kal spoke quickly, worried she'd start asking questions. Questions he couldn't answer while having the brig's security team listening in.

"Huh," Nicole said, mouth pursed. "And what makes you think that I would want to do this?"

"You said you wanted to help. You said you wanted to try and make up for the mistakes you made. Was that a lie?"

"No, but am I going to just end up back in this cell?" Nicole sat back in her chair.

"Maybe. Probably. But at least you would be doing *something*. We need you; we need your help. I'm asking you because I know that you care and want to the right thing. But

173

if nothing else, do it for yourself. Do something that will make up, at least in some small way, for what you did before."

Nicole sat quietly, biting her lip and cracking her knuckles as she thought. "Okay, I'll do it. But during the mission, I want to be free. No restraints, and no locking me in a cell." She smiled sweetly. "I promise I'll be a good girl."

"Fine," Kal hoped that the audio of his conversation with Nicole wouldn't reach Sato before they left. He had a feeling the general wouldn't agree to unrestricted access for her considering her past crimes. "I'm going to get your release authorized." He winked. "Wait here."

Nicole didn't laugh at the joke.

Kal walked to the passageway outside and contacted General Sato's new aide for final approval. After a few minutes, it came through with the general's authorization. After five minutes for out-processing, they were walking out the door, headed to the landing bays.

"So, what aren't you telling me?" Nicole asked once they were out of sight of the brig. "Captain Ruiz was asking a lot of questions around my experience with the Kurz, and now you show up for a last-minute mission that just happens to need that same expertise."

"Of course, there's more. But I'll tell you later, once we're gone."

"I just hope I haven't signed up to be accused of committing treason again."

"No, this time you would have plausible deniability." Kal kept up the pace after they took the lift to the dome containing the landing bays. They arrived at the *Oruc's* bay to find the ship's engines already active.

"Looks like we're just in time," observed Nicole.

They entered the ship to find Lieutenant Colonel Zhou, Captain Ruiz, and Staff Sergeant Jones waiting for them in the cargo bay.

"Sir, we have everyone accounted for and are ready to depart," Zhou reported.

"Okay, let's get going. I'm going to head to my stateroom. Ruiz, can you join me? I have some questions regarding the soldiers' equipment. Zhou, I will leave it up to you regarding our departure from the station. Garcia should already have the coordinates set."

"I'll head to my stateroom," declared Nicole.

"I've got a detail ready to escort the prisoner," Jones said.

"That won't be necessary," Kal replied.

"Sir?" Zhou frowned at Kal. "She's a confirmed traitor to the UEG. You're going to let her walk around the ship?"

"Yes." Kal met the man's eyes. "I agreed to let her remain free during the mission. Besides, the ships security protocols will prevent her from doing anything."

"But—"

Kal cut off the colonel. "Ruiz, where is Ms. Bergeron staying?"

"Same one she was imprisoned in," Ruiz responded, her face flat.

175

"There you go. Zhou, let me know when we reach our first fold point." Kal walked the familiar path to his stateroom with Ruiz behind him.

"I don't like her," Ruiz spat as soon as they were through the door. "She sold our secrets to the Ukhel. She has blood on her hands."

"Perhaps," Kal said. He still didn't know how he felt about the entire situation. He did know that he believed Nicole when she said she wanted to make amends. But even though she hadn't realized who she was spying for, she had still betrayed the UEG. "Either way, there's nothing we can do about it now. We're committed."

"Yes, we are. Finally." Ruiz smiled broadly.

Chapter Sixteen

"Colonel Norman, we're ready to fold." Zhou's voice came through the speaker in Kal's stateroom.

Kal pushed himself out of his desk chair. "Okay, I'm heading to the cockpit now."

The departure from Kapustin Station had been relatively smooth. He half expected to receive an urgent message from General Sato asking what he was doing but he'd been left undisturbed. Kal took the time to put away his clothes and personal items as well as write a short message to General Sato that would be sent as they folded. Once the *Oruc* left the area with the other scout ships, thirty-five civilian ships would depart. Kal felt he owed it to Sato, and his staff, to let them know what was going on.

Every head in the cockpit turned to face him as he walked through the door. Colonel Zhou leaned back in his seat, blissfully unaware of the enormity of their actions. The rest of the flight crew was clearly nervous, knowing that they were about to fold out of system and trigger a mass exodus from the station.

"You still ready to do this, sir?" Lieutenant Park looked over his shoulder, the subtext plain in his words.

"As ready as I'll ever be." Kal gave a smile. "Captain Garcia, go ahead and proceed."

Garcia announced they were about to fold over the intercom and then let Kapustin Station control know. His hand danced over his console as he made final checks and activated the fold drive.

The stars blinked several times, indicating a small series of folds. After it stopped, the flight crew took a moment to review the sensors, checking for other ships and confirming their locations.

"We have one other ship in the area...Confirmed that it is the *Lagos*," reported Chief Kanumba.

"Excellent, make contact and find out their situation. Colonel Zhou, can you come with me to my stateroom. We have some things to discuss." Kal had brought his sidearm with him, just in case.

"Sir, what is going on?" Zhou looked back and forth at the monitors and Kal's face. "You knew they were going to be here?"

"I did—we all did. I think it's better if we talk in my quarters."

"General Gbeho didn't brief me on this—is this some sort of black ops mission?" Zhou looked around the cockpit, studying their faces.

"I'll explain. Follow me," Kal said as he ushered Zhou out of the cockpit. He made sure Zhou went first. He was clearly a career EDF man and most likely wasn't going to do anything rash, but he couldn't be too careful.

"Sit down." Kal motioned to the seat as they entered his stateroom.

"Sir, this isn't what was in the briefing I received. What's going on?" Zhou remained standing, his hands on his hips.

"What we're doing is in the full interest of saving the Human race. We are dedicated to fighting and destroying the Ukhel." Kal paused. "Every soldier aboard this ship has realized that our leaders have frozen. We've been sitting at Kapustin Station for almost three months and have yet to make a move or do anything."

"We've been planning, sir. Figuring out how to balance risk of attack with moving on the enemy."

Kal shook his head. "I can tell you that's not the case. I've been in the daily briefings with General Sato—at least before they were cancelled. I have nothing but respect for the general, but him and his staff don't know what to do and so have stopped doing anything. We've been slowly suffocating ourselves. A group of us felt it was time to take action." Kal outlined their plan to Zhou, who grew more frantic with each word.

Once Kal was done, he took a long draw of water from a glass, his eyes still on the colonel.

"This is crazy. This is insane," Zhou declared, wringing his hands.

"I promise you, not doing anything would be much more insane."

"Sir, I'm not sure if we're committing treason, but we're certainly close. What happens if the Ukhel find Kapustin Station?"

"If they find Kapustin Station, there is nothing we can do to stop them from destroying it. Forty or so scout and cargo ships certainly aren't going to make a difference."

"But you're talking about trying to infiltrate, to spy—what happens if they capture a ship? They'll find the location of Kapustin Station. We'll lead them right to us."

"There's always the chance. But the coordinates for the station are not in any of the ships—the flight crew for each ship has memorized them. They can still be retrieved through torture or somehow decrypting our neural implants, but you keep talking about the risk of taking action. What about the risk of inaction? If we continue to do nothing, how long until the Ukhel find the station or completely consolidate their hold on the planets they have conquered? How long until we run out of supplies?"

Kal placed his arm on the man's shoulder. "I'm sorry you got caught up in all of this. But this is where we are. If you don't want to be a part of this operation, then I'll respect that and leave you in your stateroom. However, if you want to join, then I need your promise you will do anything you can to help accomplish the mission. Nothing less will do."

Zhou met his gaze. "Sir, I will not commit treason. You are betraying the oath you took as an officer and you will face court martial when we return to Kapustin. This war will be won with discipline and training, not rogue officers with their own vendettas."

"I respect that." Kal stepped back into the doorway. "You're confined to your stateroom in that case. Please understand that everyone on this ship has committed to this operation, so there are no allies for you here. We're all in, to the end."

Zhou shook his head ruefully. "I want you to know that I will testify to how I am treated in confinement. I fear for your future when this all fails."

"Lieutenant Colonel Zhou, if our plan fails, we'll all be dead."

Kal called Captain Ruiz to take the man to his stateroom and enable the security protocol for the room. He couldn't say he was surprised by the colonel's response, but he had still held out hope. Lieutenant Colonel Zhou refused to bend, instead clinging to the traditions and norms of the EDF—he reminded Kal of Staff Sergeant Jones in many ways.

After Ruiz left with Zhou in hand, Kal made an announcement over the ship's intercom for key leaders to meet in the ship's galley. It took several minutes for everyone to trickle in. Kal looked at his co-conspirators as they entered, trying to sense their state of mind. On the bulkhead viewscreen he could see the crews of the other ships that made up their small flotilla—the *Lagos*, *Pittsburgh*, *Hannibal*, and *Han Xin*. Captain Garcia, Chief Kanumba, Lieutenant Park, Captain Ruiz, Staff Sergeant Jones, and Nicole Bergeron were all seated around the galley table with him.

"Thank you all for volunteering," Kal began. "I know the decision to join this venture wasn't an easy one."

"Pretty damn easy for me," Ruiz muttered under her breath.

"But I believe what we're doing is essential. We can't wait for the Ukhel to make the next move. We can't afford to sit in our station, waiting for a miracle."

"This fleet of scouts, along with the civilian cargo ships that left Kapustin Station immediately after us, will be traveling to known systems throughout the universe. We have three goals. The first is to better understand our enemy, their locations, and their capabilities. We know next to nothing about the Ukhel, which makes it hard to understand how to defeat them. The second is to find other species who are still willing to fight and see how we can work together. Finally, we need to report back as to what is going on around the galaxy. Kapustin has been operating almost completely blind for nearly a month. This blindness has been used as an excuse for inaction. We have to force them to see what is going on—no more excuses."

Kal sensed the unease around the room with his last sentence. It reminded them all that what they were doing went against the letter, if not the spirit, of the oaths they had sworn.

"You all have been given your orders and provided the resources to carry them out. We've gone over the plan in detail multiple times. After this discussion, we'll not be able to talk until the mission is complete."

Kal went through the plan a final time, outlining where each ship would be heading and their goals. The *Oruc* would travel to Kurz space to try to contact their government, talk to locals, and scan the Ukhel presence in the area. The other ships would be conducting the same missions in Qudoru, Tounous, and X'Ado space.

"Any questions?" Kal waited for a moment to see if anyone was going to speak up, but there was only silence and nervous expressions. "Alright. Again, thank you all. As of this moment, we are no longer operating on behalf of the EDF or the UEG, but on behalf of Humanity. Good luck." Kal cut the line to the other ships and then turned to the soldiers in the galley with him.

"So, Ms. Bergeron, any questions about the plan or why we asked for you?"

"No question," she replied.

"This is the last time you will commit treason; I swear." Kal put his hand over his heart. "But since you're here, we need your help. We know that the Kurz home world, Gorash, was destroyed. We need to figure out where the Kurz would still have some governmental presence."

"Well, their government is relatively centralized, but they do have regional offices on some of their other planets. If your aim is to make contact with some sort of leadership, I would suggest Tamulk. The planet has several industrial and mining facilities and is far away from Gorash. I know people there, and more importantly, they know me. No guarantees, though—the Kurz very well could have a secondary headquarters, like Kapustin, that's hidden."

"Okay, well it sounds like our best bet. With a complete absence of information, I don't think there are many other options."

"That seems like a theme," Nicole quipped.

"Sir, anything the Tac-I squad can do to prep?" Jones asked.

"I want you to work with Ms. Bergeron here to learn more about the Kurz. We'll be infiltrating their planet, and the knowledge may come in useful." Kal stopped for a moment. "Also, I think we can drop the courtesies. We are so far beyond regulations at this point. Just call me Kal or Norman or whatever you want. You and your soldiers are here of your own volition. I can't and won't give you orders to do something you don't want to at this point."

"Sir, I appreciate the gesture." Jones looked him in the eye. "But those courtesies are there for a reason. When a soldier is nervous and facing the unknown, there is a reassurance to what is normal, to following one's training. I would rather still call you sir and keep the discipline as it stands."

"I respect that, Sergeant Jones—it's ultimately your decision. I hope everyone here understands that to me, you're a volunteer and I appreciate it."

"You too, sir." Jones slapped Kal on the back.

"Captain Garcia, can you set us on a route to Tamulk?"

"Roger that."

Kal looked around the table. "Okay then, let's start getting ready. The soldiers should be training while we are folding, not only in combat but also learning as much as they can about Tamulk and Kurz. We're at war, entering hostile space, and we need to be prepared for anything."

Chapter Seventeen

After wishing the other scout ships good luck, Garcia set the *Oruc* on a path to the Tamulk system. Normally a ship underway had an air of indolence as the soldiers waited to arrive. However, everyone on the *Oruc* was busy, motivated by their mission and relieved to finally have a sense of purpose again.

Aside from monitoring their progress, the flight crew prepared for what was called a staged arrival. This would allow them to investigate Tamulk from a distance with minimal chance of discovery. They would fold in a couple of light weeks from the planet and examine it with long range sensors, then continue to progressively fold closer, each one being only a light day or so in distance. Due to the limitations of the speed of light, the ship's long-range sensors would see the planet as it had appeared days prior. This would give them some idea of what to expect, but there was always the risk of folding into a situation that they had not anticipated if an Ukhel ship had just folded into the system.

It was riskier than a normal entry. The folds they made on approach were shorter than what was standard, increasing the potential for error. Also, the gravitational pull of planets and star systems attracted debris, increasing the chances of fold drive malfunction due to an unexpected gravitational field, especially as they moved closer to the planet.

The crew used the data they had on the system in to plan their approach to the planet. They wanted to make sure that they avoided gravitational interference by confirming that any known asteroids or other objects were far away from any fold points.

Jones and the Tac-I squad conducted combat drills using a variety of preplanned scenarios. The squad leader had them executing drills that required the squad to operate both in their battle suits as well as in civilian clothes in order to prepare them for both conventional and undercover operations.

Kal was surprised to see Ekon on the Tac-I squad—normally it required years of training. He found out later that Jones had accepted him into the squad due to his performance at Base Camp and their history facing the Ukhel on Caracas Station. Not to mention there was no funnel of new recruits and no way to replicate the Tac-I training with the EDF gone.

Every day Nicole held informal classes on the Kurz and Tamulk, which Kal attended whenever possible. The complexities of the Kurz caste system went over his head, and Kal struggled to remain engaged since he knew Nicole would most likely handle any of their interactions with the locals. Her overview of Tamulk was much more interesting, and he felt probably more applicable. Tamulk was the Kurz's mining and agricultural center. The planet's land was covered with large swathes of forest and farms, with occasional large cities dotting the land. It had a relatively small population, which made it surprising that their military and government had such a large presence.

Captain Ruiz surprised Kal with her dedication to the classes. She was a very engaged student, often interrupting Nicole to challenge her on a particular point or to ask detailed questions. She also wasn't afraid to challenge the attaché or argue with what she saw as inconsistencies in instruction. Nicole handled these outbursts much better than Kal would, letting Ruiz state her case and then calmly clarifying the point she was trying to make or agreeing with some of the captain's assertions.

A side effect of this back and forth was a growing sense of ease between the two women—almost to the point of friendship. Although Ruiz clearly could never forget what Nicole had done, she seemed to accept she was remorseful and was trying to redeem herself. Ruiz appreciated anyone who was driven, and Nicole certainly was that.

Kal periodically stopped at Zhou's stateroom to talk and ask how he was doing. He had instructed the rest of the crew to treat the colonel with the utmost respect. Ultimately Zhou was doing what he thought was right and following his oath. Initially, the colonel refused to address any of Kal's questions, instead staring straight ahead, mouth closed. After several days, though, Zhou's demeanor began to change, and he answered basic questions. Still, he refused to even discuss the idea of joining their mission, his manner growing cold and hostile when it was brought up.

After almost two weeks of folding, the crew of the *Oruc* was ready to begin their entry into Tamulk space. They were two light weeks away and prepared to begin their staged arrival.

"You ready?" Garcia asked.

 Kal stood behind the flight crew as they prepared to conduct the first fold in the approach. All materials had been secured and the Tac-I squad was in their battle suits—just in case.

"Yes, go ahead."

Chief Kanumba conducted an optical scan of the planet. Unfortunately, they wouldn't be able to intercept transmissions or take full advantage of the ship's suite of sensors, but the scan would reveal things such as capital ships or extensive physical damage.

"Clearly the Ukhel have been here," Kanumba reported. "There is significant damage to the orbital station and evidence of bombardment on the planet's surface. It looks pretty recent, but we're too far away to detect much more than that."

"Damnit," Kal swore. He'd been holding out for a miracle.

"There is no evidence of any Ukhel ships remaining in the system. We are pretty far out, so I can't confirm for sure, and we are of course seeing the system as it was two weeks ago." Kanumba sounded surprised.

"That's odd. Why wouldn't they try and hold on to the planet once they had captured it?" Kal asked.

Kanumba gave a shrug.

"Let's keep going in." Kal knew that they could be entering a trap, but he was desperate. They'd burned too many bridges not to continue if they had any chance of success.

Over the next couple of hours, the ship conducted several small folds toward Tamulk. As they grew closer time seemed to speed up on Tamulk and the smoking craters that dotted the planet's surface extinguished and signs of rebuilding began to spring up. Surprisingly, there was no evidence of Ukhel ships returning to the system. With a final fold, they were close to the wreck of the orbital station.

"Okay, we need to find a place to land." The sensor data that they'd collected painted a grim view of what had happened. The station was completely destroyed, just a wrecked hulk of metal at this point. On Tamulk itself, most of the major cities had been bombarded or destroyed by the Ukhel.

Nicole pointed to a large city on the viewscreen. "Land here. It's close to the Counselor's Palace. I have some contacts in the area, and there's an open space port and market nearby as well." Every Kurz planet was led by a Chief Planetary Counselor. They reported directly to the Kurz Chief Counselor, the head executive of their government, who was selected through a vote in the Kurz senate.

The *Oruc* descended quickly through the atmosphere to avoid being detected by local security or the Ukhel and flew toward the space port. As they soared over the planet's surface, Kal gazed out the viewscreen to admire it. Bright yellow, purple, and red foliage stretched across the ground as far as he could see, only broken up by an occasional river or stream. The land was flat with some small hills undulating across the terrain—the colors made Kal think of the patchwork blanket that Stephen had had as a child. None of the craters they detected from space were visible as they had been concentrated in the urban areas.

A large metropolis grew on the horizon. The city was a sprawling mass of low-slung buildings that took over the entire horizon. There were gaps in the skyline where buildings had been destroyed.

The public port was located near the outskirts of the city. A large tower stood in the middle of several landing pads, almost all of them occupied by different models of merchant ship. The Kurz only allowed non-citizens to land at designated public ports, so it was filled exclusively with ships from off-planet.

Despite the carnage they had seen from space, the port seemed to be operating normally, and a Kurz attendant was waiting for them as soon as they landed. A simple exchange of credits ensured they would have their space for as long as they needed and prevented any questions about the ship or their intentions.

"Okay, I was able to get in touch with some of my former Kurz colleagues via neural net," Nicole announced. "They'll be meeting us at a restaurant in an hour. In the meantime, I suggest we look through the market and see what we can learn."

Their away team consisted of Nicole, Ruiz, Kal, and a few members of the Tac-I squad as security. They had changed into civilian clothes to draw less attention. Slipping into the free merchant clothes was liberating for Kal, not to mention a thousand times more comfortable. He'd already briefed the squad members that Nicole would lead the mission; she was the expert on this planet and they needed to follow her lead to avoid notice.

"Okay everyone, you ready to go?" Nicole asked.

They all nodded, and Kanumba hit the button to drop the back ramp. A heavy floral aroma struck Kal as he walked out of the bay door—the trees that covered the planet were known to be a primary component in Kurz perfumes. Nicole had told them the smell was everywhere—even in the center of the largest city it smelled like a garden. Aliens of all shapes and sizes loitered around the ramshackle port with an air of boredom. Kal guessed that they were stranded on the planet, unsure of where to go now that the Ukhel had arrived.

Nicole led them to a large market, bustling with activity, which was a short walk from the port. There were several large craters, the size of several buildings, scarring the area. The debris and bodies that Kal assumed would have filled the streets immediately after the Ukhel bombardment had been removed, and construction equipment was already filling them in.

The market's layout was chaotic—clearly there had been no central plan when the area was established. Food stores, small merchants, pawn brokers, and the like had sprung up with little rhyme or reason. Streams of pedestrians were broken up by hover sleds speeding through the crowd, around Kal's waist level. There were no defined avenues for transit, and so Kal found himself continually running into aliens as they walked through the market.

He was surprised to see how busy the area was. He expected empty streets and refugees on every corner. But except for the bombardment craters, there wasn't anything that hinted at the trauma the city and planet had been through recently.

"Strange," Kal said to Nicole as they made their way through the crowd. "It's almost as if nothing happened."

"Not too surprising. The Kurz are a pragmatic species. They would observe the one-day period of mourning dictated by the code and then immediately get to rebuilding." Nicole turned to look at him. "Though, even for them, this is a surprisingly quick recovery."

A variety of alien species blended in with the crowd of Kurz locals. As they walked, Kal connected his neural implant to the local net to see if he could learn anything from the news there. The news, entertainment, and other systems on the local net were down—only basic mapping and communication functions were still available.

Nicole led them through the bustling walkways, occasionally stopping at a stand and pretending to be interested in an item by picking it up and showing it to some of the other members of their group. While she was talking to the shopkeepers, Kal hovered close by, trying to eavesdrop.

They were able to find out that the Ukhel fleet had arrived on Tamulk about three weeks before—the battle had been bloody but short, with the Ukhel fleet quickly subduing both the planet's populace and the station above with very few casualties. They had lost some of their assault craft in the initial hour of the battle, but that had been it. After that, there had been several days of intense orbital bombardment and then, almost magically, the Ukhel left. Since then, all communications to and from the planet had been cut off, frustrating many of the merchants.

After an hour of talking to the locals, Nicole led them into a small restaurant near the center of the market. Kal blanched as they walked through the door, his nose assaulted by the stench of rotting flesh. Racks filled with dead animals were strung on the wall. The animals all looked to be in various stages of decay, their skin taking on an unhealthy rainbow hue. The restaurant was filled exclusively with Kurz, happily gnawing at the rotten carcasses as they talked.

Nicole scanned the restaurant, looking for her contacts. Finally, she saw what she was looking for and instructed the group to grab a table while she and Kal went over to join the two Kurz.

As Kal and Nicole approached, the two looked up and stopped talking. They were both dressed in formal Kurz uniforms, with green tunics around their midsections that stretched all the way to the tip of each of their claws. Kal wasn't the best at reading Kurz mannerisms, but even he could tell they were frustrated about something.

"Greetings Emissaries Torkav and Noram." Nicole held up her hands, fingers splayed in the Kurz greeting, and Kal quickly mimicked her.

"Greetings Attaché Bergeron. Who is your compatriot?" Both Kurz held up their hands, splaying their claws in greeting.

"I am Colonel Kal Norman of the Earth Defense Force." Kal gave a small nod.

"Greetings Colonel Norman, I am Senate Emissary Torkav and this is Senate Emissary Noram." He made a gesture for them to sit down. Kal reluctantly took the proffered seat; the difference in Kurz and Human physiology made their chairs extremely uncomfortable.

"Thank you for meeting with us," said Nicole, wincing slightly as she eased into her chair. "I'm sorry for what your people have suffered here. We wanted to talk with you to learn more about what happened and see if we can speak with the Planetary Chief Counselor to understand what the Kurz senate is doing about the Ukhel invaders." The two Kurz inclined their heads slightly.

"It is good to see you," said Torkav, his skin reddening. "It is a dark day for both our species. Before we speak can you tell us what has happened to you and your species?"

Nicole quickly went through the destruction of Earth and capture of the Human colonies. Kal noticed that she left out several key bits of information including the existence of Kapustin Station, instead only alluding to a secondary EDF headquarters.

After she was done, Torkav tilted his head in sympathy, his skin turning a light orange. "I'm sorry for your species. It is sad to be under the control of another."

"Thank you. Can you tell us about what the Kurz senate is doing to fight the Ukhel invaders?" Nicole asked.

Torkav let out a high-pitched whistle of frustration. "I don't know what the Kurz senate is doing about these Ukhel, nor will the counselor. Since our occupation, we've not been able to send or receive transmissions off planet. I don't even know if the senate still exists. The destruction of Gorash was sudden. Noram and I have not been allowed to visit other Kurz planets; the counselor has forbidden it."

"I understand." Nicole tilted her head, mimicking the Kurz gesture for sympathy. "Can you also tell us what has happened on Tamulk? We've heard stories from the locals, but I'm hoping you have a more detailed and accurate understanding of what occurred."

"It was tragic," Torkav responded. "The Ukhel came and attacked with four ships. Our ships and station were almost immediately overwhelmed. When they launched their assault craft, the soldiers in the station resisted but were overrun. At least our honorable soldiers were able to destroy it, rather than let the Ukhel gain control."

Nicole tilted her head again. "They followed the code well."

Torkav continued, "The Ukhel began to bombard the planetary defenses and population centers. They also sent several assault craft onto Tamulk, to seize key defense assets.

The remains of our once-proud defense force were able to bring down a few of the assault ships before they landed, but they were ultimately overwhelmed. Once the invaders destroyed our means to resist, they sent emissaries to meet with the counselor. The Ukhel demanded that she surrender the planet to them, but she refused. Unfortunately, they began to bombard the planet, and did so for days, until she finally relented."

"What concessions did the Ukhel demand from the counselor?" Nicole asked.

Noram turned a shade of green. "That's not something we are permitted to speak about—you will need to talk to the counselor. I will let her staff know you are coming; she is still in the Chief Counselor's Palace."

"Thank you for the information," Nicole said. "Remember that this is not an end but a beginning."

"Well spoken," agreed Torkav.

They stood up from the table and made their way outside. "Looks like we're not going to be getting any assistance from the Kurz," Kal said. It was frustrating to see just how complete the Ukhel victory was. Nothing had been spared in their onslaught.

"Do you still want to meet the counselor?" Nicole asked.

Kal thought about it. Despite their lack of ships or soldiers the planet was clearly under the control of the Kurz. Seeing the Chief Planetary Counselor was a risk, she may be under surveillance or even be working with them. However, they had to pursue every opportunity they could. He nodded. "Yeah, let's go."

The palace was in a traditional Kurz style, large minarets topped each of the eight corners with a large geometric dome in the center. Nicole explained that the building had several floors beneath the ground, as was traditional for any official Kurz building.

As they approached the compound's main gate, a bot floated toward them. The shiny sphere hovered directly in front of Nicole's face and a Kurz voice came from the loudspeaker.

"This is the residence of the Counselor of Tamulk. State your name and business."

"I am Attaché Nicole Bergeron of the UEG. I wish to speak to the counselor. The Senate Emissary Noram has announced us to her."

There was a pause and then the droid responded. "Yes, we've heard the announcement. Proceed through the gate and along the path, and there will be a steward there to escort you to the counselor."

Kal looked around the palace grounds as they walked up the path. Small, manicured trees were arranged in neat geometric patterns with paths twisting through them. The planet's floral scent was even stronger here than it had been in the market. There weren't any obvious signs of security, but

Kal was sure their every move was being monitored. A large Kurz wearing a powered exoskeleton, their version of a battle suit, and holding a plasma rifle stood at the entrance to the building.

"Stop there. Do not move from your current position."

The guard walked to a viewscreen on the outside wall of the building and studied it closely. Kal could see an image of them on the display with Kurz symbols around them—it was clearly some kind of scanner.

"You're carrying multiple sidearms and rifles that are military grade. Only two of you were announced to the counselor and may proceed. You must relinquish your weapons before you do. The rest of you must remain outside the residence."

"We're the ones who were announced." Nicole motioned to herself and Kal. They handed over their weapons to Ruiz and the others for safeguarding, and then followed the Kurz guard as he led them through the door. The main hallway traced the outline of the building, with portals opening to rooms on the outside perimeter. The walls were a light tan color and inlaid with intricate patterns that traced sconces and door frames. Kal looked around to admire the detail as they followed the guard to the other side of the building. Their escort stopped in front of a lift and gestured with his claw tipped arm for them to enter.

They descended what felt like several floors into another hallway, almost identical to the first except the patterns on the wall were now gilded with thin strips of metal. Kal suddenly realized the patterns were in fact complex pictographs. He marveled at the level of artistry that had gone into the building.

The guard led them to a large set of double doors and pressed his eye against a sensor nearby. The doors opened and Kal and Nicole followed him through into an enormous room, with an array of floor-to-ceiling windows on one wall. The other walls, to the left and right of the entrance, were lined with racks containing tattered scrolls. Kal had once carried a load of the ancient scrolls to Gorash, and he couldn't help but goggle at them and wonder how much they would have fetched on the open market. In the center of the room stood a Kurz female wearing a russet-colored robe with intricate gold stitching along the hem.

"Greetings, I am Chief Counselor Rohr."

"Greetings, I'm Attaché Nicole Bergeron and this is Colonel Kal Norman of the—" She paused, "Human forces." *We're not really EDF anymore*, realized Kal. They both raised their arms and splayed their fingers in the Kurz greeting.

"You are both welcome on Tamulk." Counselor Rohr returned the greeting. "It's good to meet people from off planet. Please let me know how I may be of service." She sat down on a padded mat on the floor. Kal and Nicole followed suit.

"Thank you. As you may know, our home world was destroyed, and our forces are in retreat. We're here to learn more about Tamulk and what's happened to the Kurz. We hope for an exchange of information."

"That would be most desirable," Counselor Rohr replied. "We have not heard any news from outside the system since the Ukhel invaded. They forbade any communications with the outside world, and our code demands we obey their rules now."

The Kurz code had many strict rules regarding diplomacy. It strictly forbade them from violating any agreement, whether made in duress or not.

Nicole informed Counselor Rohr of the EDF's alternate base—without divulging specifics—and their hopes to launch a counterattack. She was generous with the truth, exaggerating the size and capabilities of the base and the remaining EDF while downplaying or ignoring the issues they faced. Counselor Rohr periodically interrupted to challenge or question something Nicole said. Kal realized how the woman had been able to so deftly handle Ruiz; the captain acted almost exactly like the Kurz counselor. Rohr was especially interested to learn if they'd had direct contact from any of the remaining Human planets—and was disappointed to find that they had not.

"Thank you for being so forthcoming with your information, Attaché Bergeron. It saddens me to know that our two civilizations have suffered much at the hands of the Ukhel." The counselor turned a shade of red. As far as Kal could tell, Counselor Rohr seemed to be genuine.

"What about you? What has happened here? Emissary Torkav told us about how the Ukhel took the planet," said Nicole.

"Yes, we also fell to the Ukhel." Rohr bowed her head in sorrow. "They attacked quickly, sending missiles at our fleet before we even knew they were in the system. Our capital ships were able to destroy one of their ships before they were destroyed, and we were able to destroy our station before it fell into Ukhel hands at least."

Kal was glad to hear that they had at least taken out one of the Ukhel ships. The Ukhel had shown that they were ruthless and powerful, but they were not invincible.

"Their attack also took out all of our planetary defenses. First, they bombarded our bases and defensive batteries, then they sent down assault ships to eliminate the military targets that they were not able to hit from orbit. After eliminating any means of defense, they contacted me to talk terms of surrender. I refused to parlay, hoping we would receive reinforcements of some sort. The Ukhel promised to eliminate five percent of the planet's population every day until we agreed to their terms."

"What were their terms?" Kal asked.

"They required a tribute of fifty percent of our raw materials in perpetuity and for us to secede from the Kurz empire and close all communication for the near future. I waited for seven days, and they Ukhel kept their promise— around thirty-five percent of the people on this planet were killed. Finally, they gave their final ultimatum. If I did not agree to their terms immediately, they would destroy the entire system, as they did with Gorash." Counselor Rohr turned a bright yellow color.

"I realized there was no choice. I could not doom this entire planet." She paused for a moment. From what Nicole had told Kal, the decision must have been difficult for her. "They created a small military base outside this city and now have it occupied by a group of their soldiers. They watch over us and ensure we comply. As if they needed to."

"How many people and how much equipment are at the base?" Kal asked. They had just landed in their public port with an EDF scout ship. The Kurz garrison very well may be on their way to the ship now.

"There are not very many soldiers there—perhaps a hundred or less. The base is only there to send the daily report, not to enforce their rules. If we break the agreement, they will just leave the planet and return with their fleet. They were very clear about this."

"Do they have fighters or assault craft?"

"The Ukhel only have atmospheric fighters and assault craft Colonel Norman; they rely on their capital ships' armaments in battle, which has so far proven effective. In terms of what they have on Tamulk, they have several unarmed assault craft and two or three atmospheric fighters."

Kal was not aware of any other species that relied solely on their capital ships in combat. Why wouldn't the Ukhel have fighters? However, he couldn't argue with the results. He guessed fighters weren't as critical if you could immediately annihilate anything that stood in your way.

"Do you think the Kurz government will help your planet now that you are independent?" Nicole asked. Kal knew that she was disappointed with the counselor's revelation of their independence. They had hoped to meet with someone who could represent the interstellar Kurz government. Clearly Counselor Rohr couldn't provide assistance to their cause.

"Perhaps. Perhaps the Kurz empire, or what is left of it, will accept us back, but already I see signs that Tamulk will go its own way in the future," Rohr replied.

"Is there any aid or assistance you can provide to our people?" Nicole pleaded. "We're dedicated to fighting the Ukhel and will be back one day to help you win your freedom."

"That is very nice of you to say, attaché. There is not much I can do to help you at this time. The Ukhel tribute leaves us only enough material and food to survive, so we have nothing extra to provide. I can offer you a small bit of information though. I have heard that the Alliance was able to obtain some of the Ukhel wreckage from their initial assault. I have not seen it myself, but I have heard that there are materials that may be of value."

"Thank you. That is valuable information," Nicole said.

"And now, I must ask you to leave." Counselor Rohr stood up to her full height. "I fear that my palace is being monitored by the Ukhel troops remaining on Tamulk. The very fact that we have met puts us all in danger."

"We understand, Counselor," Nicole replied, holding her arms in front of her in a symbol of respect. "We thank you for your time and hope that our people and the citizens of Tamulk may work together in the future to destroy the Ukhel."

"As do I." Rohr said as her aide came into the room. "Escort the Humans back to their companions."

Kal and Nicole followed the steward through the building to the entrance. The rest of the group stood anxiously looking at the grounds and the city waiting for them.

"Let's go," ordered Kal. "We've got a lot to discuss."

Chapter Eighteen

"So, where do we go from here?" asked Ruiz.

They'd returned from the palace and were sitting around the table in the *Oruc's* galley when Garcia reported there had been no activity in the landing port. Kal hoped that meant they would be able to leave the planet without being attacked, but he wanted to get off planet as soon as possible just in case.

"I do not think we have long before the Ukhel realize we're here." Ruiz looked around the table. "When they do find out, I think their small force on Tamulk will come after us, guns blazing."

"About that—isn't it interesting the Ukhel left only a small contingent on the planet?" Kal asked.

"What do you mean?" Nicole asked.

"We've been operating under the assumption that the Ukhel are invincible, unassailable, but this isn't true. I saw their ships get hit in the attack on Caracas Station, and Counselor Rohr told us that they lost a ship in the invasion here. I think the Ukhel are more vulnerable than we realize."

"I certainly like the sound of that," Garcia said after a moment. "But they've not only been kicking our asses, but those of several other species as well."

"Yes," agreed Kal, "but why? Their ships are definitely more powerful and more advanced than our own. But their real advantages lie in surprise and ruthlessness. They came out of nowhere and attacked mercilessly, destroying our home world before we had time to react. What would have happened if we had a traditional war with them? If they hadn't immediately destroyed Earth?"

"They would have kicked our ass," Kanumba replied.

"Well, yeah." Kal chuckled. "But they wouldn't have been able to take on us, the Kurz, the X'Ado, the Tounous, and the Qudoru at the same time. They're hoping to overpower all of us before we can mount a response, and it's working. They don't have the ability to fight a prolonged war, so they rely on ruthlessness; they are decimating populations and threatening to destroy systems because they don't have the numbers to hold on to a large group of planets." Kal looked around the room, trying to gauge the reactions.

"Interesting theory," Jones mused. "Unfortunately, we can't prove it."

"Yet," Kal replied, holding up a finger. "But if we gather all the video we have of Ukhel attacks, we can start cross-referencing their ships and see if the same ones are showing up in multiple locations. Should give us some estimate as to the size of their fleet."

"I have some of them," said Garcia, "but only a few. We would need more. Also, the ships may be hard to identify over simple video. From my experience, all ships look the same on holo unless they have identification markings."

"Yes, but every ship has unique scarring from the wear and tear of space travel. Each ship would be distinct in that sense," Park said. "We just need video at a high enough resolution."

"Exhaust signatures too," Chief Kanumba added. "Each ship has a slightly different one based on their engines. As a ship ages, the engines wear in different places and cause minute changes to the pattern of their exhaust—like Human fingerprints."

"Which would require thermal imagery. Again, something we don't have enough of." Garcia shook his head.

"I may be able to get the holos you need," Kal said, holding up his Alliance chit. "The counselor said the Alliance may have some debris or material from these Ukhel ships. I may also be able to get some more holos of the Ukhel attacks from them as well."

A few people looked at him askance. His relationship with the Alliance hadn't been known by everyone.

"Makes sense, but you'd better hurry," Ruiz urged. "We don't know if, or when, the Ukhel are going to figure out we're here."

"Captain Garcia, can you work to prep the ship and get us ready to launch?" Kal asked. "I need everyone else to be ready to go at a moment's notice. The Alliance security protocol will only allow me to enter their front, so I'll need to go alone. If you see anything out of place while I'm gone— get out of here."

"Yessir." Garcia gave a nod.

Kal left the ship and walked out of the space port. After Counselor Rohr's warning, he could not shake the prickly feeling of being watched. He took out the Alliance chit and pressed the button to locate the closest front.

As Kal weaved his way through the market, he continually changed his direction, veering through crowds, in order to lose anyone who might be tracking him. Occasionally a shopkeeper would call out to him if he accidently ran into their stall, causing him to jump, but the rest of the market ignored him.

Following the arrow on the chit, Kal found his way to the front of a small pawn shop. The inside was a jumble of weapons, drugs, and various pieces of junk piled in disorderly heaps based on size—as far as Kal could tell. He activated his chit to provide access to the back room of the store located behind the counter. The back room had the same ornate furnishings and blast-proof doors as all the other Alliance fronts Kal had seen. He found it reassuring that every front was the same as the others inside—even down to the service bot waiting for him in the back room.

"Greetings. We are currently operating in enhanced security mode. Any potentially hostile action will be met with overwhelming lethal force. Also, we have detected that Ukhel forces are currently en route to this location." Kal started to sweat. "Current estimate is five minutes until arrival. To expedite your departure, we are connecting you directly with the local Alliance member."

Kal wondered how the Ukhel had been able to track him. He realized there were probably several—they'd landed on the planet using an EDF ship, they'd met with the Chief Planetary Counsel, they'd used their implants over the net, and he'd gone to an Alliance front. He wanted to smack himself. He should've just made a planetwide announcement that Human spies were there, it would have been simpler.

The droid's pleasant holographic face disappeared, leaving empty air in its place. A high-pitched, modulated voice came from the speaker in the bot. "Colonel Normal, what do you need?"

It took Kal a moment to recover from the shock of the Alliance knowing his name and rank. He shuddered to think how far they had infiltrated the EDF.

"I...I need two things. First, I've heard that you may have debris from Ukhel ships that were destroyed on this planet. The second is a complete set of holos of all known Ukhel attacks."

The response was immediate.

"We'll transmit the coordinates of a facility where we are holding the Ukhel technology outside the city. Due to our current limitations in communications, you'll need to travel to one of our consolidated centers on Forha in order to get the holos you require. We'll transmit the location of a space port that is close to the location to your ship as well. Once there, you can restock and repair your ship as well as use your chit to find the center's location."

"How much do I owe you?" Kal asked, hardly believing his luck.

"The price of the information and materials we are offering is more than you would be able to pay in ten lifetimes, Colonel Norman. We offer them free of charge. Our organization is not comfortable with this Ukhel force. Their actions are disrupting our business, and we're willing to provide assistance to destroy them, no matter how small the chance."

That the Alliance was feeling the effects of the Ukhel invasion wasn't surprising. That they would offer up materials and information for free was. Kal wasn't going to ask twice though, and was gratified to know that the Alliance thought they had some sort of chance against the Ukhel.

"You have less than two minutes until the Ukhel kill team is at this location. I'm going to open an escape door—get out as fast as you can. We will prevent the Ukhel from entering this facility at any cost."

A piece of the far, fresco-covered wall slid back and to the side, revealing another hallway. Kal ran through the door and down the corridor, his footsteps reverberating off the metal flooring. The hallway ended at a thick blast-proof door that let Kal out into a back alley.

Oruc, this is Norman, can you hear me? Kal hailed the ship using his implant.

Roger, what's your status? Captain Ruiz responded.

I was able to make contact with the Alliance, and they agreed to help. Unfortunately, I have an Ukhel kill team en route to my location, ETA less than a minute.

Roger, we're sending the Tac-1 squad to your location. Proceed directly to the ship and we will intercept.

Copy. Kal closed the communication line and focused on figuring out where he was. His implant superimposed a map of the market over his vision. The path from the alley he was in to the *Oruc* was convoluted, zig-zagging multiple times through the stalls and rough buildings. Kal ran back toward the landing pad, looking around for any Ukhel soldiers.

An explosion lifted him off his feet and sent him sprawling, face first, into the compacted dirt ground. Pushing himself up, he ducked into a side building, a large tent-like structure that provided concealment but no protection against attack. Screams and shouts, combined with the booms of explosions and hiss of plasma, sounded from outside. Hell had broken loose.

Get ready to run, Ruiz said. *Okay, go!*

Kal could hear and feel the concussive blasts of kinetic rocket fire ripping through the streets outside the building he was in. He leaned his head out of the tent flap and saw several Tac-I in full battle suits advancing down the street, leapfrogging from building to building using their suit's thrusters.

He couldn't determine where the Ukhel were, so made an educated guess based on the trajectory of the Tac-I team's fire. Cutting a hard right out of the flap of the building, he ran down the street in the direction of the *Oruc.* As he ran, Kal weaved, trying not to endanger civilians while using buildings and debris for concealment.

His right leg gave out, and a sharp pain caused him to cry out. Kal fell—face first again—into the street, the loose gravel scraping away a layer of his skin on his hands. While getting up, he saw an Ukhel soldier landing a hundred meters down the street. It was pitch black and stood out against the tan

211

colored building. The lithe figure ran towards Kal, its weapon extended. There was a grace in its movements that Human's in battle suits couldn't match.

The high-pitched whine of a rail gun rang out in the street, and several slugs hit the Ukhel, knocking it off of its feet. A loud thump sounded next to Kal, and he turned to see the welcome sight of a Human battle suit.

Sir, Jones called through the neural net, *we're only able to delay them from advancing—there are too many for us to stop them completely. Grab on, I'm taking you to the ship.*

Kal didn't have time to respond as the sergeant quickly picked him up, tossed him over his shoulder, and activated his thrusters. As they rose, Kal looked back to see the anarchy that had descended upon the Kurz market. The Tac-I squad set up positions between where Kal had been and the *Oruc*, using buildings and equipment as cover. At least three of the twelve Tac-I soldiers were down, one of them grotesquely cleaved in half. Using his heads-up display, Kal saw that the other two were only wounded. Approximately fifteen Ukhel soldiers were advancing on them, leapfrogging by fire teams, with one team providing suppressive fire while the other advanced. Kal gave a small cheer when two Ukhel were hit by a kinetic rocket, their bodies flying several meters through the air.

Kal switched his implant to the open tactical channel to hear what was going on. The chatter was sparse and direct as the Tac-I squad tried to conduct a staged withdrawal back to the ship against the superior Ukhel firepower.

212

Alpha squad, this is the Oruc. We are airborne and are going to provide close air support on your location. Get ready to get the hell out of there, Garcia announced over the net.

Kal felt a jolt as they touched down on the half open ramp of the *Oruc*. Jones gently set him down, and he turned over so he could get his bearings. The ship was airborne and hovered directly over the Tac-I squad's position. The *Oruc's* position allowed them to provide covering fire for the soldiers to assist in their escape. The side gunner's door of the cargo bay was open and Kanumba was positioned behind a large kinetic machine gun, which was spewing out an almost uninterrupted stream of kinetic slugs.

Sir, I'm going to recover the wounded—sit tight. Jones jumped off the ramp and dove back on the street. Kal opened the tactical map on his implant to see what was going on. Out of the twelve-soldier squad, three were now killed and two wounded, marked on his map with red and yellow dots respectively. He sat up and grabbed the kinetic rifle that he'd strapped to his body. He watched as the Tac-I team slowly exfiltrated back into the *Oruc*, moving in pairs to cover each other.

Jones rushed through the market, making his way to recover one of the wounded soldiers. Kanumba continued to provide covering fire from the *Oruc*, her normally pleasant face twisted into an expression that Kal could only describe as terrifying. Ruiz found a defensible position on the roof of one of the taller buildings in the market and was raining fire down on the Ukhel, trying to pin them down.

The *Oruc* rocked violently and dropped several meters in the air as a rocket detonated against its side, near Kanumba's position. The blast threw her across the cargo bay as the shrapnel pierced the ship's energy shield and lacerated her face. As one of the Tac-I soldiers rushed toward her motionless form to render first aid, Kal crawled over to the gunner position and maneuvered himself into the chair.

The weapon's automatic targeting system highlighted at least four Ukhel surrounding Jones and the wounded soldier. Kal pressed the trigger and began to fire on the Ukhels' positions—alternating fire between each one—to prevent them from getting a clear shot. Jones reached the wounded soldier and picked him up, slinging him across his shoulders as he had with Kal. Kal noted the last wounded soldier's dot had turned red on his neural map.

Oruc, I'm coming in, Jones announced.

Gotcha covered, Kal and Ruiz responded almost simultaneously.

Kal continued to spray the Ukhel positions with fire as Jones activated his thrusters and soared toward the ship. He had clearly maxed his thrust and was traveling toward the *Oruc* faster than a rocket. Kal's constant barrage was having the intended effect of pinning the enemy down, preventing them from getting a clear line of sight and causing their shots to miss the mark. Kal gave a small whoop as one of the Ukhel went down, a hole in their chest where one of Kal's rounds had pierced the armor.

Jones launched into the ship without any deceleration, turning his body to absorb the impact and hitting the far bulkhead with a clang. Out of breath, he called out that he was onboard.

Okay, I am coming in. Ruiz activated her thrusters and started back toward the *Oruc.* Halfway to the ship, her suit jolted from the impact of an Ukhel round. Her icon on Kal's suit's tacmap turned from green to yellow. Despite the wound, Ruiz continued to fly upward, her speed unchanging as she got closer. She hit the top of the cargo bay and her thrusters continuing to fire, launching her into the bay floor and then the back bulkhead, denting a series of electrical conduits. Luckily, the impact was enough to trigger the suit's failsafe, cutting off the thrusters and causing her to drop against the bay door.

Everyone is in, Kal called to the flight crew.

The *Oruc* immediately turned and started to climb, heading to space.

Hold on, Kal instructed through the neural net, *we have to make another stop here on Tamulk. The Alliance should have transmitted a series of coordinates.*

You nuts? We barely made it out of there. Kal could sense the incredulity in Garcia's words.

We have to pick something up from the Alliance, Kal answered. *Otherwise this is all for nothing.*

Okay, but they'll follow us, Garcia warned.

I know—we'll be as quick as possible, Kal responded. *Hopefully, it will take them a moment to regroup.*

Hold on.

Chapter Nineteen

The *Oruc* flew nap-of-the-earth, treetops almost touching the *ship's* underside, over the Tamulk countryside. Kal leaned forward and tried to extricate himself from the gunner's seat but felt pain explode in his leg as soon as he put weight on it. The throbbing continued to get worse as his adrenaline high began to dissipate. Nicole hurried over from the other side of the bay, her face white.

"That leg does not look good," she said. "Let me put something on it." Kneeling, she placed a bandage over the wound. Kal felt the pain reduce as its numbing agents went to work. Standard-issue EDF bandages contained a cocktail of chemicals to promote faster healing, reduce pain, and prevent infection.

Jones had exited his battle suit and was assessing Ruiz's condition. Her helmet was already off and he was reviewing the medical indicators on her suit.

"How is she?" Kal asked Jones as Nicole helped him into a standing position.

"Not good," Jones replied, looking grim. "She took a kinetic round in the chest, and it didn't come out the other side. It looks like she has several fragments in her abdomen."

"Shit," Kal swore under his breath.

"My thoughts exactly." Jones called out to one of the soldiers, "Hey Kimathi, get the medbot over here now! The rest of you, prep this area for a sick bay." The soldiers scrambled, quickly clearing the bay and setting up a makeshift hospital zone.

Nicole strained to keep Kal upright as he limped through the ship and made his way to the cockpit. Lieutenant Park was on the controls while Captain Garcia reviewed the tacmap, trying to determine if they were being tracked or followed. Park had doubled back multiple times, going in and out of flows of traffic before they left the city in order to lose anyone who might have a read on them. Their low altitude would hopefully make them harder to spot, but Kal knew it wouldn't take too long for the Ukhel to distinguish them from other ships flying over the surface of the planet.

"We should be low enough that the Ukhel have a harder time tracking us. But they'll eventually figure out where we are," Garcia said.

"How's chief?" Park glanced over, his eyes leaving the screen for only a moment.

"I'm not sure," Kal admitted. "She got hit with shrapnel while manning the door gun." The pilot shook his head.

"How far are we from the objective?" Kal asked.

"About five minutes. Do you know what we're looking for?" Garcia replied.

"No idea. I'm probably going to need to go in there myself, though."

"Grab a battle suit. That should support your weight while you walk and keep the pressure off your leg."

"Good idea." Kal watched as they sped across the planet's uninhabited countryside. The landscape flew beneath them, an endless blanket of orange, purple, and red. The *Oruc* arrived at the coordinates the Alliance had provided and there was nothing that Kal could see to indicate they were anywhere special.

"You able to detect anything in the forest?" Kal asked, squinting as he tried to see a clearing or structure among the trees.

"Nothing yet...wait...there's something, almost directly underneath. Not a structure necessarily, but some sort of concrete pad, perhaps a bunker. Completely flat—it's not natural." Garcia squinted at the viewscreen in front of him.

"We can't land here; I'll need to just drop out. Nicole, can you help me to the cargo bay?" Kal stood up with Nicole's help and they made their way to the bay. The bandage was working, and he was able to walk without aid for most of the trip.

The Tac-I squad had removed their suits and were helping to administer first aid to the wounded, taking readings and configuring the medbot. Ruiz's battle armor had been completely removed, and a large bandage, already tinged red with blood, was affixed over her torso. From this distance, Kal couldn't tell if she was dead or alive.

He stepped up to one of the suits lining the wall. The suits were stored in standing position, with an open seam splitting the back and down each leg. With Nicole's help, Kal stepped into a pair of boots and then placed his arms into the sleeves of the suit. He connected his neural implant to the suit and activated it. Clamps tightened down on each of his joints, and the gauntlets and shoes constricted until they were snug. The exterior armor then started to knit itself back together, beginning at Kal's feet and ending at the base of his neck. After the suit was completely sealed, Kal grabbed the helmet strapped to the wall and put it on.

"Wait, we need something to carry the parts in," Kal announced to the soldiers in the bay. Carrying anything in the bulky suit would be impossible—he would need a bag or carton of some sort. Hearing his comment, the soldiers in the bay scrambled, looking around for anything that could be used.

"This is the best we have, sir." One of them handed Kal a large duffel bag. It was big enough to carry a week's worth of clothes and at least had a strap so Kal could carry it across his body.

"That's it?" Kal was in disbelief.

"That's all we got, sir."

The back cargo bay door was already open, and his suit's heads-up display was tied to the *Oruc's* computer, with the structure highlighted in his field of vision. Using the suit's thrusters, he left the ramp and slowly made his way through the canopy of the forest, landing on the soft earth.

The understory of the forest was made up of a dense network of gray bushes, their square leaves rustling slightly from the downdraft of the *Oruc's* thrusters. The forest floor was littered with a blue moss, and Kal felt his feet sinking into the ground.

He ran through the forest, heading toward the structure highlighted on the heads-up display. The battle suit's interior skeleton supported his leg, and combined with the anesthesia in the bandage, eliminated the pain as he ran. Finally, he came upon a concrete slab embedded in the forest floor. A large, reinforced metal door lay in the middle.

Kal quickly stepped out of his battle suit so he could get to the Alliance chit in his pocket. He pressed the pad on the chit to identify himself and got back into the suit as the door swung upward, revealing the dark interior of the bunker.

There's a ship coming toward us, Garcia announced over the net. *Unknown type—but it is moving faster than any atmospheric ship we know of, so safe to assume it is Ukhel.*

Damn, okay, I've gained access to this structure and am going in.

Hurry up, we've got about two minutes.

Kal dropped through the opening into the Alliance storage bunker. His suit automatically switched to night vision, allowing him to see in the dark chamber. It was about the size of the *Oruc's* cargo bay and littered with the Ukhel debris. The matte black parts were mangled and ranged in size from a centimeter to Kal's entire body.

He started to stuff whatever pieces were closest to him into the duffel bag. As he collected the pieces, he noticed some of them had a semi-transparent material running through them—nothing he had seen before. The battle suit hampered his efforts, as the large arms made grabbing items and placing them in the bag extremely difficult.

221

They're engaging us—get the hell out of there, now. There was a hint of panic in Garcia's words.

Kal ran underneath the doorway in the ceiling and activated the thrusters in his suit, shooting out of the bunker. He could see the *Oruc* hovering just above the treetops and angled himself so he would exit the canopy of the forest right at the vessel's cargo bay.

The *Oruc* suddenly shifted 90 degrees as incoming plasma bolts saturated the energy shield around the ship.

We can't take another blast like that—hurry! Garcia yelled through the neural connection.

Hold still so I can get in.

As Kal's momentum shot him over the ship, plasma bolts streaked around him. He cut the vertical thrusters and directed the energy laterally, causing him to drop onto the top of the *Oruc*, directly above the cargo bay. He grabbed a hold of the lip of the bay entrance with one arm and swung himself into the ship. Plasma fire streaked around him as he came down into the bay, so close he could feel the heat on his shoulders.

I'm in! Get us off this planet.

The cargo bay doors shut and the ship accelerated at such a speed that many of the soldiers standing in the bay were thrown to the floor. Kal lay still for a moment, shocked and grateful he had made it. He tried to push himself up so he could get the suit off and head to the cockpit, but the right arm of the suit wasn't responding to his commands.

222

Kal checked his suit's diagnostics and felt his stomach sink as he saw the right arm marked as 'missing.' With a growing sense of shock and dread, he slowly turned his head and saw a charred stump coming from his shoulder. He stared at the space where his arm should have been. Unable to take his eyes off the stump, he saw where the metal of the suit had fused with the tissue in some places. Strangely enough, he couldn't feel a thing.

"Sir, you're gonna be fine." Kal saw Staff Sergeant Jones standing over him. "Let's just get that helmet off you."

Jones gingerly pulled the helmet off Kal's head. The nauseating smell of burnt flesh and metal flared in his nostrils. A wave of pain radiated from his shoulder and images of the blackened, dead stump of his arm hovered before his eyes. As the pain grew to a disabling crescendo, he felt something give and threw up, the vomit coursing down his face, some hitting the floor and the rest pooling inside the collar of his suit. Kal tried to say something, but the world went black before a word came out.

Chapter Twenty

A kite floated on the wind. The air, still damp from a storm a few hours earlier, felt like a blanket covering his body. The wind was the only respite from the stifling heat of the sun. The kids were holding on to the string, laughing as the kite dove and twisted in the wind. Li Na sat on a blanket and took food out of the picnic basket with a smile. *Whose birthday is it again?*

The wind gusted, sending the kite soaring upward and tearing the string from the kids' hands. Kal watched its flight as it sailed above them, heading to a nearby copse. Following its trail, his eyes caught the sun, blinding him to everything else.

"Can you hear me?" The words were faint, but the voice was familiar. *Who is that?*

Kal tried to speak but nothing came out. He tried harder and felt a dry groan escape his lips.

"No need to say anything." The voice was nice, calm. "Not sure what you were dreaming of, but you seemed happy. I was jealous."

"Wha…what happened?" Kal remembered landing in the *Oruc's* bay. His family. They were dead.

"Don't worry about anything right now. Just recover."

"No, tell me."

A pause. "Fine. Then you should know the truth—no nasty shocks when you recover. You took a kinetic round straight through a tendon and bone in your leg. The medbot

224

was able to save the leg, but you are going to need some surgery before it will work correctly again. And a plasma round hit you when you were coming back into the ship—took off your right arm at the shoulder. Lucky for you, the round partially cauterized the wound, and your suit's auto med system was able to seal the rest, so you didn't bleed out."

The voice paused. "Others weren't so lucky. We lost five soldiers in the Ukhel assault—the one Jones rescued died later of her wounds. Chief Kanumba took shrapnel to the face, but the medbot was able to reconstruct most of it—she'll still have some gnarly scars though. And also…Captain Ruiz. She fought hard, she really did—but it was too much, her body was hemorrhaging in so many places. She never recovered."

Nicole, that's who's speaking. It's Nicole. Kal's mind started to put the pieces together—Earth gone, Ukhel, going to Tamulk. He imagined her face looking down at him with concern.

"We got away, barely. Luckily, the counselor was right—the Ukhel ship couldn't leave the atmosphere. Their base did fire a salvo of missiles to stop us, but Garcia and Park were amazing. They got us out and we were able to fold away."

Kal's mind raced as he processed all the information. They had started with, what, twenty people, and they only had fourteen left. Their mission was not yet complete, and they had already lost over a quarter of their team.

"We've been out here in deep space for about two days. We kept you under while you got worked over by the medbot and Park and Garcia worked on getting the ship mission capable again." There was a brief snort. "Only thing is, Kanumba is the one who actually knows how to maintain the ship—they just fly it.

"We're going to have a ceremony today for those who died. I figured you would want to be there. Right now, everyone's in shock." She sniffed. "I mean what's the point? We got a few pieces of junk and instructions to go to another system."

Kal sat there and wrestled with the question. It was one he had asked himself every morning for almost a decade—yet he still got up. *What is the point now? We have lost so much, and what do we have to show for it?* Kal thought of Ruiz—she had been the strongest person he had known, yet still she had fallen. *What is the point?* He thought of the other soldiers who died; he'd never gotten to learn their names. *They died, but for what? If we can't win, why try to win and lose so many people?* He thought of Li Na, of Stephen and Lan Fen—they were so sweet and innocent. Yet they were gone, and Kal was still there.

Kal heard sobbing, and he opened his eyes to see Nicole's face above him. Her eyes were ringed in red and her blonde hair matted and knotted around her face. "Why should we keep going when we've lost almost everything?"

The answer was there in Kal's mind; he had known it every morning when he had forced himself to get up. *Because we haven't lost everything. There are still things that are worth fighting for.*

"We go on because they haven't won yet. We have lost a lot...but we haven't lost everything." Kal's voice came out as a hoarse whisper. "We have each other. We still have hope."

Nicole grabbed his hand and held it. "I didn't realize how much I liked Ruiz until she was gone. Then, when I was staring down at her body, I realized I didn't even know her first name."

Kal forced himself to smile. "Esperanza—she hated it. Told me that she didn't care about my rank, but she would gut me if I called her that."

Nicole smiled tearfully back. "That sounds like Ruiz. She...she would know what to do here."

"First thing she would do is to kill us both for calling her Esperanza." They both gave a tearful chuckle at the thought.

Nicole looked him in the eyes. "I was never really close to anyone. In hindsight, maybe that's why I...did what I did. I was always studying, working—making sure I got out of the communes and made something of myself. But Ruiz, she was easy to talk to. No bullshit. She let you know what she thought. It's funny, I feel like I'm closer to the people on this ship than I have ever been to anyone except my family."

"That's why we keep going—not for the people we lost, but for the ones who remain." He squeezed Nicole's hand and she squeezed back. Kal felt something as he looked at their interlocked fingers. It was strange that only a few weeks ago he had nothing but contempt for her due to what she'd done. Now they were friends; she was one of his only friends.

"Chief Kanumba is back up and is fixing the repairs that Park and Garcia tried to make. She said it would take a few more hours. I'll let you know when we are ready for the ceremony." Nicole patted his chest with her arm and then turned and started to walk out the door. Kal lifted his head to watch her as she left his stateroom. There was still a spark of hope inside of him, and it seemed like not even the Ukhel could extinguish it.

Kal spent the next hour trying to sit himself up and getting acclimated to his wounds. His leg felt tender as the painkillers were wearing off, but he could at least put weight on it for now. A metal frame supported the limb, allowing him to walk. His entire right arm was gone—the area was still tender, but the medbot had done its job well. It was hard to believe the injury had occurred only a couple of days ago.

He walked around the room, trying to get used to walking with the metal device on his leg. As he paced back and forth, he thought about the past several months. His entire world had changed, his meaningless drifter routine upended. Kal now found himself in a position of responsibility unlike anything he'd held before. The Ukhel had not only changed Kal's life, but the entire galaxy.

They had clearly been waiting and planning for years and struck quickly and without mercy to disable Humanity and its neighbors. They had then moved to capitalize on their advantage, attacking and conquering worlds and then moving on, using the threat of annihilation to keep them in line.

To Kal, it seemed like a strategy born of desperation. Otherwise, why destroy the most valuable asset in each civilization? The population and output of Earth rivaled all its remaining colonies. If the Ukhel were invulnerable, as some soldiers thought, why would they simply destroy those riches? They were trying to subdue Humanity and its neighbors before they had a chance to strike back. That thought gave Kal some hope. If Humanity could last, if they could survive, they had a chance to defeat the Ukhel. It wasn't about winning the battle; it was about surviving it so they could win the war.

A small chime sounded, indicating someone was at his door. "Come in," Kal called through the intercom.

Nicole walked back in. Her hair had clearly been washed and she had it pulled back, accentuating her high cheekbones. The utilitarian shirt and trousers she had been wearing for most of their voyage were now covered by a red shawl, embroidered with a fine gold thread in a floral design.

"You ready?" Nicole asked.

"Yes, though I feel a bit underdressed." Kal gestured to his own clothes, crumpled from two days of sleeping in them.

"At least you don't have blood on them."

"Yeah, thanks to whoever changed me while I was out."

They walked out of the stateroom and down to the cargo bay in the lower deck. The remaining soldiers were standing in formation, dressed in the gray garrison uniform of the EDF. Kal was surprised to see Lieutenant Colonel Zhou standing with the officers—in garrison uniform as well—opposite the enlisted soldiers. Kal took his place next to Zhou with Nicole on the other side of him.

In the middle of the bay were two utility boxes that had been converted to coffins along with four sets of boots, signifying the soldiers whose bodies they'd been unable to recover. Captain Garcia moved to the back of the bay, standing directly behind the two coffins, his face a mask.

"Today we are here to remember our comrades who have fallen in battle, dedicating their lives so that Humanity may never forget their names. Captain Esperanza Ruiz, Sergeant Stacy Raymond, Private First Class Mohammad Baqri, Private Sofia Schneider, Private Mahir Varma, and Private Luciana Altshuler. They each fought, and died, for something bigger than themselves—that we may all live—and we must continue to honor their memories through our fight against the threat we face today. Now we will have someone who knew them speak a little bit about each one of these soldiers so that we can remember them as the person that they were. Ms. Bergeron, would you please come up to tell us about Captain Ruiz."

Nicole stepped forward to speak. Kal assumed that everyone on the ship had learned of her betrayal to the Ukhel. During their first few days folding toward Kurz space, there had been some open hostility toward the woman, which Kal understood. However, over time, much of that had dissipated. Her classes had especially helped the soldiers on board to get to know her better, and though Kal knew there was still a deep reserve of distrust, the open hatred had almost completely vanished.

Nicole tearfully spoke about meeting Ruiz. She talked about their different upbringings and how despite that, they'd faced many of the same obstacles in their lives. Several times during her speech, Nicole had to stop to contain her emotions—hiding her mouth behind the ornate scarf she was wearing. After she spoke, a procession of soldiers walked to the center of the room to speak about each of the others they had lost. Kal felt guilty, knowing he had never been able to appreciate the person each soldier had been.

Captain Garcia opened the bay ramp and the interior bay lights dimmed. The brilliance of the stars against the pitch-black of space were breathtaking, haunting pinpricks of multicolored lights stretching to infinity. Kal wondered what else was out there besides what they knew already. *Are the Ukhel the worst thing we'll ever face?* He hoped so.

"Thank you all for attending." Captain Garcia continued to speak as the ramp closed behind him. "I ask that each of you remember your comrades and remember what they were fighting for. It was a tough loss we took today, but never forget why they were willing to lay down their lives and what they were fighting for."

As the group started to disperse, Kal turned to Zhou. "Thank you for coming. I know you don't agree with our mission."

"These soldiers died fighting an enemy the likes of which we've never seen before. They've earned my respect. I've been talking to the crew—they told me about the details of what happened on Tamulk."

"Yeah, it certainly didn't go how we'd hoped," Kal said, looking away.

"Maybe, but you did something. The information and parts that you gathered may prove invaluable in the future." Zhou grasped Kal's left shoulder. "I don't agree with what you did, but I want you to know that these losses were not meaningless. You accomplished what you set out to do, whether you feel like it or not right now."

Kal looked the man in the eyes. "Does that mean you are reconsidering joining us?"

"Perhaps…but only reconsidering. When we get back to Kapustin Station and General Sato, I feel like it is my duty to speak on your behalf. I can say this—the crew of this ship believes in what you are doing. That means something, at least to me."

"I understand," Kal replied. He held no ill will toward Zhou. The man had been placed in a difficult situation through no fault of his own. "The offer remains, though."

Kal walked through the bay, offering condolences. Ekon was standing with two other soldiers—a man and a woman, their faces streaked with tears. They all looked over as Kal approached.

"Good to see you back up again, sir." Ekon raised his eyebrow and pointed to the place where Kal's arm should have been. "Looks like we have another member of the club too." He pointed at his legs.

"Guess so." Kal still hadn't fully processed his loss. There was no pain, for which he was grateful, but several times he had found himself trying to pick up something with his arm, only to realize that it was gone. He thought he should feel a sense of loss but so far he hadn't felt much of anything other than the minor annoyance of having to do everything with his left arm. "How are you all doing?"

"It was a tough loss, sir." Kal looked down at the soldier's nametape—Private Stevens. "We'd only been together for a bit, but going through everything that has happened, we felt like family."

"Argued like family too," Corporal Wang interjected with a smile. "Raymond was tough and had no sense of humor, and man did Baqri like to tease her about it." She turned to Ekon and Stevens. "Remember when he rigged her battle suit during training? She shot up straight into the bay ceiling." They all chuckled.

"Remember when Altshuler couldn't find her rifle for a day? Had to sleep with a metal rod for two weeks," Stevens added.

"Man, she was pissed." Ekon laughed, and then paused for a moment. "But she was there for Sergeant Raymond when she found out her husband had died on Earth."

"I'm sorry that you lost them." Kal felt his words were inadequate.

"You shouldn't apologize, sir." Ekon looked him in the eye. "You didn't kill them—the Ukhel did. You gave us hope when you offered us the chance to go out and do something rather than sit around and wait."

"Thank you." Kal searched for the right words. "We'll do what it takes to honor their memory."

"Kick the Ukhel's asses sir—that will honor their memory." Wang looked him dead in the eye. "We're soldiers. We're here to fight."

"You got it." Kal stepped away from the group and moved on to rest of the crew. As he walked through the bay, he found himself gaining strength from the women and men under his command. Rather than needing to console them, he found that they were even more committed than ever and were in fact consoling him.

"Captain Garcia, I want us all to meet up in an hour. We need to discuss what we do next."

"About time, sir." Garcia smiled. "You've been resting long enough."

Chapter Twenty-One

After the memorial for their fallen comrades, Kal returned to his room inspired. The soldiers were right, the best thing he could do to honor those who'd died was to continue to fight. After a quick wash and a new uniform, Kal sat at the galley table with the rest of his small team's leadership. They were down but they weren't out.

"So, how's it look?" Kal asked Lieutenant Park.

"The *Oruc* is pretty banged up. We took multiple plasma bolts to the port side. Shields stopped most of them, but we had some damage to the engines. Chief Kanumba has made some temporary fixes, but we really need to dock and replace some of the major components. Other than that, there were some minor issues in the electrical systems from kinetic rounds—nothing major." Park brought up a schematic of the ship on the galley wall, showing where the damage was.

"Jones, how are the soldiers doing?"

"They're hurting sir. But more than anything, they're pissed. We had six killed in action and two injuries—they want payback. We also lost six battle suits, which puts us down to eight remaining."

"Chief, I understand you got to look at the debris we recovered from the Alliance. Anything interesting?"

Kanumba's face now bore two deep scars running across the side in parallel from her jaw to her hairline. They gave her face a severe warrior aspect, which Kal knew was misleading, since she generally was one of the warmest people he knew—when she wasn't on the job.

"Sir, I'm not an expert on other species' electronics and materials, but I've seen some and this is completely different. Their hardware seems to be architected in a manner very similar to our own. However, they rely on bionic relays and processors instead of the minerals we use. Based on what I've seen, their ships may *grow* their electronics. It is not an exaggeration to wonder if their ships could be considered living beings—perhaps not with higher-level cognition, but still living."

"So, do you think you could hack into this equipment? Is there any way to get information out of it or potentially intercept their communications?" Garcia leaned forward, his eyes fixated on Kanumba.

"Right now? No. But we found several components that look to be some sort of processing or memory system based on the architecture and number of leads coming from them. Unfortunately, I've reached the limit of my capabilities—we would need to run more tests to be able to understand them enough to look at penetrating their security or getting information."

Despite Kanumba's admission that she had reached the extent of her ability, her report was still interesting. She hadn't said it was impossible, which meant they had a chance. The ability to hack into the Ukhel ships would be a huge equalizer.

Kanumba continued, "Additionally, we did find a piece of the hull. What surprised me was the relative lack of armor. We

236

know that their energy shields are almost impenetrable, but it appears they have relatively thin conventional armor plating on their ships. This is only a small piece, so I can only hypothesize for now."

"Back in the New America system, we saw an EDF missile breach their hull. That would lend credence to your theory." Kal felt himself getting excited.

"Ms. Bergeron, any insights on the Ukhel in terms of behavior or values?"

"Unfortunately, nothing new. I have a lot of theories based on what we have seen—but nothing confirmed. They're clearly aggressive and, based on our conversations with Counselor Rohr, and our own experience, we know that they're completely ruthless. One thing I think will be important for us to consider is that this Ukhel invasion is shifting allegiances, and movements that already existed are finding new life. The interstellar governments may not exist anymore. Already we know that Tamulk is no longer a colony of the Kurz. We have to assume that the Human colonies may have had to make the same agreement with the Ukhel. If there is no Earth and the colonies are independent, then the entire concept of the UEG and EDF are no longer valid."

"So, what? Each planet is on their own?" Park asked.

Nicole nodded. "Exactly. The political structure of this portion of the galaxy is based on sovereign governments aligning to a particular species. The Ukhel seem to be fracturing this order. I think we will see a new order, based on planets rather than species."

"So, a bunch of little planetary governments. That's a scary thought. I mean, think just about the people in this room—we are all from different planets. Do we now have different alliances? And some are from Earth, so where does that put them?" Jones raised his hands in the air.

"They can always join us in New America," Lieutenant Park said as he mimicked a hug.

The thought of a splintering of these multi-system governments was indeed frightening. Kal thought back to his childhood on Mariga—he knew several people he'd grown up with would welcome the change. But the thought of a Humanity no longer united was a tough pill to swallow. Kal filed his thoughts away—the threat to their existence was much more pressing than what they would look like later.

"Well, I guess we'll have to figure that out when we get to it." Kal looked around the table. "Each of you has done more than I could have ever asked. You've excelled in the toughest imaginable conditions. The Alliance can provide us additional intel on Forha. We may also be able to get some repairs to our ship before heading back to Kapustin Station."

"What about heading straight back to Kapustin?" asked Jones. "If we're captured or destroyed, then everything we've done so far is lost."

"If we go to Forha, it'll add at least a week to the mission," Park agreed. "We've already got a lot of good intel."

"Who knows how long the Alliance will be around?" said Garcia. "We have to get that info—if we can confirm our hunch, then that will be huge. It can change our entire strategy."

"I agree," said Nicole. "It's a risk, but one worth taking."

"What do you think, Chief?" Kal asked. All eyes turned to Chief Kanumba, who sat quietly biting her lip, deep in thought.

"I think we have to go to Forha—the mission isn't done yet."

"T—look, we can always stop by Kapustin and then head to Forha," Park said.

"I doubt it, sir," Jones said. "Or did you forget how we left? I'm guessing they'll make sure we don't leave for a while."

"Or ever," Garcia added.

Kal held up his hands. "We head to Kapustin Station and this mission's over. The Ukhel is hunting down the Alliance and we'd better take advantage of their generosity while we can. Captain Garcia, plot a course to Forha. I'll head down to the planet with a security team and get the holos. While we're there, see if we can get additional fuel and parts for the ship—perhaps we can make some quick repairs." Kal stood up to indicate that the decision was made. "You can initiate the fold sequence when ready."

As the *Oruc* was underway, on its ten-day journey to Forha, Kal sat quietly in his stateroom, sipping a glass of tea and looking at the stars through the viewscreen. The instant shifts in their locations made it appear as if he were watching a slideshow, the stars blinking out and then reappearing in slightly different locations every couple of seconds.

A chime sounded, pulling him out of his thoughts. His implant notified him that Private First Class Ekon Kimathi was waiting outside. Kal was surprised—Ekon had never willingly started a conversation with him. Kal called for him to come on in.

Without saying a word, Ekon sidled in and slouched in the chair across the room. He had been through hell, and it showed. The bloodshot eyes and unshaven face gave him an air of age and weariness. Kal waited, letting the man speak when he was ready.

Finally, Ekon took a deep breath and spoke. "Was your time in the service like this before?" he asked. "Uh, sir?"

"No, nothing like this. I sat behind a desk, occasionally took trips to visit and inspect orbital supply stations. I saw some bad stuff and we faced some tough odds against the Torgham, but this is something different." It seemed like everything that had happened the last few months was finally catching up to Ekon. Seeing his comrades die on the streets of an alien planet had been too much for him to just accept and move on.

"Yeah...I guess that was a dumb question. It seems like every time we're getting somewhere, it just gets worse." Ekon looked down. "I don't know if I can handle it."

"You can. I know you can. I hear you. This is more than any of us have faced. But you are strong enough, I have seen what you can do."

Ekon shook his head. "I don't know. I don't know." He paused for a moment and then kept speaking. "How do you do that? How do you seem so calm, so confident?"

"All a facade." Kal gave a small self-deprecating smile. "It's a survival technique. If I can't remain calm, then I can't do what I need to. Sometimes the only way to keep going is to pretend that I'm okay, act like it and push everything aside. Eventually, is becomes true." *Kind of.*

Ekon considered the logic. "That doesn't make sense."

"Maybe, but it's true. You do it already. When you saw the Ukhel back there in the marketplace, what did you really feel like doing?"

"I mean"—Ekon shifted in his chair uncomfortably—"honestly? I felt like running. I felt like saying screw this."

"So did I, so does any sane person. But you didn't do that. You faced the Ukhel multiple times and never ran, even though I bet you felt like it every time. It's the same for me. I might be a little more used to it than you, but that feeling never goes away."

"So, you're just pretending that you know what you're doing?"

"Basically, we all are. We're all making this up as we go along. Even Sergeant Jones." Kal thought about the sergeant. "Well maybe not him. But the rest of us are. You've already been doing it. You might be scared, but I haven't seen it from

241

you." Kal got up to put his cup of tea in the room's recycling unit.

Ekon's head followed him as he walked gingerly across the room, but his eyes were focused on the wall behind him. He waited until Kal sat back down before speaking again. "What do you really think happened to them?"

"Honestly, I'm not sure." Kal knew he was talking about his friends—Sandra, Klarissa, and Li Wei. "But I would guess that they're okay. Based on what we saw on Tamulk, I would guess they're at least safe for now."

"We grew up together, Li Wei and me. He was supposed to enlist and enter Base Camp the day after I did. I don't know if he was on Caracas Station when the Ukhel came."

"Li Wei is strong. To survive the Rapturium the way he did—that takes a lot. After what he's been through, the Ukhel are nothing." Kal tried to be as reassuring as possible, but he *also* wondered what happened to the station.

"Maybe he got away on a ship before the Ukhel captured the planet." The doubt in Ekon's tone betrayed his true thoughts.

Kal was doubtful as well. "Who knows...we did."

"It's funny to think of what you were like when we met and how you are now." Ekon turned his gaze to the floor. "I mean, you were so..."

"Wasted," Kal finished for him.

"Well, yeah, I guess. I mean, your ship was a mess, and you reeked."

"I tried not to care, it just didn't stick. Funny thing, though." Kal looked directly at Ekon.

"What?"

"I don't think you're the type of person who can't care either. I think you want to be but just can't do it. You and I are cursed in that way." Kal wasn't sure how Ekon would react to him comparing the two of them, but the other man didn't say anything.

The two sat silently in their chairs for a while, alone in their thoughts. Ekon eventually asked more questions about what would happen on Forha and when they got back to Kapustin Station. Kal tried to be as forthcoming as possible, but he also wondered what would happen, especially if they were able to make it back to Kapustin. They could be promoted or kicked out an airlock—both were equally likely.

They talked for another hour with Ekon continually jumping from topic to topic. Kal could tell he was still trying to process everything he'd seen and done in the past few months. What Kal didn't want to tell him was that he'd never truly accept what had happened and he didn't have that luxury anyways. If he was lucky, they would fade in his mind and become images lost in a fog. Kal had been a young officer during the Torgham War and had seen some awful things. It had only been through Li Na and time that he had been able to fully set aside those awful memories.

After Ekon left, Kal activated the viewscreen on his desk and started to draft a mission report. Part of the standard operating procedure of the EDF, a mission report was intended to provide superiors and intel with the details of what had occurred, the potential implications, and the performance of the soldiers and leaders during the mission. Many times, especially for a logistics officer, these reports were dull formalities. Kal found them to be valuable; they helped him to think about what had happened during the mission. He used them as a tool to gather and organize his thoughts, to make sense of everything that had gone on. He had the strange feeling that they were beginning to learn the truth of the Ukhel, though he had no clue yet what that truth was.

Chapter Twenty-Two

There was a somber undercurrent on the *Oruc* during their journey to Forha. Kal stayed in his stateroom much of the time, eschewing the daily stand-ups he'd previously held in favor of electronic status reports. The rest of the soldiers and crew stayed in their quarters as well, only coming out for mandatory training or meetings.

Occasionally, someone would stop by his stateroom. Staff Sergeant Jones came by a few times; their conversations centered around the EDF that they had both grown up in. Considering what they faced now, their problems then seemed miniscule. They chuckled at how so many of their experiences were the same despite the differences in their postings and ranks. Kal was impressed by the breadth of knowledge and experiences the sergeant had in the service, and frankly shocked that an NCO as skilled and experienced as Jones was still a staff sergeant.

Nicole also stopped by periodically. They reminisced about what Humanity had been like before the Ukhel arrived. Despite the depressing subject, Kal found himself laughing and lighthearted most of the time they were together, talking about how much they had taken for granted and how much they wished they could go back to the problems they'd had before.

Occasionally, Kal felt a pang of guilt during these talks— as if finding happiness in talking to Nicole was a betrayal of Li Na and his children. He knew it was irrational, that Li Na would want him to be happy, but the guilt still came up, causing a laugh or smile to cut off abruptly.

Kal mostly talked about his career in the EDF, the Torgham War, and his childhood on Mariga. He had spent much of his youth wandering around the warrens that dominated the planet. Mariga's icy surface was inhospitable to Human life, so the first Human settlers had taken over the large underground warrens that had initially been dug by native creatures, called Murghins. Humans eventually expanded the warrens to cover almost the entire planet, creating huge underground cities. Kal's father had been a doctor and his mother had died when he was young—leaving him plenty of time to explore his small town as well as the dark tunnels on the periphery that were off limits.

Nicole told him about her family's life in the communes of Earth. The communes were government-created cities-in-a-building holding the population that was too poor to rent or purchase their own living quarters. Inhabitants would enter agreements with the government to perform labor as needed, and they would then be allotted the relatively sparse homes, often smaller than thirty square meters for a family of four. Nicole's father was not able to pay off his debt to the state and so was obligated to work or be thrown in prison. Luckily Nicole had the intelligence and drive to escape these conditions, though her story was the exception to the rule.

Listening to her talk, Kal was amazed at how little he knew about how much of Humanity lived. He had been blissfully isolated on Mariga and then in the EDF. In many ways, he had been tasked with protecting Humanity without understanding what it truly was. He wondered, if they survived, what Humanity would look like in the future.

His instincts told him that the concept of a United Earth Government was dead and that they were now irrevocably fractured. The crew and soldiers of the *Oruc* came from all five UEG planets—Earth, Mariga, Patagonia, New America, and Wudexingqiu—would they end up serving in different militaries? What about the Earthlings who were now orphaned? What would they do?

Nicole wondered aloud many of the same things. They often found themselves talking about what they would do if they did defeat the Ukhel. Their musings ended in laughter as they started coming up with increasing silly hypothetical futures.

The *Oruc* arrived two light weeks away from the Qudoru planet of Forha. Again, they arrived by staged approach, and again they found a planet's surface with the same signs of bombardment as Tamulk, leaving dark scars on the otherwise pristine surface. Thankfully, there were not nearly as many craters and fewer signs of damage. Kal guessed the Forha government had quickly given in to the Ukhel demands, saving much of their population and infrastructure. He was also glad to see the Ukhel had left long ago, based the scaffolding and reconstruction they saw as they approached the planet. Using the coordinates the Alliance provided, the *Oruc* landed in a small landing port in the large conglomeration of cities at the northern pole.

Kal wondered how the Qudoru were adapting to the Ukhel occupation. They were a religious species, believing in the concept of the Eternals. According to the Qudoru belief, each sentient species in the galaxy had their own Eternal who had created their world. The Eternals placed each creature in existence to fulfill a part of their plan and to make the universe better. The Qudoru believed that one could be reborn to a new life if they fulfilled their purpose in the current one. This meant excelling at one's profession and working to make the universe better for all. They also believed that the Eternals punished their creatures for sins they committed in the past by having bad things happen to them. It was a nice idea, though like with most religions, Kal found that the practice of it was often lacking.

This belief system always made the Qudoru seem fatalistic to Kal. They tended to accept negative events as a deserved punishment for some past sin. He couldn't anticipate how the Qudoru on Forha would be able to accept the loss of their home world, Norto, and the occupation of Forha as part of their Eternal's plan.

Forha was a tropical planet—hot and humid compared to Earth and other Human planets, but ideal for the Qudoru. The surface was covered with oceans and dark blue rain forests, with mountains and volcanoes stretching upward at the planet's equator. The Qudoru had settled the entire planet, but their major population centers were located near the poles, where the temperatures averaged only 40 degrees Celsius. From orbit, the Qudoru cities created a reddish halo at the top and bottom poles of an otherwise blue planet.

Port control informed Garcia that they were expected and that all services would be taken care of, free of charge. Kal, Nicole, Jones, and two Tac-I soldiers—Sakata and Robinson—stepped off the cargo ramp and into the humid Forha air. The landing port was clearly restricted for private use, and there were no attendants or crowds of merchants inhabiting the terminal. The landing pads were clean and immaculately maintained, with service bots efficiently offloading materials and conducting repairs.

I just contacted the port control and it looks like they can conduct at least some of the repairs here, and for free, Garcia told the away team as they entered the city.

Another thing we owe the Alliance, responded Kal. He didn't like the feeling of being in their debt.

They walked out of the port and were greeted by a maelstrom of activity. Enormous buildings, which Nicole said were called shoupas, stretched several thousand meters into the sky. They looked almost like giant trees with small, tapered bottoms but expanding out hundreds of meters at the top, creating a red-colored canopy that enveloped the entire city. Underneath the canopy, circular domes, each hundreds of meters tall, covered the landscape. Their outsides were plastered with digital displays that broadcast an ever-changing rotation of products and services. Large, elevated walkways stretched between domes and carried Qudoru pedestrians, slithering from one to the next.

Kal saw very little of the damage and devastation he'd seen on Tamulk. As far as he could tell, only one of the shoupas had been destroyed by the Ukhel; everything else looked untouched. It looked to have been hit at its base, causing the enormous building to topple over on its side, crushing several smaller structures underneath.

Kal used the Alliance chit to lead the away team through the city, weaving through the crowd on the walkways.

Qudoru were about three meters long from the head to the tip of their tail. Their heads were pointed and covered in a hard shell with eyes on the top and a wide, toothless mouth below an impressive, pointed snout. Most of the pedestrians wore typical business attire, the top half of their body covered in colorful shirts that extended down to cover much of their tails. Kal noticed that every single Qudoru they saw had a yellow band across their head. He had never seen the Qudoru wear them before so was guessing they were some sort of sign of mourning.

The citizens all moved slowly through the street, the normal buzz and chatter of the large city seemingly muted by the tragedy they had just faced. The garish advertisements were jarring after the quiet of their voyage, and in stark contrast to the somber tone of the pedestrians. Kal's chit led them to the base of a shoupa, and its cavernous entrance led to a large corridor lined with restaurants and high-end shops.

Small children scrambled around playgrounds while their caretakers watched from garden areas.

Kal guessed that this shoupa was designed to cater to tourists and non-Qudoru. Peering into the front windows of the bars and restaurants, he could see there were meal options for non-Qudoru, who mostly ate grubs and raw grains. The furniture in the corridor looked to be adaptive, meaning that it could alter its shape to conform to a variety of body types.

The corridor ended in a central atrium that spanned the entire height of the building, letting natural light flood into the chamber. Intricate, vermicular carvings crawled up the side of the room. A circular desk stood in the center of the atrium, with kiosks placed at regular intervals around it. A Qudoru attendant stood in the center of the table.

"Hello loves, how can I help you today?" the clerk asked, sliding to face them.

Kal hesitated, unsure of how to ask. "Umm...we are looking to speak with certain associates who...wish to remain unknown."

"Smooth, sir," Jones whispered in Kal's ear.

"Well, I don't think I can help with that particular problem. I might recommend using any sort of chit you have on one of these monitors." The attendant placed her hand on the kiosk in front of them and wrinkled its snout in a conspiratorial manner.

"Of course, of course," Kal replied thankfully. He saw that there was a small receptacle in each kiosk that seemed to fit the Alliance chit. Kal awkwardly used his left arm to place the chit into the kiosk, then pressed the identification pad.

The floral logo on the screen was replaced with the image of what looked to be two mountains. Seeing Kal's puzzled expression, the clerk said, "That is the lift over there, love. It is only for special people…like you."

The away team walked to the lift the clerk indicated. A Qudoru guard stood by the door and placed a hand in front of Kal as they were about to enter. "Sorry buddy, but only two people can go up. Your friends will need to wait down here. There are several great restaurants, bars, and other recreational activities down here in the atrium. So sorry."

"We'll wait here," Jones offered. "You and Ms. Bergeron head up there."

Kal nodded, and he and Nicole stepped into the lift. The doors closed and Kal felt the floor start to rise beneath them. The far wall disappeared, revealing the city stretching out as they streaked upward. The view was breathtaking, a mosaic of light created by gaps in the shoupa's canopy blanketed the domes and walkways.

"So, anything you can tell me about who we're about to meet?" Nicole asked as they stared out the window.

"Nope, I've never even heard of the Alliance having anything but fronts. I have no idea who we will meet, or what will happen."

"It certainly seems like they are going through a lot of trouble just to deliver some holos to you." Nicole looked at him with a raised eyebrow.

"Agreed—I think we can expect that there's more to this."

The lift slowed when they were near the top of the canopy. Kal realized that as they had been traveling, the car had been not only moving vertically but horizontally as well, edging out to trace the expanding canopy of the building. The window was now at a 45-degree angle to the lift floor, extending out over the bustling city below them.

Stepping out the door, they were greeted by another Qudoru guard. This one was clothed in a soft, maroon-colored, fabric vest—the same color Kal had seen in the other Alliance fronts he had visited. It dropped the front half of its body in a bow, its rear tail remaining on the floor.

"Humans, welcome to the Alliance," the Qudoru greeted them. "We're honored to have you here. Please follow me."

Kal and Nicole followed the attendant as it slithered down the hallway. Kal smiled as he realized that in addition to the color of the guard's vest, the decorations and fixtures were also nearly identical to those of other Alliance fronts. However, the hallway was slightly more opulent—the fabrics softer and the gilt decorations more fashionable. Were they at some sort of Alliance headquarters? The idea would have seemed humorous to Kal months ago, but now anything was possible.

Their guide stopped in front of a set of platinum-gilded doors. As they approached, the doors swung open to reveal an office big enough to fit the *Oruc*. A Qudoru stood, clearly waiting for them, with its arms outstretched. Kal couldn't be sure, but he had the impression this Qudoru was elderly. There was a hint of white around the eyes and a general sense of age. Qudoru lived to be several hundred years old—much more than the hundred-twenty of the average Human—which meant that most of them were ancient from Kal's perspective.

"Welcome, welcome." The Qudoru wrapped his arms around Kal and embraced him. Kal awkwardly patted its back with his left arm. After giving Nicole the same warm embrace, they were ushered into the room, the doors closing behind them.

"We are so happy to have you here in my office. My name is Administrator Yitari Tkash Nervoroon, but please call me Yitari. It has been ages since I have talked with a Human, and I am beside myself."

Kal stole a sideways glance at Nicole; she shrugged. Yitari gestured to a grandiose seating area in the center of the room then slid to a credenza against the wall and picked up a wooden tray filled with sweets.

"I had these chairs brought in years ago and almost never have a chance to use them," Yitari said as he slithered to the seating area. "I just hope that I honor you and your Eternal through these chairs and Human food." He set down the tray in front of them. Kal's mouth watered as he saw the variety of Human delicacies—shingen momo, chocolate trifika, fekkas, and many more that he wasn't familiar with. He selected a fekka from the tray and took a satisfying bite of the biscuit.

"You truly honor us and our Eternal," Nicole replied as she took a chocolate.

"I know you've come here for the holos of the Ukhel," Yitari said, setting the tray down on an end table. As he turned around, his face became serious, the eyes focused intently on Kal. "And we will get to that soon enough. But the Alliance has asked me to talk with you. Given the state of Humanity and the Ukhel's clear dislike of your species, we feel it is important to understand who we're dealing with."

"You said clear dislike—what makes you say that?" asked Kal.

"Two reasons. First, the Ukhel attacked five species—Humans, Kurz, Tounous, X'Ado, and Qudoru. These species are not very similar—we occupy roughly the same portion of the galaxy, but there are other species that also exist in this region of space. We have different values, technologies, and dispositions. The only thing that the other four species have in common is that they are aligned, in some way, with Earth."

"Could be coincidence," Kal replied. "Perhaps just dumb luck or something we are not thinking of."

"Maybe, but there is a second, more convincing reason. All five of our species had our home worlds destroyed by the Ukhel. Since then, the Ukhel have been systematically capturing all the remaining colonies of each species. When they do this, they treat all non-Human systems the same. They ask for 50 percent of all raw materials, make the local government declare independence, and set up a local force to report infractions. Other than that, they leave the planet and its inhabitants alone. This is not what they are doing on your Human colonies. There they require a much heavier

255

tribute, keep capital ships in orbit, and have troops actively patrolling—looking for rebellion. Also, your local leaders have not only been forced to declare independence but have had their authority overridden by the Ukhel. They seem to have what one might call a vendetta against Humanity"

"But why? We've never seen them before."

"Does the Alliance know anything else that we do not about the Ukhel?" Nicole interjected. Kal could tell she was troubled by Yitari's revelation.

"Unfortunately, no. They are completely unknown, even to the Alliance. They seemed to appear as if from nowhere." Yitari slid toward Kal and raised his head in question. "Do you know of any way that you Humans have angered your Eternal? Has your species committed any great sins recently?"

"Uh…well, I mean I think Humanity definitely committed a great many sins. But I'm not sure if we're any worse than any other species," Nicole responded. Kal nodded his head in agreement. He thought back to Nicole's stories of her time growing up on the commune.

"It may also be an ancient sin that you are paying for. These things are hard to know." Yitari leaned back and seemed to brood on this thought for a moment. "There are indeed many ancient sins in your species, as there are in most—slavery, war, corruption, genocide."

Kal squared his shoulders in his chair. "Yes, we made mistakes, but that was long ago. Humanity has evolved, we have become peaceful to one another and the rest of the universe."

256

"Ah, Colonel Norman, don't make false statements such as that. Your species fought against the Torgham very recently, did they not?" Yitari chided him.

Kal felt his face flush. And he bit back the childish retort he wanted to say.

Yitari continued. "All sentient species commit sins; it is a part of living. But I forget that you Humans don't truly understand Eternals. They do not forget, and you can only be absolved of sin and past mistakes through a trial that you must master. It seems that you are now paying for a sin that is ancient, and this is your trial."

"What about the Qudoru, the X'Ado, and the other species who were attacked?" Kal asked. "Aren't you also paying for a sin then?"

"Indeed, we are," replied Yitari. "That is why we wear these bands on our heads. To signify our desire for atonement. There has been much discussion about what we might have done to cause this horrible tragedy."

"Any thoughts?" Kal didn't believe in the Qudoru philosophy, but he couldn't help asking.

"My guess is that it is due to the destruction of the Rudoru. Before our species evolved to the point that we were traveling throughout the galaxy, we fought a terrible war with ourselves. The Rudoru were members of our species who did not believe in the Eternals. They splintered off, changing their names and taking over a portion of Norto for their own. Our ancestors fought against them, converting them to our beliefs when we could and eliminating them when we could not."

Yitari's mouth curled downwards in a frown similar to a Human's.

"That may be the case, but can we not reduce our suffering? Or is it already decided?" Nicole asked.

Yitari gave the Qudoru version a smile, his nose twitching. "Ah, that is a wonderful question, Ms. Bergeron. Of course, you can reduce it—through hard work to show your Eternal that you are worthy. Just as I dedicate my life to the Alliance to honor my Eternal, you must work diligently to defeat this attack, and then you may earn a respite from your species' pain and master the trial before you."

"You say that you are working for the Alliance—are you their leader?" Kal asked, seeing an opportunity to change subjects. He was not big on religion or philosophy.

"Ha, no, I am an Alliance Administrator for the Qudoru. I do not know who the leader of our organization is. I am responsible for our dealings with my people. It is my duty, and thus I honor my Eternal by performing well."

"And in this case, doing well is to determine if you can trust us," asked Nicole.

"Not trust you, but determine if we think you will succeed. Humanity has been hit harder than most, and we wonder if you'll survive."

"But why us?" Kal asked, pointing to Nicole and himself. "There are still a lot of Humans out there."

As soon as Kal said it, he wondered if it was true. Earth had a population of fifteen billion, but the combined colonies were about the same. Kal estimated that there still should be a large portion of Humanity still alive, although trapped under the Ukhel's thumb.

"Because there are not many Humans left with the resources to fight, other than you. But let me ask, what do you plan on doing? How can you defeat the Ukhel and honor your Eternal?"

"Right now, not much," admitted Kal. "But we're trying to understand them, figure out their motivation, technology, and weaknesses. Then we can begin to fight back."

"And that is why you want the holos," finished Yitari. "To confirm your hunch about how many of them there are. Perhaps, one of their weaknesses lies in their numbers."

"Yes." Nicole's mouth twisted. "That's what we are hoping."

"Well then I can confirm for you. They are few in numbers—only twenty-three capital ships that we have seen. However, they are very willing to destroy worlds and systems if they feel it will serve their goals." Yitari made a clicking noise indicating disapproval.

"If you know this already, I imagine that you have capabilities that we do not. Why don't you attack them or at least broadcast this information so others can use it?" Kal felt annoyed at having their intentions so easily guessed.

"Again, a good question. I do enjoy you Humans. The answer is simple. The Alliance are not warriors; we conduct trade. We would provide this information, but to whom? There are few who can make use of it, and the risk of the

Ukhel learning more about us is great." Yitari made a gesture that Kal could not interpret.

"So, what is the Alliance doing?" Nicole asked, her face growing red. "What are you doing to honor your Eternals?"

"The Alliance is a much larger organization than you might imagine in some ways, and much smaller in others. I am not fully aware of how far our influence spreads, but I do know that we have fronts on planets that have yet to be discovered by any of the species that you are aware of. I also know that we do not have the power to match your EDF or other militaries head on. We chose information over power because power invites challenge and conflict—we wish to avoid those."

"What about Forha and the Qudoru?" Kal asked. "Do you know what they are doing?"

"Yes, but unfortunately it is little. Forha is under the Ukhel. Much like other planets, it capitulated to the Ukhel and has declared itself independent. The other remaining planets have declared themselves independent as well. So, I fear the concept of the Qudoru as a sovereign empire no longer exists." Yitari shook his head sadly. Kal and Nicole sat quietly, waiting for him to continue.

"Alas, that is the way of the Eternals—we also have sins to atone for. Perhaps through my information I can help to atone for some of the Qudoru's sins." Yitari stiffened for a moment; he must have received a message through his implant. "I am sorry my dear Human friends, but our time to chat must end."

"Why?" Kal knew he was in no shape to fight any Ukhel soldiers.

"It seems the local Ukhel security forces have a suspicion that Humans are on this planet and are actively looking for you."

Kal and Nicole bolted up.

"I am notifying your ship that they will need to pick you and your team up directly from this shoupa. You will need to take our lift to the top, and they can extract you from there. Also, I am allowing your friends to enter and meet you."

"Thank you for your help," Kal said.

"Yes, this has proven to be invaluable," Nicole agreed.

"I hope it pleases my Eternal that I have been able to assist," Yitari said. "One last thought, though. You have said that Humans do not know the Ukhel—and this may be true—but the question you should be asking is: how do the Ukhel know you?"

Chapter Twenty-Three

The *Oruc* folded a final time, arriving in the space around Kapustin Station. The eleven-day journey had been quiet and routine, with most of the crew keeping to themselves.

During their journey, Kal found himself continually circling back to Yitari's parting words. It seemed the Ukhel had targeted Humanity for some specific reason, but Kal didn't have a clue what it might be. He and Nicole went back and forth, discussing what had happened, but neither of them had any insight. Their best guess was that a dark ops mission had gone wrong and somehow brought the wrath of the Ukhel upon them.

Kal also felt wary about how they would be greeted when they returned to the station. In some ways he didn't care as long as there was some emotion. Nothing would be as bad as the lethargy they had left weeks ago. His apprehension over having to look General Sato in the eye wore on him more and more as they neared the station. He also wondered what insights and intelligence the other ships might have gathered and how many of them survived their missions? They still did not have a comprehensive understanding of where the Ukhel were and how much of the galaxy was under their sway, though he knew it was significant.

There also still was the question of the other powers in the galaxy, farther away from Humanity. Would the Ukhel attack species like the Z'Ta or Killari? Would those species attack the Ukhel in response to their aggression? With the communications net in disarray and the *Oruc* travelling between stars, he was stuck in the dark.

Prior to their final fold, the *Oruc* stopped one light week away to conduct a staged approach.

"Sir, something's wrong," Lieutenant Park said in a worried tone. "The fleet around the station has disappeared almost completely. I see a few large capital ships, but that is it."

"Maybe they sent the fleet out," Garcia offered hopefully. "Some of the other ships came back with intel and they took action."

Kal wanted to believe that, but he had strong doubts. What had happened? Were they too late? "Maybe. Can you see any damage or evidence of a battle?"

"No, but we are still pretty far out," Park responded.

"Okay, let's keep folding closer," Kal instructed. He also sent a ship-wide message to be prepared for emergency maneuvers. If there were Ukhel at the station, they would need to leave immediately.

As they continued to fold closer, the ship's sensors told a grim story. Kapustin Station had been hit in multiple places with large-bore kinetic rounds. The ships they had seen were actually derelict hulls, floating coffins created by the Ukhel. Whatever ships had done this had since moved on, leaving only the wreckage. After an informal conference, the crew of the *Oruc* decided to investigate.

They neared the disabled station and Kanumba hunched over her monitor, taking detailed scans of the station, looking for survivors. "I think the entire station has been decompressed…wait, there may still be a small section with atmosphere in the command dome. Looks like the entire station has active emergency power."

Kal wanted to fall on the deck and scream. They'd lost everything. Humanity's final stand, wiped out. They were all that remained. He struggled to think of what to do next.

"Dammit! Just detected something folding out of the system." Garcia looked like he wanted to hit something. "The signature was small—a drone of some sort." Kal had to assume that it was reporting their arrival to the Ukhel. Now the clock was ticking.

"We have to expect that we're going to have company soon," Park advised.

"Another drone just folded out of the system," Garcia announced to the rest of the cockpit.

Despite everything, Kal knew they still had a mission. If they'd survived, perhaps there were others out there. Perhaps there were others still on board the station. It was a long shot, but there was still hope. There had to be.

"We don't have much time. We need to get in that station to see if there are any survivors. Also, if the central servers are not destroyed, we may be able to get their data backup and have an idea as to what happened." Kal swore under his breath as he thought about the lives that had been on the station.

"Staff Sergeant Jones, Kapustin Station has been attacked. Prepare your squad for insertion. We are going to the command dome—expect two to be joining you," Kal called out over the ship's intercom.

"Lieutenant Colonel Zhou, please come to the bridge—there's something you need to see now," Kal called directly to Zhou's room.

Zhou was in the cockpit only a few moments later, his mouth agape at the scene of destruction before him.

"Colonel Zhou, we don't have a lot of time, but now I'm begging for your help. There's a small portion of the command dome that still has atmosphere and may have survivors. We need to get in there to find out if that's the case. We also need to access to as much of the station's central database as possible. Two probes have folded out of the system. I can't confirm who they belong to, but I expect we're in a race against time."

Zhou continued to stare out the screen of the ship, his face frozen in shock. His mouth started to move, but no words came out, just a jumble of sounds. Kal grasped Zhou's shoulder—snapping him out of his stupor.

"Yes…yes, I will help you. The area that still has some atmosphere is on the command deck. We can enter the station here." He pointed at a point on the central dome between two of the spokes on Garcia's screen, "and then maneuver through. Good news is that there is a backup data removal unit very close."

"Okay, great. Garcia, you got that?" Garcia nodded. "Perfect. We are going down to the cargo bay to get suited up. Remember, stay vigilant and let us know if you see anything—the Ukhel could show up at any point."

Kal and Zhou headed to the lower deck. Jones and five of the Tac-I soldiers were competing the final checks on their suits when they arrived. Because they would be entering a zero-gravity vacuum, the soldiers were double and triple checking of all their systems. Kal stepped into one of the remaining battle suits and put his arm in. The suit automatically sealed itself and Kal clumsily put on the helmet with his left arm. The right sleeve hung limply at his side—he knew that he could control it even without an arm of his own, but didn't have the training to even attempt it.

Garcia, how far out are we? Kal asked through his neural implant.

About a minute. I'll go ahead and open the bay from here. As soon as Garcia finished speaking, the back cargo bay door opened—an energy shield stretched over the opening, keeping the atmosphere inside the ship.

Listen up! Jones's instructions were sent to the subnet for all the soldiers in the away team. *Do not jump off the ramp; step very lightly. We'll be moving directly into zero gravity.*

I should go first. I have access to the external doors of the station, Zhou said.

Roger that. Colonel Zhou is on point, Jones acknowledged.

Once Garcia gave word that they were in position, the away team started to walk off the cargo ramp single file to the empty space outside the hull of Kapustin Station. Zhou took a moment to find the entrance, and was able to open it through his neural implant, giving them access to the airlock inside the station.

They floated into the airlock, the magnetic soles of their battle suits locking them to the floor. The room was large enough for the entire eight-person team to stand comfortably, and soon everyone was inside.

Can you override the station's security protocols to keep the interior and exterior hatches open? Jones asked Zhou.

Yes. Since it's already decompressed, the system should allow me to do it. It took a few seconds, but the interior hatch slid open to reveal a utility corridor, dimly illuminated by emergency lights on the ceiling. Kal expected to see traces of explosions or other damage, but it looked much as he remembered. He did see a few pieces of debris floating in the air—a plaque from a wall, a tablet, some sort of machine gear—but otherwise the space seemed untouched.

The group started to traverse the corridor, forgoing walking and instead using their thrusters to speed ahead. They were all aware the probes that had folded away were notifying *someone* of their presence. As they turned a corner, they came across a body floating in the center of the corridor. It was a female captain, her face frozen in pain, her body bloated from the vacuum of space. Kal hoped the end had come quickly, but was sure it hadn't been quick enough.

Zhou gently pushed the corpse aside and continued down the hallway until they reached a large security door. It was designed for rapid decompression situations; and would have slammed down as soon as the station sensed atmosphere leaking from an adjacent section in an attempt to isolate the leak. There was a small airlock in the center to allow people to pass through without allowing atmosphere to escape.

Okay, we'll need to go one at a time, Jones said. *I'll go first and give the all clear. Private Kimathi, I want you to cover the rear and come through last.*

Jones made his way through the airlock and called out the all clear a minute later. Kal was in the middle of the column and waited for his turn to cycle through. After passing through the airlock, he quickly double-checked the atmosphere with his suit's sensor—even though he already saw a few soldiers with their helmets off—before taking off his own. The air was tinged with the smell of stale smoke. He could hear the faint sound of an alert going off in one of the rooms further down the corridor. Otherwise, it was identical to the hallway they had just come from.

"Okay, listen up, we have to be quick. Kimathi and Chen, cover the airlock we just came through; Khan and Sakata, you cover the far one." Jones pointed down the corridor, opposite from the way they'd entered. "The rest of you, fan out and look for any survivors. If you find any, give me a holler."

"Can you go to the data removal unit and see what information you can get?" Kal asked Zhou. "I'm going to take a look around."

"Yes, sir." Zhou gave a nod and then started down the hallway.

Kal realized he was familiar with this area. It was the exact section of the station where his stateroom had been. He started studying the doors—General Sato's office should be in the area.

Finally, he saw a nameplate with General Albert Sato stenciled on it, framed squarely in the center of his battle suit's light. Kal awkwardly pulled the door's override lever with his left hand. The door jerked open as the emergency release caught and Kal's nose was slammed with the acrid smell of decay.

General Sato's bloated body floated above his desk. His face was peaceful, looking almost asleep, except for the circular entrance wound of a kinetic slug and bruising on the general's temple. He was wearing his dress whites— immaculate, except for a few drops of blood on the front. Kal shook his head sadly as he advanced into the wood-lined office. The memorabilia and belongings that had lined the general's shelves now floated around the room—a few plaques, some small pieces of art, the general's whisky that he would offer visitors.

Kal used his thrusters to maneuver closer to the desk, gently nudging the general's body out of the way as he got close. Despite the main power being off, it appeared that the general's personal desk monitor was on, seemingly tied to the backup power grid. Kal had his suit open the gauntlet covering his left hand, exposing his glove underneath. He gently tapped the monitor's surface and was relieved to see that the general had disabled the security protocols on it.

The screen immediately opened to the communications folder. It was a catalog of all the general's correspondence with the other soldiers in the station. The very top message had the subject line, in all capital letters, *READ THIS FIRST*.

The message was very simple, only one sentence, which read, *So that you know what happened here. - AS*. Kal read through the general's correspondence since they left, trying to understand what had happened.

After the *Oruc* left with thirty-nine ships instead of four, the general had flown into a rage. Protocols had been tightened around the station and boards of inquiry were held. However, their departure had inspired other ships to leave as well. The messages between Sato and his staff became more and more paranoid and depressed. General Lee in particular began to see plots and insubordination all around him.

Officers submitted letters of resignation or sent suicide notes as they were no longer able to take the strain. The final message in the folder was from the general to a junior captain, ordering her to take control of the station.

Kal wondered how long the general and his staff had been dead before the Ukhel arrived. He wondered how many people had been left at the end—it seemed like not too many, thankfully. He couldn't imagine the depression and horror of those final soldiers as they saw the Ukhel fleet descend upon the station. They'd only been gone five weeks; the decline was swift.

Colonel Norman, Jones called, *our troops have completed their sweep. They found no survivors, though they did find the bodies of several members of the command team—all of them committed suicide.*

I found General Sato, also dead. Kal responded. *Zhou, any luck with the data removal units?*

Yes, sir. I've located them. It appears that they're in good shape. Heading back to the main corridor now.

Roger that. I'll start heading back as well. Kal left the general's office and maneuvered back through the corridor.

The away team gathered in the center of the command deck and Jones conducted a quick accountability check, while inspecting each suit's propellant and oxygen levels at the same time. "Sir, we need to head back. We're good on oxygen, but with all this maneuvering in zero gravity, we're running low on propellant."

"Agreed—let's get back to the *Oruc* and we can decide what our next steps are. We need to take a look at what Zhou was able to pull from the station's systems."

The team donned their helmets and began to reverse course back to the *Oruc.* The reason for the lack of bodies was clear to Kal considering General Sato's note. Thankfully, most of the occupants had probably left by the time the Ukhel attacked—a blessing for which Kal was very grateful.

The team returned to the ship and Captain Garcia immediately maneuvered the *Oruc* away from the station, to allow them to fold away quickly. Kal stepped into a charging cradle at the side of the bay and got out of his battle suit. The cradle would automatically repair minor damage as well as refill the suit's energy, oxygen, and propellants.

"Zhou, please join me in the cockpit. I need you and Chief Kanumba to see what you can get from those data backups. We need to figure out what happened to Kapustin as soon as possible." Kal beckoned with his arm as he started moving to the upper deck.

"Will do, sir." Zhou fell in step with him. "Sir, I heard you say you found General Sato—what happened to him?"

"He committed suicide. I'm not sure if you were close to him, but I respected him. He just couldn't handle it all—losing everyone, the fear and uncertainty, and then our departure." Kal felt a stab of guilt as he said the words. "It all dragged him down. It could have happened to anyone."

"I didn't know him too well. Talked to him a few times at the operations center. He seemed like a good officer." Zhou's face betrayed his disgust at the general's fate. Most military officers viewed suicide as a coward's way out. To have an officer of Sato's stature do it must be hard for Zhou to swallow.

As they reached the cockpit door Kal stopped, blocking the door, and turned around. "He was. He'd gone through a lot. I don't agree with what he did, but I sure as hell understand it."

Kal turned around and walked into the cockpit without giving the colonel a chance to respond. As he sat down in his chair, an alarm went off.

"Another ship just entered the area. Scanning now…" Park's face had gone white.

"Damnit! Starting up our fold drive now." Garcia furiously tapped on the console in front of him. One of the great advantages of a deep station like Kapustin was that you could fold from almost any point within the area, allowing quick escape.

"Don't do anything yet," Kal counseled. "We need to at least know what type of ship it is."

They waited several precious seconds before another alarm went off on the dash. "They're hailing us. Looks like the ship is the EDF *Hannibal*."

Everyone in the cockpit exhaled in unison. The *Hannibal* was one of the scout ships that had participated in the mission.

"Bring them up on the main viewscreen," Kal instructed.

The face of Major Lucinda Bankole appeared on the main viewscreen. "Colonel Norman, pleased to see you again." Kal nodded. "I'll make this brief since we don't have much time. We came back from Tounous space with several EDF ships a few weeks ago. When we arrived, Kapustin Station was in the state you see here. The Ukhel set up drones to alert them whenever a ship folds in, and I can guarantee they're on their way now. There's a small EDF fleet, led by the *Ofira*"—a carrier, Kal remembered—"that's not far away. They set up drones as well so they can warn friendly ships. I'm sending coordinates to the EDF fleet to the *Oruc*. You need to fold away now."

"Thank you. We'll rendezvous with you at the coordinates." Kal replied.

"See you there, sir." Bankole cut the connection and the *Hannibal* folded away.

"Should we fold, sir?" Captain Garcia asked.

"Wait…I want to see what ships the Ukhel send. Also, make sure we're tracking exactly when and where they arrive in the area."

Kal knew he was taking a risk. Even though they were in deep space, they ran the risk of the Ukhel folding to a point that blocked their escape or even right on top of them. He had to take it though. If the Ukhel had this place set up as a trap, it could also be sprung on them. Kal had found a place where he could lure in the Ukhel and gain the element of surprise.

"Roger, sir. I have the fold drive primed and ready to go as soon as they enter the area. We're in a location with minimal gravitational disruption." Captain Garcia's voice practically dripped apprehension.

After several minutes, alarms blared in the cockpit, announcing the arrival of the Ukhel ship. It was close enough that they could see it through the viewscreen—also close enough to cause gravitational interference and prevent them from immediately folding.

"Shit! They're way too close. We need to get away from that ship before we can fold." Captain Garcia's hands flew across his console as he increased throttle to full speed.

"Kanumba, make sure you run full diagnostics on that vessel. I want you to light that thing up with every sensor suite we have." Kal instructed.

The Ukhel ship looked to be roughly double the size of a Human battleship—the *Oruc* would be no match. It took a moment to determine where they were and then started to rotate and fire its main thrusters, heading at them. As it moved, the Ukhel ship fired a salvo of plasma rounds from its front cannons.

"We have two rounds heading straight toward us, break left!" Park called out.

The ship banked quickly to the left and then settled on a line traveling away from the Ukhel battleship. The process continued, with the Ukhel firing at the *Oruc* and Garcia navigating away from the rounds while keeping a general outward trajectory.

"Okay, we're clear enough. Activating the fold drive." Garcia slammed his hand down on the panel in front of him.

Chapter Twenty-Four

"Running scans now." Kanumba called out as the stars shifted and the Ukhel ship disappeared. "I see multiple EDF and Human ships in the area—a small fleet, in fact. We have a carrier, a battleship, and multiple civilian and scout ships!"

Kal couldn't keep the smile off his face. The sight of other Human ships was a welcome relief from the despair of Kapustin Station. Kanumba turned to him. "The carrier *Ofira* is hailing us and asking us to land."

"Absolutely." Kal was beside himself, slapping everyone in the cockpit on the back.

Garcia navigated the *Oruc* toward the landing bay of the *Ofira*. Relief flooded through Kal's body—there were other Humans still fighting the Ukhel besides them. After weeks of touring Ukhel-captured worlds and wrecked stations and ships, this small fleet reignited a glimmer of hope. Once the commanding general saw his report and he was able to talk with them, Kal hoped they would be able to begin a strategy to take the fight to the Ukhel.

A few minutes later, the *Oruc* touched down in the *Ofira*. Kal walked through the ship, thanking every crew member and promising to make sure their actions were known by every single flag officer in the fleet.

Stepping off the back ramp, Kal was greeted by a lieutenant colonel with shoulder-length brown hair and a small smile on her otherwise tired face. She saluted smartly and then abruptly put her hand down when she saw Kal's missing right arm.

"Pleased to meet you, sir. I am Lieutenant Colonel Irina Petrov, Executive Officer of the *Ofira* and acting commander of Samsara Fleet. I, uh, see you have…seen some action. We have a medical facility that should be able to help with your arm."

"Thank you. Good to see you and this fleet. But what do you mean acting commander? What is Samsara Fleet?"

"Sir, it would probably be best if you followed me, and we can discuss in private." Petrov extended her arm toward the door of the bay. Kal followed her lead. Soldiers walked past them in small, placid groups, talking quietly to each other. He noticed that there was a certain carelessness in the attitude of the crew. Uniform regulations seemed to be more of a suggestion than an actual rule on the ship.

They arrived at a lift bank and Kal stepped in with Petrov. The lifts in large capital ships such as this one not only went to other decks but to various sections of each deck, traveling vertically and horizontally, and allowing one to travel quickly between opposite ends of the large ship.

Petrov turned to Kal as they started to move. "Happy to have you aboard, sir. Morale has been suffering, but once soldiers know that you're onboard…well, you inspired a lot of people when you decided to set out on your mission."

"Glad that I inspired, but it was never my intention to even indirectly support insurrection." Kal shifted uncomfortably and felt guilt creeping over him. *You never*

thought about the people you left behind. What your
departure would do to them.

"Sir, when a senior-level officer departs with a small fleet of ships, it's bound to cause some people to think." Petrov looked at him with raised eyebrows.

Kal didn't know what to say to that and so kept his mouth shut.

After a minute, the lift doors opened as a pleasant voice announced that they were in the fleet command cell. A carrier like the *Ofira* was designed to be a flag ship, acting as command and control. As such, it had a separate portion of the ship intended for the fleet generals and their staff—all of them who would outrank the ship's commander and officers. The hallways were slightly more sumptuous than the area around the bays, with wood and platinum highlights as well as viewscreens with holographic recreations of famous battles from both modern-day and ancient times.

Kal followed Petrov to an unmarked door. Walking through, Kal found himself in a small waiting room, lined with empty chairs. A sergeant sat behind a desk at the back of the room, his uniform rumpled and missing the nametape. He was clearly looking at something on his monitor and failed to notice them entering the room.

"Sergeant Trabelsi!" Petrov raised her voice in a sharp bark, causing the sergeant to quickly jump up into semi-attention.

"Yes, ma'am." Trabelsi tried to feign interest but was betrayed by his stifled yawn.

"Pull yourself together. This is Colonel Norman—you'll be working for him now." Petrov's admonishment was delivered in the half-hearted manner of someone who has been through the same conversation before; Kal felt it was more for his benefit than anything else.

"Yes ma'am. Pleased to meet you sir." Trabelsi held out his hand, trying to stifle yet another yawn.

Kal took his hand and looked him directly in the eyes. "Sergeant Trabelsi. Get your shit together." He walked into the office, past the shocked sergeant, with Petrov following behind him, the corners of her mouth ticked up.

"I can't recall the last time I saw Trabelsi at a loss for words."

Kal couldn't hide his annoyance and frustration. He had not realized he would be assuming command of essentially the last remaining element of the EDF. It was a huge burden, and one that he didn't feel especially qualified to take on. However, if he was the senior officer remaining, then it didn't matter what he wanted; he was in charge. He could delegate his authority, but it would still ultimately be his responsibility as the senior officer. "Lieutenant Colonel Petrov, I need to understand what is going on...now."

Petrov's smile disappeared as she sat down in the visitor's seat in front of the desk. Kal sat behind the desk, the sumptuous chair moving to mold itself to his body. He noticed that the desk had what he assumed were a few of Petrov's personal effects on it—a picture frame with her and a man during happier times, some small bit of memorabilia, and a drawing made by a small child with the words "I love you mommy" on it. Painful reminders of a life that was no longer reality.

"Yes, sir. After you left Kapustin Station with your fleet, General Sato tried to pass it off as some grand strategy on his part. However, behind closed doors, he raged against you and Captain Ruiz, saying that you were undermining his authority. It got out pretty quickly that he had nothing to do with your mission, and soldiers began to grow disillusioned. People started to leave, wanting to do anything other than sit around waiting for the Ukhel to attack. At first it was a few small scout ships and civilian merchant vessels, but then the *Bahia* left with almost eighty percent of her crew aboard." Petrov paused.

The *Bahia* was a heavy destroyer, smaller than a battleship or a carrier like the *Ofira*, but it still carried a significant amount of firepower, and its loss must have been a heavy blow to the station.

Petrov detailed the final days of Kapustin Station. The air of hopelessness that had overtaken it during Kal's time there had turned to lawlessness. Major General Gbeho had been found shot in her quarters. Brigadier General Lee had instituted random searches of soldiers' quarters, trying to catch the culprits behind the wave of murders. It seems like this crackdown had led to the complete collapse of morale and doomed the station. The trickle of ships became a flood. The flag officers, rather than trying to rally the troops, began to succumb to their hopelessness and commit suicide or drowned themselves in drink or drugs.

Colonel Stanković, the former commander of the *Ofira*, saw the situation was hopeless and ordered his ship to leave the station. They'd travelled to New America to conduct reconnaissance and determine if the planet had been destroyed. An Ukhel battleship was waiting for them in orbit and dealt heavy damage before the *Ofira* was able to escape. When the *Ofira* returned to Kapustin Station, the crew found the station destroyed and another Ukhel battleship waiting there. Rather than fight, the *Ofira* had folded away, but not before sending out probes to alert them when any Human ships folded into the area. In the past couple of weeks, they had built up their current fleet from various ships that had come to Kapustin, although Petrov admitted that the Ukhel destroyed many Human ships before Samsara Fleet was able to contact them.

Kal sat back in the chair, lost in thought. The events of the final days of Kapustin Station were tough to hear. Things had spiraled out of control after they left, and they were culpable in some of it. That being said, he knew it ultimately vindicated his decision to leave as well—many more could have died in the Ukhel attack. Would anything have changed if they hadn't left? Probably not, but the doubt remained.

"Thank you, it seems like your crew has been through a lot since we left. You mentioned Colonel Stanković—what happened to him?"

"The colonel decided to pilot one of our fighters himself in the battle at New America." Kal raised his eyebrows at the breach of protocol—a carrier commander would normally never pilot an individual fighter. "I think he was tired of it all and decided to leave his life to fate. He didn't make it."

"I'm sorry to hear that. Where does the fleet's name, Samsara, come from?" Kal asked.

"One of our crew members came up with it—it's from an ancient religion. I'm not totally sure what it means, but something around rebirth. We felt it was appropriate for our current situation." Petrov shrugged. "At this point, any little bit of hope helps."

Kal gave a quick nod. "I saw that there's at least one other capital ship in the fleet—a battleship. What is its status?"

"Yes, that's the *Merrimack*. She's fully functional, with all systems online. Right now, she is being commanded by Major Pham. He is a good officer—decided to leave Kapustin Station with the ship after their commander decided to drown herself in drink."

Kal had to pause before speaking again. "That's tough. I can't imagine how morale is right now."

"It has been better, sir."

Kal drummed his fingers off the desk. The small ray of hope that had almost been destroyed by the events at Kapustin returned. "I want you to let the officers and non-commissioned officers know that I will be holding a ship-wide briefing tomorrow at 0900. I will be laying out the plan for the fleet—we are done sitting around and waiting to be destroyed."

Chapter Twenty-Five

Kal sat in the fleet commander's conference room surrounded by several officers from the *Oruc*, and the command staff of the *Ofira* and *Merrimack*. They had eight hours to develop a plan to take the fight to the Ukhel. Kal had an inkling of what he thought they should do, but it wasn't fully fleshed out. The one thing they all knew was that if they didn't have a victory soon, however small, there was no hope.

Kal flexed his new cybernetic arm. It looked almost identical the arm he'd lost, merging seamlessly with the brown skin of his shoulders. According to the ship's doctor this was cutting-edge technology, with a host of features that made it better than the real thing. Ironically, the new prosthesis made him miss his arm more than when there had only been a stump. It finally hit home that he'd lost a part of himself and that there was no way to ever get it back.

After his talk with Petrov, Kal had made his way to the medical center, where a tech had fitted him for the new limb. Normally, he would have gone through a week-long rehabilitation program to help him adjust. However, there simply wasn't time, and so he was learning as he went. In the hour since he'd had it, a glass and a monitor screen had been casualties of his learning process.

"Okay, listen up everyone." The chatter in the room died down. "We have eight hours to figure out exactly what our next steps are. Whatever, they are, I can tell you this—we *will* take the fight to the enemy. I'm done waiting, done scouting, done running. We will strike, and we will put it all on the line—we're suffocating and it needs to stop. Our target is the Ukhel ship that is monitoring Kapustin Station. Our objective is to destroy or disable it so they cannot prey on any more of our ships."

Kal's pronouncement was greeted with nervous smiles. "Hell yes!" Jones shouted.

"So, now the hard part. How do we destroy one of these ships? They've laid waste to multiple fleets in a short time with only twenty-three of them. Chief Kanumba, you've had some time to study their technology, what are your thoughts?"

"The Ukhel ships run on a fusion of biometric and gallium systems. They're highly advanced and use mechanical and biological components in ways we've never seen before. There is no known way to hack or infiltrate these systems, though we have some pieces that the science team is reviewing and attempting to understand."

Kanumba took a breath and continued, "Offensively, their weapons far outpace our own. From personal experience, I can say that our capital ships can only take a few direct hits from their cannons, so evasion will be required. Their defenses are quite good as well. They have energy shields that are more than adequate against even our largest plasma cannons, and their point defense is almost impenetrable. Bottom line—our conventional tactics will not be effective."

"Always can count on you to cheer us up, Chief." Garcia slapped her playfully on the back.

"There is one bright point though," Kanumba added with a mock stern look at Garcia. "Based on what we've heard from eyewitnesses as well as our analysis of the small bit of hull we have been able to recover, it's a safe assumption that their armor plating is very weak. I can't put an exact number around it, but their hulls have roughly half the strength of a typical EDF ship."

"So, if we can get past the shields and point defense system, then it should be easy going," summarized Garcia.

"Pretty much," Kanumba replied.

"Lieutenant Colonel Petrov, what assets do we have available?" Kal appreciated Garcia's ability to lighten the mood but wanted to move the conversation along.

"Our fleet consists of two capital ships—the carrier *Ofira* and the battleship *Merrimack*. The *Ofira* has severe degradation to both kinetic and energy defensive systems as well as operating at only seventy-five percent of our normal power. We took heavy casualties to our fighters as well—we have about fifty percent operational at this point."

"How many is that exactly?" Lieutenant Colonel Zhou asked.

Petrov checked the monitor before her for a moment. "Two hundred and three. Luckily for us, the *Merrimack* is fully operational. Also, the fleet has thirty-four smaller civilian ships and EDF scouts—none with weapons that can do damage to a capital ship, though."

"So, we know that any ship that launches into the space around Kapustin Station triggers the Ukhel probes. And we discovered that the Ukhel battleship takes about thirty minutes to arrive," Garcia said.

"So, that answers how we make contact, but we still need to figure out how we destroy that ship?" Kal asked the group.

"Sir, if I may." Lieutenant Colonel Zhou stood up. "As Chief Kanumba has already mentioned, we cannot take on the Ukhel using our traditional techniques. But we may be able to defeat them another way—though not without a heavy cost. One thing that we've discovered is that the Ukhel do not have individual fighter ships. Their advanced point defense systems and energy shields make up for this, but not completely."

"Go on," Kal instructed.

"I think we have to assume we're at a decisive point. We need to do something to show our soldiers that we have a chance against what they see as an unbeatable enemy. If we can't prove to them the Ukhel can be defeated, then this fleet will be a repeat of Kapustin Station." Zhou got out of his seat and walked toward the viewscreen at the far end of the table.

"Agreed. What's your point?" Petrov asked.

"My point simply is that we need to be clear about how much we're willing to sacrifice for victory. We have only one operable capital ship, which won't stand a chance against the Ukhel. However, we have almost 250 fighters, merchants, and scouts. The Ukhel do not have any fighters of their own, which gives us an advantage." Zhou activated the viewscreen so that he could draw out his strategy.

"We split our smaller ships into two groups, the fighters in group alpha and the scouts and merchants in group bravo.

When the Ukhel fold into the Kapustin area, the fighters immediately begin to ram the Ukhel ship. They can use—"

"The point defense will just destroy them all," interrupted Chief Kanumba.

"We go through the point defense," responded Zhou. He had drawn an illustration with the Ukhel ship, marked as the target, on one side of the screen and the *Merrimack* on the other. A circle labeled group alpha surrounded the Ukhel ship. "The fighters attempt to get as close as they safely can and then try to use the fold drives to bypass the point defense. If only one of two ships are able to penetrate the Ukhel hull, they should disable or destroy it."

"That's suicide," called out Major Pham. "We'll be condemning hundreds to death no matter what. The margin of error on such a short fold make will make it a crap shoot for the pilots."

"True, but I think the soldiers will understand that we would not ask this of them unless we had to," Zhou responded. "At the same time, group bravo will be positioned between the *Merrimack* and the Ukhel ship, acting as a point defense system to block any missiles. It's a strategy that we can use only once, the cost will be too high to repeat. But, it can give us the victory we're desperate for."

Garcia nodded his head. "It makes sense to me, sir. But what is to prevent the Ukhel ship from just folding out of the area?"

"It's a risk, but I think the very presence of the *Merrimack* will keep them in the system. I expect them to believe the risk is worth the destruction of a major EDF capital ship." Zhou finished the illustration on the board showing group bravo as an oval between the Ukhel ship and the *Merrimack*. "The *Merrimack* will keep retreating at full speed from the Ukhel ship to make sure they remain out of plasma fire range. However, I expect the Ukhel ship to be faster and to eventually catch up. If we don't destroy it before that happens, it's game over."

Zhou turned himself to face the room squarely. "I know that this is a costly plan, but I think it's the best we have. We would be asking for the ultimate sacrifice from many of our pilots. But I think it's something they will gladly give. We're all tired or running and hiding. We have an opportunity, and I think this is how we take it."

A blanket of silence covered the room as they considered Zhou's plan. It was audacious and risky, but Kal couldn't think of anything better. He was right—they had to take this opportunity, otherwise their morale and forces would continue to be hacked away.

"So, we doin' this or what?" Sergeant Jones asked.

The room erupted and soldiers started to talk over one another, arguing for or against the plan. They were roughly divided into two equal camps. The group that was against it continued to call out the risks and the casualties, but in the end, they couldn't think of anything that had a better chance of success.

"There has to be a better way," Lieutenant Park beseeched the room.

"If there is, I'm not sure what it is," Zhou replied calmly. "We've been talking for two hours and no one has come up with any other ideas. Ever since the Ukhel first attacked, I think we've been subconsciously hoping that it wasn't actually happening, that we were in some sort of dream. We need to face facts. We're fighting for our survival, and we have to act like it."

"Final call. Does anyone have a better idea?" Kal asked calmly. He waited for a few moments, looking each person in the eye, and then continued to speak. "We'll go with Colonel Zhou's plan in that case. Colonel Zhou, grab who you need and draw up the detailed orders. I want them distributed to key leaders in the fleet by the time I speak in six hours. Also, Zhou, you will be taking command of the *Merrimack* for this mission. Major Pham, you will be his executive officer."

"Roger, sir," both Pham and Zhou responded.

With the meeting adjourned, Kal paced the hallways of the *Ofira*. He walked aimlessly, thinking about what the next day would bring. His meandering path eventually took him to the soldier's quarters. As he walked past the open doors, he could hear discussions of lost family and friends and plans being made for when this was all over, and Humanity finally won. Kal felt his heart lighten, just a bit, listening to the optimism inherent in the soldiers' plans for the future. He knew that there was a large amount of wishful thinking in these types of conversations, but he also knew that sometimes that was necessary.

"Nice to hear people talking about the future." Kal turned around to see Nicole behind him.

"Have you been following me?" he asked with a smile.

"Not at first, but when I saw you wandering the corridors, I thought you looked like you could use someone to talk to." She stepped next to him, and they began to walk beside one another.

"I think you give people hope. Strange, since you tell me that you don't have any yourself." Nicole glanced at him out the corner of her eye.

"Maybe—I'm not sure. I don't think this will be over for a long time, though." Kal shrugged.

"You went from being an independent merchant, carrying junk through space, to commanding the last known Human fleet in the universe."

"Yeah, I guess."

"Do you think you'll ever go back to being that simple merchantman again?"

"Probably not. I don't think I could if I wanted to, though. But I don't want all of this either."

"I don't think anyone wants this."

"I mean command. I've never commanded a fleet before. But they're all looking to me, even Petrov and Zhou."

"What do you want?" Nicole asked, an eyebrow raised.

"I really don't know. I know I don't want to go back to the way I was, though." Kal saw a slideshow in his mind of the dingy chem bars he had made his home the last ten years.

"I hear that," Nicole nodded. "The only way is forward."

Chapter Twenty-Six

"One hundred and forty-three days ago an alien species called the Ukhel attacked Earth and destroyed the home of Humanity. Then they laid waste to the home planets of our allies and captured our colonies. The Ukhel have not given mercy or quarter, killing innocents and enslaving planets throughout the known universe."

Kal sat at his desk in full dress uniform, looking directly at the monitor fixed to the wall. His image and voice were being transmitted to every single ship in the fleet. Although there were officers with more experience than Kal, he still was the ranking officer in the fleet and had the responsibility to let the soldiers know what their mission was. Normally, a fleet commander wouldn't send out a speech like this, but nothing about their situation was normal.

"They've killed countless—our children, parents, brothers, and sisters. We've been beaten back by these invaders, but I am here to say that today it ends. Today, we are going to launch an attack on the Ukhel to prevent them from killing any more of our comrades at Kapustin Station. At seventeen hundred hours, we will be folding into the space around the station and will destroy the Ukhel battleship that is preying on ships that enter the space. The same battleship, I might add, that was part of the original force that destroyed Earth."

Kal paused to let his message sink in. "This will not be an easy battle, but it is one that we must fight. We can no longer sit and wait for a salvation that does not come. We will seize the opportunity and strike at our enemy with everything we have. Your leaders will be briefed shortly on our plan of attack. I ask that each and every one of you have faith in your leadership and in the soldiers next to you. The victory that we will win today will be remembered as the day Humanity stood up and declared that we will not be defeated. Thank you."

Kal cut off the feed and sat back in his chair. This kind of inspirational speech did not come naturally to him, and he felt beads of perspiration already forming on his brow. Nicole gave a small round of applause from the other side of the desk.

"Thank you, thank you." Kal gave a small faux bow, remaining seated.

Nicole's face grew serious. "Do you think it will work?"

"I honestly don't know," Kal admitted, "but I have no idea what else to do."

"Not the most reassuring answer from the fleet commander." Nicole picked herself out of her chair and started to head toward the door. "Whatever happens, you did the best you could. You didn't give up." Nicole turned around before she left. "That's a pretty amazing feat considering all that you have been through."

After she left, Kal quickly changed into his flight suit and headed out the door. The bright lights of the hallway splashed across his face, waking him up and reminding him of what was to come. He headed to the landing bays. Soldiers were deliberately walking around their aircraft with tablets in hand, making final checks. Their actions were quick and efficient—these were checks and procedures that they had performed countless times before. Kal could see they had already completed them but were trying to cover their apprehension through staying in motion, waiting to be told that it was time to go.

Captain Garcia stood on the back cargo ramp of the *Oruc*, elevated above a crowd of junior officers, non-commissioned officers, and civilians. These were the pilots of the scout ships and civilian ships that would be integral to their mission.

"Does everyone understand the plan? Any questions?" Garcia looked down at the crowd and a civilian raised his hand.

"We're not in school—just ask the question," Garcia chided.

"So, who's gettin' the first round when we get back?" The man looked around at the rest of the pilots, earning a laugh from the group.

"I will, and you can have as much as you want." Garcia smiled. "If there's nothing else, get in your ships and make sure you're ready. We only get one chance."

The crowd dispersed into small groups milling around, talking to each other. Kal approached Garcia as he stepped down off the half-raised ramp.

"You sure you want to be in the *Oruc* with us, sir?" Garcia furrowed his brow. "We'll be in the thick of it."

"Yes—I started this on the *Oruc*, and I intend to finish it on the same ship. Zhou is commanding this operation anyway. My job is done." Although Kal was the commander of the fleet, he had quickly relinquished control of the mission to Zhou, since he had devised the plan and was an operational officer. Kal had wrestled whether to stay on the *Merrimack* but he couldn't justify remaining on the capital ship, twiddling his thumbs, when so many of his soldiers would be in harm's way on the small vessels. It didn't feel right. He wondered if Colonel Stanković, the former commander of the *Ofira*, had had the same thought. Kal had been quick to condemn his actions, but he wondered if he was just doing the same thing.

"I bet Petrov gave you an earful." Garcia knew she'd lost her first commander the same way.

"She wasn't happy, but she understood. Truth is, I will not be the one to win or lose this battle. It will be the soldiers and pilots and the commanders making split-second decisions like Zhou." Kal shrugged. "Besides, a logistics officer should not be commanding a fleet in battle."

Garcia smiled as Chief Kanumba came running up to them. In her hand she had one of the Ukhel parts that Kal had recovered on Tamulk. "Gentlemen, good news. We think we may have been able to make this device work with our communications system. As far as we can tell, it is designed to decrypt communications between ships."

"So bottom line, what will this do?" Kal asked.

"Well, bottom line—we don't know, and frankly we should spend about another month testing it before we power it up. But what we hope is that it will allow us to listen in to Ukhel transmissions. Without more information, we're just guessing, but we ran some tests on it and were able to at least get it to connect to our communications systems through this interface we rigged up." She pointed at a dull metallic gray box that had been spliced onto the Ukhel piece.

"Is there any risk to the ship if we plug this thing in?" Garcia looked askance at the box as if it might explode at any time.

"Well, nothing is certain, but I will install it on its own circuit on the ship with a parallel communications line going in and out. That way it can't trip the ship's electrical or be a point of failure for our communications. Honestly, it's interesting how similar some of their technology mirrors our own. They're light years ahead of us, but a lot of it is very familiar."

"Let's get the thing installed then—we're going to be folding soon," Garcia instructed.

Kal looked across the bay at the ships and the soldiers who would be piloting them. The bay was charged with a sense of excitement. Soldiers laughed nervously to each other as they purposefully went about their final checks.

"Attention all personnel, this is Lieutenant Colonel Zhou on the battleship *Merrimack*. We will be folding in approximately five minutes. All crews should immediately make their way to their ships and prepare for departure." The announcement sent everyone hurrying to their stations.

Zhou's plan required him to be on the bridge of the *Merrimack*, since the *Ofira* would be folding out immediately after it launched its fighters and ships.

Kal made his way into the *Oruc*, following Garcia. Lieutenant Park was already in the cockpit—Kal was guessing he'd been waiting there for at least an hour, ready to go. Chief Kanumba was at her station with one of the access panels opened as she attempted to connect the Ukhel box into the ship's systems.

"Ready?" Garcia asked the group.

"Does it matter if we're not?" Kanumba smiled as she closed up the access panel.

"No, but I like to give you the option to voice concerns—even when they'll be ignored." Garcia smiled back as Kanumba gave a playful slap at the back of his head. Kal made one last check, feeling around in his pocket for the picture of his family. It was still there.

"Prepare to fold." Zhao's voice was broadcast to all the ships in the fleet. "Folding in…three…two…one…"

Kal didn't feel a thing as the *Ofira* folded through space with the *Oruc* inside, but he saw the tacmap change on the cockpit viewscreen. The bay doors immediately opened to reveal the energy barrier that kept the atmosphere inside. Peering through it, Kal saw waves of fighters depart the ship in staggered columns hurtling out into the stars. Soon the command came from the operations center for the scout ships to depart. Garcia activated their thrusters and the *Oruc* slid through the bay and past the energy shields.

"Okay, fighters are positioned where the last Ukhel ship folded," Kanumba reported. "The scouts and civilians are making their way next to the *Merrimack*."

After a few minutes, all ships had left the *Ofira* and were in position or making their way there. Lieutenant Colonel Petrov's voice came over the comms. "Samsara Fleet, this is *Ofira*—we're folding back to our position. Get the bastards!"

The *Ofira* blinked out of existence as it engaged its fold drive, leaving behind the *Merrimack* and the rest of Samsara Fleet. In their condition, they would only be a liability. It was agreed that if Petrov did not hear anything from them after one day, she would fold back to look for survivors.

As they waited for the Ukhel to arrive, Kal felt a knot of apprehension build in his stomach. He nervously zoomed in and out on the tactical map, fidgeting to keep his mind occupied. He kept reviewing their plan, thinking of all the things that could go wrong. There was nothing that could be done now, though.

"They're here!" Park's shout caused Kal to jump.

"Looks like they folded in exactly where we thought they would," Kanumba added.

The *Merrimack* turned itself directly away from the Ukhel ship and began to engage its thrusters. After a brief pause, the Ukhel ship turned and gave chase. It launched a wave of ten missiles towards the departing battleship. Kal knew that if just one or two of them hit the *Merrimack* it would be catastrophic.

"Buckle in, folks," Garcia warned as he changed course, aiming the *Oruc* toward the Ukhel and the oncoming missiles. Kal saw all the scout and civilian ships following the same course of action on his viewscreen.

As they closed the distance with the oncoming missiles, Park's hands flew across his console, trying to get a lock on them. "Damn," he swore, "the computer just can't lock on to these things. We're going to have to go manual."

A stream of plasma fire shot out from the cannons on the side nacelles. The first volley missed the missile by a wide margin as it shot past them. Another was following fast, and Park reoriented the cannons to focus them on the new target.

"Yes!" Park gave a whoop as the plasma fire hit the incoming missile, obliterating it. Garcia turned the *Oruc* away from Ukhel and back toward the *Merrimack* to prep for the next round.

Kal looked at the viewscreen—eight of the missiles had been destroyed, and the ninth went out as he watched. The fighters were trying to fold past the point defense of the Ukhel ship with little to show for it. One of them exploded, the gravitational fields of the Ukhel ship causing the fold drive to fail spectacularly. Folding such a short distance was a guessing game, and most of the ships folded past the Ukhel battleship, though some got caught in the point defense and were instantly destroyed. Looking at the situation report, Kal saw that they'd already lost a quarter of their fighters.

"Someone got the last one," Park called out as the tenth Ukhel missile disappeared from the tactical map. "Wait, there's another wave coming up."

Sure enough, Kal's tactical map showed a wave of another ten missiles headed toward the *Merrimack*. The Ukhel had already significantly closed the distance between the two ships, so there would be even less time for their motley point defense system to stop them.

"Here we go again," Garcia announced as he turned the ship back toward the Ukhel.

As the battle had shifted, the *Oruc* was no longer in the front of the ships firing at the Ukhel missiles. They watched silently as several of the Ukhel missiles met their end, destroyed by plasma fire. Kal glanced at the tactical map— about half of the fighters were left with nothing to show for it.

A small explosion blinked into existence as one of the fighters successfully folded directly into the Ukhel ship, exploding as it hit the side. Kal zoomed his viewscreen to see what damage had been done. He smiled when he saw that it had left a gaping hole in the side of the ship. He could see debris shooting out, buffeted by the expulsion of the ship's atmosphere.

"One of the fighters got through," Kal announced.

Park and Garcia didn't respond, as they were completely focused on the incoming wave of missiles. "Stay on your current course; we'll be in range shortly," Park called out. Kal could see him adjusting the targeting to anticipate the trajectory of a missile.

Plasma bolts fired out from the *Oruc* and streamed toward it, missing by what appeared to be a hair's width. After muttering an oath, Park adjusted the cannons to target the next incoming missile and fired off another stream of plasma bolts—missing again.

"Losing your touch, Park?" Garcia asked.

"Sir...please shut up," Park responded without taking his attention off the targeting screen in front of him. There was only one missile remaining in front of them. Park, concentrated on his console and fired the plasma cannons. Kal watched, holding his breath, as the rounds flew past the tail fin of the missile, again missing by what looked to be centimeters.

"Damnit, is there anyone else who can get that missile?" Garcia asked.

An alarm blared and a new ship appeared on Kal's tactical map. The map adjusted to show Battleship Alpha, the original Ukhel battleship, and Bravo, the new ship that had just appeared.

"Damnit! Another battleship just folded in!" Kal swore as he saw the ship. He wasn't sure if it was intentional or pure luck, but the new battleship was positioned directly in the path of the *Merrimack*.

A loud voice suddenly rang out in the cockpit. It was deep and guttural, the words flying out of the speaker with a staccato rhythm. It took a moment for Kal to realize that they were hearing the Ukhel transmissions. Then he realized that he could understand what they were saying without his neural implant. They were speaking Human Standard.

Chapter Twenty-Seven

"What the hell?" Garcia asked.

Kal tried to understand what he was hearing. The language they were using was an ancient, stilted version of Human Standard, a different dialect than what he had ever heard. As he listened, Kal began to be able to make out words, though he couldn't understand everything.

closing in...Merrimack... fighters attempt...defense.

... move to intercept...Merrimack.

"How is this even possible?" Park looked around the cockpit.

"I have no idea," Kal replied. "But we need to let Zhou know that the Ukhel speak Human Standard."

Kal made a private call to the *Merrimack*, informing Zhou of what they had learned. Zhou gasped audibly through the comms when Kal told him.

"Thank you for the update, sir," the colonel said after taking a moment to process. "I am not sure what to do with that information right now, but please let me know if you hear anything more over the Ukhel communications net."

"Will do," Kal closed the communications channel.

The *Merrimack* quickly turned 90 degrees, splitting the difference between the two Ukhel battleships that were closing in on it. The fighters—which were still attacking battleship Alpha—would have no chance at reaching Bravo in time before it got close enough to the *Merrimack* to obliterate it.

"Damnit, we are going to have to abort the mission." Kal swore. "No way we can take more than one—we are already down to a quarter of our fighters."

Calls went out over the Samsara's battle net as the Ukhel missile that had flown past them hit the rear quadrant of the *Merrimack*. Kal zoomed in on the ship and saw that the blast had not been fatal; it appeared to have detonated before making contact with the hull. He rewound the sensor feed to see what had happened. The *Hannibal* had rammed the missile with their ship a few hundred meters prior to it hitting the *Merrimack*—sacrificing themselves in the process.

*… detonation complete…*The Ukhel's words rang out in the cockpit as their sensors registered the hit.

Zhou's voice suddenly rang out over the Samsara command net. "This is the *Merrimack*—we are without fold capabilities. Any ship that is available, move to block incoming fire from Ukhel Battleship Bravo."

"Damnit, this is going from bad to worse," Garcia muttered under his breath as he adjusted their heading to put the *Oruc* directly between the *Merrimack* and Bravo.

A volley of missiles launched from both Ukhel battleships simultaneously, streaking toward the *Merrimack*. Kal saw half of the vessels that had been blocking the missiles launched from Alpha turn and follow the *Oruc*.

"Can we go any faster?" Garcia asked, turning around to look at Kanumba.

"Well, I can try. I may be able to bypass some of the safety devices." Kanumba bent down and opened the panel where the Ukhel device was.

The *Oruc's* speed accelerated—Kanumba's efforts had obviously paid off. Kal could see warning icon's flashing on her viewscreen as she pushed the engines past their normal limits. She left the panel open and got back to her station. The *Oruc* was well ahead of the other Human ships—most, if not all of them, were not going to make it in time to get a shot off on the missiles streaking from Bravo toward the *Merrimack*.

"Looks like we aren't going to have a lot of backup," Kal advised Park. "Most of the other ships won't be able to help."

"I thrive under pressure," Park answered, wiping sweat off his face.

As they sped toward the new onslaught, Kal studied his viewscreen, looking for some way to salvage the situation. With their limited forces, there wasn't any way for the *Merrimack* to evade the combined Ukhel battleships. Their fold drive was down, and the battle would be over in minutes.

"Have you ever wanted to be a fighter pilot?" Kal asked Garcia.

"Wha...oh," Garcia stuttered. He closed his mouth as he realized what Kal was asking.

"There's no other option. The *Merrimack* can't fold, and our fleet can't survive against two battleships for long. We could always fold out of here, back to the rendezvous point— but I think we all know that's not an option."

No one spoke, and Kal took their silence as agreement. The cockpit was quiet except for occasionally garbled messages from the Ukhel ships or updates on the Samsara net.

"This is a way to go," Kanumba said softly. "I mean, I always thought it would be in my sleep."

"Okay Park, you're up," Garcia said as the targeting computer began to designate the incoming missiles as in range. He reduced the throttle, allowing Park more time to target and fire on the projectiles.

Park methodically trained the cannons on the first incoming missile. Small beads of sweat had formed on his forehead, but his face was calm—a mask of concentration. The targeting reticle moved smoothly across the viewscreen as he lined up the shot. The plasma bolts streaked out and hit the incoming missile, obliterating it.

"Nine more to go," Kanumba called out.

Park proceeded to systematically destroy the next three Ukhel missiles. His demeanor was one of perfect calm, except for the sweat now trickling into his eyes.

"Damn!" The plasma blast missed the fifth missile and it hurtled past the *Oruc*.

"Don't worry about it," Garcia coached. "Another ship will get it. You're doing perfect."

Park nodded and then put his head back down, proceeding to destroy the next four missiles before they could get past the *Oruc*.

"Take us to full speed toward them," Kal commanded Garcia. "We can't wait for them to launch another barrage."

"Roger, been nice knowing you all." Garcia set the thrust to maximum, and the *Oruc* catapulted toward the looming Ukhel battleship.

The tenth missile flew past them, the *Oruc's* cannon fire missing by a wide margin. The Ukhel ship continued to grow on the main viewscreen as they headed on a collision course.

"When I count to three, start firing the plasma cannons," Garcia instructed Park. "If we're able to slip through their point defense, I want to make sure we do some damage."

"Got it," Park responded.

"Okay, get ready to fold in three…two…one…"

The noise was unbearable, a combination of screeching metal on metal, parts ripping, and small explosions. The inertial dampeners on the *Oruc* were overtaxed and unable to adjust to a sudden loss of velocity. Kal was flung from his seat onto the floor of the cockpit, hitting his head in the process.

Looking up, he saw that they had managed to fold *inside* of the Ukhel ship. Its interior was made up of a nearly black material that appeared almost organic in nature due to the sweeping lines and delicate accents that adorned the walls and ceilings of the room. A translucent fiber was interwoven with the brownish-gray walls. It was luminescent—a multi-hued glow emanating from the inside. They were in a landing bay of some sort; the room was filled with assault ships, arranged in a haphazard manner. The *Oruc* had already burst through several of the interior walls and supports of the ship, the light construction giving way without destroying them. The collision had greatly reduced their speed though they were still hurtling forward, their inertia continuing after they had successfully folded.

Garcia picked his bleeding head up from the viewscreen in front of him and put the thrusters in full reverse, trying to stop their progress before they hit the far wall of the enormous bay. Their plasma cannon was laying waste to the interior of the bay, destroying vessels and tearing through the bulkheads of the battleship.

Kal saw Humanoid figures scurrying through the area, trying to avoid the explosions and debris caused by the *Oruc*. They were a light purple in color with dark black markings curling around their bodies and wore uniforms that looked similar to the standard EDF ones that the *Oruc's* crew had on. Even though they were far away from the *Oruc*, Kal saw that they moved with a certain feline grace that he had never seen in a Human before. Whatever they were, they were not completely Human, no matter what language they spoke.

"I marked what looks to be the bay doors on your viewscreen," Kanumba called out to Garcia. "I think we should be able to blast our way out of here."

"Okay, but we are going to make sure we take them out before we do," Garcia responded. "Park, can you set a timed fuse on the missiles?"

"I sure can," the lieutenant said with a smile.

The full complement of the *Oruc's* missiles shot out one by one—embedding themselves in the bulkhead. Garcia rotated the ship as they fired to distribute them around the room.

"Okay, let's get out of here." Garcia aimed the ship at the bay doors Kanumba had marked, and Park launched a volley of plasma bolts at them.

The doors blew apart, causing the atmosphere inside the Ukhel ship to expel the *Oruc*, along with several of the other ships inside the bay. Garcia tried to maintain control of the ship, but the force of the explosive decompression made it impossible. An enormous clang rang through the ship as an Ukhel transport collided with them.

"Damnit, we lost our maneuvering thrusters," cursed Garcia.

"We have about ten seconds—get us out of here," Park advised.

"Well, I have no control of our speed or direction. So, what the hell do you want us to do?" Garcia spat back.

"We have nothing to lose, just fold. Time to hope luck is on our side," Kanumba said.

"Here we go!" Garcia hit the fold button on his console and they were instantly on the other side of the Ukhel ship, with the Bravo between them and the rest of Samsara Fleet.

"Three...two...one..." Park counted down.

Everyone in the cockpit stared at the Ukhel ship, waiting to see what the effect of the entire payload of missiles would be. It continued to move closer to the *Merrimack* without any sign of distress. Kal waited a few a few more seconds and then put his head in his hands. *All those lives lost...*

The ship's viewscreen went completely white as the explosion overloaded the optical sensors. After a second it automatically dimmed and they could see an enormous ball of fire that resembled a small sun more than anything else. As the explosion subsided saw that the Ukhel ship had been split almost in half—its two pieces folded back on themselves, connected by a thin strand of metal.

"We did it." Kal was in disbelief. "I can't believe it."

"The other Ukhel ship just folded out," Kanumba advised. "Looks like our fighters were able to get a few more hits on it and then it split when we destroyed the other one."

Kal slumped limply in his seat—he felt like dropping to the floor. Everyone else in the cockpit let out whoops and calls of joy. They reached over chairs to hug each other and pat each other on the back. Tears flowed from Kanumba's eyes as she wrapped her arms around Lieutenant Park.

"Congratulations!" Zhou's voice came over the general net. "Today we have struck back for Humanity!"

Chapter Twenty-Eight

The ships of Samsara Fleet began calling out to each other over the command net. Congratulations, cheers, and calls for remembrance were bandied back and forth. The communications traffic began to slow down when the carrier *Borodino* suddenly folded into the area. At first, it was pure confusion. The carrier had left the station weeks earlier and had been presumed lost. After some tense moments, *Merrimack* was able to establish contact and explain what had just happened. Everyone on the Samsara net heard the cries of joy that came from the incoming ship's bridge crew when they heard the news.

The carrier quickly moved from celebrating to providing repairs and first aid to the survivors of the battle. Their repair crews were able to apply a temporary fix to the *Merrimack's* fold drive, allowing them to leave the system. They wanted to get out as soon as possible to prevent any Ukhel reserve forces from returning to attack them.

Several assault ships and engineers were sent to the wreckage of the Ukhel ship. They went through the remains, recording everything, and salvaging whatever parts and technology they felt could be reverse engineered. Most of the Ukhel bodies had been expelled into the vacuum of space by the explosion, but not all. They were able to collect several of them for study.

The decision was also made to destroy the remains of Kapustin Station so that anyone who came to the location would not try to look for survivors or investigate the wreck. With the station gone Human ships would most likely immediately fold out of the area, evading any sort of surprise the Ukhel might set in the future.

Kal watched as a series of strategically detonated charges destroyed each section of the station, leaving nothing but debris in its wake. He was sad to think of the lives and work that had gone into the station, but it would've only been a trap for Humans otherwise.

The *Oruc* had to land inside the *Borodino* in order to fold out with the fleet. The damage from colliding with the Ukhel ship had compromised almost every single system, and after going through a diagnostic, Kanumba said it was a miracle they were alive.

They folded back to the rendezvous point and one of the merchant ships transported the *Oruc's* crew to the *Ofira*. Kal walked down the cargo ramp of the merchant ship and into the *Ofira's* landing bay. Soldiers celebrated with each other, grasping arms, hugging, laughing, and crying. Garcia walked beside him, running his hand through his thick black hair, his face alternating between joy and disbelief.

Park and Kanumba walked behind them, their hands interlocked. Clearly Kal had missed something during his time on the *Oruc*. But then again, people were always somewhat foreign to him. His gaze swept the bay and stopped when he saw Nicole standing to one side, looking at him with a smile, making her blue eyes almost glow.

Kal ran toward her, his arms outstretched. He pulled her as close as possible, burying his head in her hair as she tucked her head in his shoulder. He could feel the sobs of relief wracking through her body, and then Kal realized he was crying too, his mind unable to handle the emotion of everything they had been through.

Around them the celebration continued. Kal tried to enjoy the moment, but his mind was already racing ahead. They'd achieved a victory today—a great victory—but it was one battle in a war they were still losing badly. He was smart enough to keep those thoughts hidden as he went around and congratulated the soldiers milling about the bay.

"We did it." Ekon walked up and slapped Kal on the back. "We won. Next stop, New America—we're taking it back."

"Yes, we will," Kal affirmed.

He continued to walk through the bay, its emptiness weighing on him. They had lost more than three fourths of their fighters in this battle—fighters they had no way to replace.

Lieutenant Colonel Petrov was talking to a junior officer when she saw Kal walking along the flight line. After patting the soldier on the back, she quickly sidled up to him and grasped his hand.

"Congratulations, sir," she cheered, "we did it!"

"Yes, we did." Kal returned the smile.

"What's next?" she asked.

"Not sure," Kal ran his hand through his hair, "but this is just the beginning. A great victory—but there's much more to do. Let's enjoy it for now."

"Sounds like a good idea to me."

Kal made his way toward the exit, congratulating soldiers as he went, and then headed back to his stateroom. Sitting on the bed, he looked at the stars in the viewscreen. He had been so engrossed in the struggle he hadn't had a chance to think about the future. Now that they had won a victory, Kal realized one thing—he didn't want to serve as an EDF officer anymore. A carrier like the *Borodino* should have a full crew of officers, many of them more senior than him—perhaps he could step aside.

Kal pulled the picture of his family out of his pocket and stared at it. Oddly, he felt as if the victory was, in some way, for them. It was strange, since they hadn't died at the hands of the Ukhel, and had never even known of them; but he still felt like he had honored his family somehow. Looking at their smiling faces, he felt peace. The loss was still there—it would always be—but he felt acceptance.

"Come in." Kal saw Nicole waiting outside of his door.

"You look like you have something on your mind. What are you thinking about?" she asked.

"Thinking about the future. I don't want to be a fleet commander and I don't think I want to be a logistics officer anymore either."

"Maybe there's something else you could do," suggested Nicole as she sat down. "Militaries win wars, but there's more to it than just that. We don't have a government. We have a military, but we need to have diplomats, politicians, and other types of leaders as well."

"True, but I don't see how I can leave when we're still at the edge of extinction."

"Perhaps there are other ways to fight." She looked him in the eye. "We won today, for the first time, but at great cost. We can't afford victories like this. We need to continue to reach out to other species and find allies."

Kal nodded and waited for her to continue. She was right, of course.

"You can't walk away from the war, and I don't think you would want to. But perhaps you can resign your commission and lead a team to go out and continue the job we started on Tamulk and Forha? Let's work together and help find allies, scout out the Ukhel, and see if there are resources that we can find for the fleet." Nicole leaned forward, grabbing his attention. He noticed that she had started to wear the starfish pendant around her neck.

Kal liked the idea—he would be away from the bureaucracy and administration he hated but he would still would be able to help the war effort.

"I'll be honest," Nicole continued, "this is an idea I've had in my mind for a while. I can't do it myself though. With my past, they would never trust me to lead a mission like this. But you, you're a war hero now. They almost have to give you what you want. What do you think?"

She was right—he had been one of the architects of the fleet's first victory. Humanity's first victory, though no one outside the fleet knew of it. Whoever commanded Samsara Fleet now would almost have to give in or face an insurrection.

"I'm in," Kal finally replied. "Now we just need to figure out how to make it work."

Nicole sat down at the desk and they began to discuss their plans going forward. Outlining what they would need and what would be their first mission. After a couple of hours, they decided enough was enough and joined their comrades, still cheering their victory.

The celebrations went on for hours aboard all the ships in Samsara Fleet. Cheers had turned to vows of vengeance, which had eventually given way to solemn remembrances of family and friends who had been killed. Kal was glad that he and Nicole had decided to stop their planning and join the crew. It had been a long time since he felt the true happiness of celebrating with friends.

He woke the next morning feeling refreshed. After his meeting with Nicole the previous night, he wanted to talk with the other officers in the fleet and propose their idea. Kal sent a message to the senior leaders in the fleet asking for a meeting later that day in his conference room aboard the *Ofira*.

He walked into the conference room and found it already filled with soldiers. A tall woman stood up and walked to him, her hand extended, when she saw Kal enter the room.

"Major General Aamina Samaha, commander of the *Borodino*. Congratulations to you, Colonel Norman."

Kal shook her hand. "Thank you, and thanks for coming this morning."

"Of course. I was going to invite you over to the *Borodino* myself anyway. You have done an excellent job with the limited resources you had available, and I commend you. I am looking forward to having you on my staff to continue the fight against the Ukhel."

"Thank you, general," Kal replied. He noted that she had already taken a seat at the head of the table.

"Thanks everyone for coming," Kal said as he sat down next to Samaha. "I wanted to discuss—"

"Before we go any further, can you tell us what you heard?" Major General Samaha cut him off. "I was told that you were able to intercept the Ukhel's comms somehow and that they were speaking Human Standard?"

"Well, not exactly. They were speaking a version of it though," Kal admitted.

"How is that possible?" asked another general to Samaha's right.

"We don't know, but we have our suspicions." Nicole swept her gaze across the room. "As you all know, Humanity has been traveling the stars for a long time now, hundreds of years. However, when we were first starting out, there were accidents and worse. Entire ships were sent out from Earth and never returned."

"We actually saw them inside their ship," added Chief Kanumba. "They looked like Humans, but appeared to have been altered or mutated in some way."

"What do you mean?" asked Samaha.

"We didn't get too close a look at them, but their skin was purple and they moved differently, not like a Human." Kanumba paused, looking for the right words. "It's the difference between a dog and a panther. They walk like dancers, gracefully, on their toes."

Samaha looked at Kanumba with her eyebrow raised. "Like a cat?"

"Exactly," responded Kanumba. "They appear to have evolved somehow."

"We were able to recover several of their bodies, and our biologists will be studying them to understand exactly what they are. I guess they could be descendants of one of the ships during the early years," admitted Samaha, "but why would they attack us like this?"

"Sins of the past," whispered Kal, thinking back to their conversation with Yitari.

"What do you mean?"

"Not all the Humans who left did so willingly. Some of them were prisoners or were willing to sacrifice their lives so their families could eat." Nicole swallowed. "People like that would have reason to hate us."

"So, they come back here to what? Take revenge?" Samaha asked.

"Yes, I think so. But I think it is more than that," replied Nicole. "They could have just destroyed Earth and then left. But they have been attacking multiple species and have been occupying planets. It seems that they are here to stay."

"If they are the Humans from hundreds of years ago, then something has caused them to mutate rapidly," Kanumba offered. "Perhaps they are trying to escape the conditions of the system or systems where they ended up."

"So, we have a working theory and a whole lot of questions," General Samaha concluded. "Colonel Norman, I would like you to investigate further and want a report at the next meeting. We need more information as to who these Ukhel actually are. Do some research into whatever histories you can find."

"Ma'am, this is the last time I'll be attending this meeting." Kal's announcement was met with surprised faces from around the table. "I am resigning my commission, effective immediately, and will return to civilian status. I plan on continuing—"

"I do not accept your resignation, Colonel Norman. You will remain an officer in this fleet." General Samaha's face was flush and her eyes bored holes into him. Kal could tell the anger was tinged with more than a little fear. She saw in him someone who knew what needed to be done, and she did not want to let that go.

"Ma'am, there isn't really anything you can do to stop me unless you want to cause a civil war within the last shreds of

Humanity." Kal looked Samaha dead in the eye. "Please stop interrupting me or I'll walk out of this room."

Samaha's eyes narrowed, and Kal could see her clench her fists on her chair's arm rests. Eventually, she leaned back in her chair, hands clasped together, and nodded for him to continue.

"We've been reeling for the past several months, against an enemy we had never heard of. Yesterday, we finally achieved a *small* victory, and now we have a chance to regroup. Fighting the Ukhel with Samsara Fleet alone will not get us far. We can take out perhaps two more of their ships with the resources we have now. We need allies and intelligence to win."

Samaha's face eased as Kal spoke, and her eyes were now looking at him inquisitively, trying to understand what was going through his head.

"What I propose is that Ms. Bergeron and myself will be the beginning of a new corps of diplomats and scouts. We'll contact other governments to establish alliances and infiltrate our planets to start revolutions. There are resources—ships, fuel, soldiers—out there. We need gain access to them and unite with other species to fight the Ukhel. At the same time, we can also look for more information on who they truly are."

"What governments would you contact?" the general seated across the table from Kal asked skeptically.

"We can make contact with Human planetary governments and other species. They may have resources that can aid our fight."

"What do you mean planetary governments?" asked General Samaha. "There's only one Human government; planets are just local administrators."

"There *was* just one Human government," Nicole replied. "The Ukhel have changed all that. They've destroyed the old system, and we need to recognize that the multi-world empires are gone, probably for good. I don't think there will be a replacement for the UEG."

"Surely, when we defeat the Ukhel, things will go back to the way they were," one of Samaha's staff officers declared.

"I doubt that," Kal replied. "I don't think the colonies will want to give up their sovereignty. I think we need to assume that going forward, we'll not have a unified Human government again."

"Then what government does Samsara Fleet report to?" Petrov asked, raising her eyebrow at Kal.

"I think for now, all of them," he responded. "In the future, it may be all of them still, or perhaps Samsara Fleet will be disbanded."

He raised his voice slightly, to make sure that everyone was paying attention. "But all of that doesn't matter right now. We don't know if there will be a Samsara Fleet in a month. That's why I am proposing this mission. We must start gathering the connections and resources we need in order to mount some sort of fight against the Ukhel. The longer we wait, the stronger they grow."

"So, with you gone, how will that affect the fleet?" Lieutenant Colonel Petrov asked.

"Glad you asked. I think that both yourself and Lieutenant Colonel Zhou have more than earned a promotion. You're the only two officers to have led a successful assault against the Ukhel. You should have your acting positions become permanent and lead the *Ofira* and *Merrimack*." Kal turned to Samaha. "Ma'am, you're the ranking officer and the commander of the fleet now that you're here. I am a logistics officer, and this mission plays on my strengths and is the best way I can contribute to our success. Let me leave with your blessing so that we can work together rather than apart."

General Samaha sighed. "Colonel Norman, unfortunately what you say makes sense. But I won't let you resign. Instead, you will still be a member of Samsara Fleet, but assigned to this special mission. Ms. Bergeron will accompany you as an official envoy of the fleet. What else do you need?"

Kal smiled. "I was hoping you'd ask."

Almost every single soldier who wasn't on watch was in the *Ofira's* bay to see the *Oruc* off. Kal stood on the ship's cargo ramp and looked out at the faces of his comrades. He smiled, proud of what this group had accomplished, and hopeful for what they would do in the future.

The *Oruc* had been completely retrofitted over the past several weeks. She now looked like a normal trading vessel from the outside, with all EDF markings and components removed. Her profile was less sleek, since the maintenance team had added additional nacelles to break up the smooth lines of the ship. On the inside, the ship's crew quarters had been reduced to allow for a larger cargo bay to maintain their cover as a trading vessel. Additionally, almost every single system had been upgraded to the most advanced technology available.

Due to his promotion to Brigadier General, Kal had been able to pull a few strings to get the best crew he could think of. Major Garcia would be piloting the ship along with Chief Kanumba and Captain Park. Sergeant First Class Jones would be leading a small four-soldier team to provide security—with Sergeant Ekon Kimathi as his right-hand man.

Kal looked to his left to see Nicole waving as well, her face beaming. Her past criminal record had been pardoned by Major General Samaha, and he knew that meant more to her than she would ever be able to express.

During the several weeks that Samsara Fleet had been retrofitting the *Oruc* and planning their mission, they received fragmented reports from the wider galaxy. The Ukhel had consolidated their hold on almost every planet belonging to the five species they had attacked. The Human, X'Ado, Tounous, Kurz, and Qudoru worlds were now all under their thrall. An uneasy standoff had arisen between them and their neighbors since they were focused on consolidating their gains and everyone else was intimidated by their lightning-fast assaults.

The biologists within Samsara Fleet confirmed that the Ukhel were in fact descended from Humans. Their genetics had been altered in many ways, such as their appearance and motor coordination, but they were still from the same family tree. The scientists had expressed disbelief that these creatures were only separated from the rest of Humanity for a few hundred years. Their genetic variations should have taken millions of years to evolve. Kal just added it to the many questions that were still unanswered about the enemy.

Samsara Fleet knew they needed to provide hope to the Humans who remained under the Ukhel's thumb. To let them know that they were not forgotten and help provide the motivation to resist. With that in mind, the *Oruc* was being sent to infiltrate New America, the largest Human colony. Some of the technical upgrades on the ship had been a direct result of the reverse engineering of the Ukhel parts recovered after the battle of Kapustin Station. Kal hoped this would give them the ability to evade the Ukhel and slip in unnoticed.

The rest of the crew of the *Oruc* stepped out onto the ramp and gave a final wave with Kal and Nicole. They turned and entered the cargo bay, the door lifting to shut behind them.

Kal stepped into the cockpit and slapped the bulkhead affectionately.

"Ready to go, boss?" asked Major Garcia.

Kal patted him on the back. "Yup, let's get outta here."

It felt like home to Kal, and the soldiers around him were the only people he had left. They weren't the Earth Defense Force anymore, they were Samsara Fleet, a new hope for a Humanity that had lost almost everything. But they were still fighting—for the Humans still trapped under Ukhel rule, for the other species who had also been crushed, and for each other. They were surviving and fighting for the ones who remained.

Authors Note

Phew, we made it!

I want to say a quick thank you to you, my reader. Writing a novel is a long and tedious process and I am grateful if even one person reads this book and enjoys it. Hopefully, YOU enjoyed the trip and are looking forward to hearing more about Kal and Samsara Fleet as they try to save Humanity and discover the story of the Ukhel.

If you enjoyed the book, you can follow my author page on Amazon or check out my webpage at www.rileycollins.info to join my mailing list.

Stay tuned for more adventures!